MW00874621

Craving His Touch

Red Phoenix

Bryan Sutton
95 Nall
Plaza
Ashley

Craving His Touch:
Brie's Submission Book 26

Cover by Shanoff Designs
Formatted by BB Books
Phoenix symbol by Nicole Delfs

Dedication

I never imagined this day would come, and yet here we are!

My beautiful series became too long to continue to thrive. Even though I have so much more to tell, I understand it is hard for new readers to jump into a super long series. Forced to confront that reality, I accepted that Craving His Touch needed to be the epic conclusion to Brie's Submission.

For years I have been taking notes that I've simply called "Ideas for Brie". They were important phrases or small snippets of scenes that my muses gave me in the middle of the night. These were ideas that had yet to be used in the series. When I set out writing this final book, I looked over the insights my muses had faithfully given me all these years and realized that many were waiting for this book. It blew my mind!

My friends, I have to tell you that the muses were powerful while I was writing this book—each one has something important they want to leave with you.

Once I let them take the lead, this book took off! I'd wake up at four in the morning and not go to bed until midnight just to keep up with them as they poured out their stories. When I wrote the final line in the book, my heart let out a sigh of joyful satisfaction.

I know you will love this book because I did while writing it!

As always, I need to thank the many people who've helped me to share Brie's journey with you.

MrRed, my love and inspiration. You supported and encouraged me to start writing and you also became the focus in my stories. So many Doms in the Brie books reflect parts of you, and I am very grateful for all the "research" we've experienced together.

To Pippa Jayne, the narrator who became the voice of the series. Your love of Brie and my fans made every audio exceptional. The fact that you and I became good friends in the process is such a sweet gift.

To Paul Salvette and his team who formatted my many books of Brie. He has dealt with my crazy deadlines and never once let me down. Truly, Paul saved my sanity every release! You may not know this, but he came up with little details in the formatting to make the Brie books extra special, such as adding my phoenix to every chapter.

To my editor, KH Koehler, you have my deepest gratitude and respect. Working with you has always been a joy and your ability to keep my "voice" while elevating my work is pure magic. Thank you for embracing the crazy schedule of this book and remaining by my side every step of the way.

To Shanoff Reads, my cover designer extraordinaire! You took on every challenge I've given you in my pursuit to create beautiful covers that reflect the words inside. From redesigning the entire set, to adding the stunning spines, you've always amazed me. I love creating covers with you and adore seeing what you create next.

To my proofers, Becki, Marilyn and Brenda, you never once balked when I had a nutty deadline during this series. You took on the challenge each and every time, pouring your energy into making sure the book was the best it could be. Thank you for being such wonderful friends and fans of Brie.

To my marketing team, Jon and Ben. You know how privileged I feel getting to work with you. Your creativity, thoughtfulness, humor and sheer brainpower always astound me. I thank you for believing in my work, for loving my fans, and for thinking of fresh ways to showcase my books.

To the admin of my Friends of Red Phoenix reader group. Felicia, Missy, Brenda, and Marilyn, you keep the magic of Brie and the gang alive by pouring your time and energy into the members of our group. Thank you for loving my fans and me.

A HUGE shout out to my Patreon peeps! Because of your love of Brie and your support of my work, you made writing this final book a joy. Just like you, I do not want these muses to die. Knowing I had your ongoing support, I was able to end this series the way it was meant to end, trusting that we will be visiting Brie and the gang again in a new series sometime in the future. You gave me hope and I will always remember you for that!

Big Red Phoenix hugs for:

Marilyn Cooper, Randi Maroney, Christal Bolotte, Melissa Guido, Lydia Schweitzer, Danyell Murphy, Crystal Smith, Krys Kielty, Lita Welch, Valerie Cosman, Yvonne Holguin, Lisa Hartman, Lynn Steller

Which leads me to the final dedication which goes to every fan who has ever picked up a Brie book. You are the reason that Brie's journey is out in the world, and the reason that it became 26 books strong.

Your love of Brie and her world changed my life. I am a better person for having written the Brie's Submission Series and for getting to know all of YOU!

I know that Brie and the gang live on and I hope that in the future we will have the opportunity to hear their voices again.

"I googled it, Sir."

Love, ~Red

Friends of Red Phoenix - Group
facebook.com/groups/539875076052037

SIGN UP FOR MY NEWSLETTER
HERE FOR THE LATEST RED
PHOENIX UPDATES

FOLLOW ME ON INSTAGRAM
INSTAGRAM.COM/REDPHOENIXAUTHOR

SALES, GIVEAWAYS, NEW
RELEASES, PREORDER LINKS, AND
MORE!

SIGN UP HERE
REDPHOENIXAUTHOR.COM/NEWSLETTER-
SIGNUP

CONTENTS

Morning Greeting

B rie woke early and turned her head, surprised to find Sir staring at her. He lay with his head on his pillow, a sexy smile slowly spreading across his lips. "Morning, babygirl."

She grinned in response. "Good morning, Sir."

Although Brie had woken up beside him ever since she'd become his collared submissive years ago, she was still as captivated by the man as she had been that first day when she met him at the tobacco shop.

She loved that chiseled jaw, those deep, soulful eyes, and his sexy lips that knew how to please and tease every part of her body.

"I don't have much time because I have to get ready for a conference call with a client in India, but I'd like to start your morning with an orgasm. Think you can come in five minutes, babygirl?"

Surprised by the sexy offer, Brie was totally game to try and answered playfully, "I will do my best, Sir."

"Look into my eyes, téa."

The moment he called her by her pet name, she was putty in his hands. Looking into those captivating eyes, Brie gladly opened her legs to him, moaning softly when she felt his fingers brush against her clit.

Even though he only had a few precious minutes, Sir did not rush. Drawing out her desire with the gentle strokes of his fingers, he swiftly made her wet before he began rubbing her clit more intensely.

Sir's touch had always had a profound effect on Brie. It felt like lightning in a bottle. That, combined with the intimacy of gazing into his eyes and seeing the look of desire for her, made her whole body hum in anticipation of a tender climax.

He slowly inserted his finger into her pussy and leisurely swirled it against her G-spot. Her inner muscles immediately tightened, and she felt the first faint pulse of an impending climax. Moaning with more passion, she opened her legs wider, welcoming the tingling feelings that washed over her.

Glancing at the clock, she smiled. With a full minute to spare, Brie let out a little gasp of pleasure as her pussy began pulsing rhythmically against his finger.

"That's my good girl…" he murmured, nuzzling her neck.

Her climax had been sweet, like the gentle kiss of a breeze.

"Thank you, Master. What a beautiful way to begin my day." Stretching in the bed, she purred in satisfaction and asked, "May I make you a cup of coffee as thanks?"

"That would be greatly appreciated, babygirl," Sir replied, winking at her before he rolled out of bed.

Brie couldn't help but stare at his fine, muscular ass as he walked to the bathroom.

"I love that man..." she said out loud.

Throwing off the covers, she grabbed her robe, tying the sash tight, before heading out of the bedroom. As the coffee was brewing, Sir joined her, already showered and dressed in a three-piece suit. Although he worked from home, Sir always dressed in formal attire for work. He'd explained once that it put him in the right mindset for the day ahead, much like a uniform would for an athlete.

Brie certainly had no complaints! She considered herself extremely lucky that suits were his uniform of choice. She had a serious weakness for them because business suits made a man look sexy and powerful.

Sir nodded to her before disappearing into his office and shutting the door. Once the coffee was finished brewing, Brie poured the liquid gold into Sir's coffee cup. He was extremely picky about the type of coffee he drank, insisting it must be the same Italian brand that his father always drank.

As for Brie, she loved the flavor of the coffee. It was a delicious blend of aromatic beans that created a deep caramel-like flavor. While Sir took his coffee black because he preferred to taste the rich flavor of the beans, Brie enjoyed a little splash of cream in hers because she felt it enhanced the flavor.

Quietly opening his office door, she walked in and placed his cup on the desk, making sure not to disturb him during his video conference as he spoke to his newest client.

Sir smiled at her, nodding his thanks as she turned to leave.

Brie then headed upstairs to check on the children and was delighted to find both still sleeping soundly. Thrilled to have a little time to herself, Brie walked back to the kitchen and poured herself a big mug of coffee.

Heading out back, she held her steaming mug in both hands and purred. Captivated by the warm colors of predawn, she listened to the sound of the waves crashing on the shore.

Curling her legs underneath her in the patio chair, Brie allowed herself to bask in this rare moment of peace…

Production on her second documentary was starting to rev up, leaving relaxing moments like this few and far between.

Taking another sip, she savored the rich caramel flavor and closed her eyes, sighing in contentment. But her eyes suddenly popped open and she let out a surprised yelp when she felt something wet and cold press against her knee.

Looking down, Brie was astonished to see Little Sparrow gazing up at her, wagging her tail.

"You scared the beejeebies out of me, girl!" Brie laughed, reaching down to pet the dog's soft fur. "I have missed you more than you know."

The dog wagged her tail more vigorously as she leaned into Brie's hand, begging for more pets. Little Sparrow held a special place in Brie's heart because of the vital role the dog had played in saving Rytsar Durov's life. The sweet dog had also helped Faelan when his heart was shattered after he lost Kylie during the birth of their daughter.

Brie scratched Little Sparrow behind the ears, cooing softly. "Do you know how very special you are?"

The dog jumped up to lick Brie on the cheek. Giggling, Brie wiped the wetness from her face. Carefully setting her mug down, she told Little Sparrow, "I'd better get you back to your master. I don't want him to worry about you."

Brie felt a thrill of excitement as she headed to Rytsar's beach house just down the shore from theirs. The place had been empty for far too long while Rytsar dealt with things in Russia. During those extended months, whenever Brie looked at the darkened house, it made her heartsick for him. So, to protect herself from falling into a depression, she'd purposely avoided looking at the beach house at all during his long absence.

Thankfully, the house was full of life again now that Rytsar had returned. Her heart raced as she ran up to the front door and rang his doorbell. Brie fully expected Maxim to answer, but she was greeted by the sadist himself, bare-chested and as hot as ever!

"*Radost moya*, what are you doing here so early in the morning?"

Brie pointed to his dog. "I found Little Sparrow wandering through our backyard."

Rytsar smirked. "She was not wandering. I sent *Vorobyshek* to fetch you."

Brie laughed as she patted the top of Little Sparrow's head. "Is that so?"

"It is," he answered in a mischievous tone. "I noticed

you sitting outside and commanded her to bring you to me."

Brie raised her eyebrows in surprise. "Why would you do that?"

His voice held a hint of mystery when he told her, "You and I must talk."

Rytsar opened the door wider, gesturing for Brie to enter. Glancing back at her own house, she asked, "Will this take long?"

"*Da*," he answered solemnly.

"Then I need to call Sir. I don't want him to worry after everything we've been through."

"Do not fret, *radost moya*. I've already texted him," Rytsar assured her as he shut the door.

Brie noticed Maxim standing in the kitchen. He nodded to her in acknowledgment.

"It's lovely to see you again, Maxim," she said, smiling at him. Brie had never forgotten the day Sir had ordered her to run for safety, instructing Brie to head to Rytsar's place with Hope in her arms.

She'd been terrified for him, but Sir had insisted on staying behind to confront the unknown men who'd spilled out of the numerous vehicles that had screeched to a halt in front of their house.

When Brie had shown up on Rytsar's doorstep unannounced, he had immediately locked her and Hope in the nursery, which had been converted into a secret panic room, in preparation for an attack. He and his men made preparations to defend her and her child at all costs.

Thankfully, it ended up being a false alarm and the

"hit men" turned out to be an army of lawyers wanting Brie to sign a lengthy production contract for her second documentary.

Although she had not been under any real threat that day, Brie had never forgotten that Maxim, along with Rytsar and his other men, had been ready to lay down their lives to protect her.

But Brie's gratitude toward Maxim had only grown deeper over the years since that incident. She could not explain why, but she always felt a deep and abiding sense of peace when she was here with them in this house.

Rytsar glanced at Maxim. "We need privacy."

"*Da, Gospodin,*" Maxim immediately responded, nodding to him before heading down the hallway.

"What do you want to talk about, Rytsar?" Brie asked in concern as she glanced around looking for a place to sit. Brie had initially thought he was just being playful, but the serious tone in his voice told her otherwise.

The Russian grasped the back of her neck with his powerful hand, causing tingles to course through her as he slowly led her to the leather couch. Rytsar then commanded gently, "Sit, *radost moya.*"

Her heart skipped a beat as she complied.

Rytsar sat beside her, his blue eyes penetrating her soul with the intensity of his gaze. "You and I have much to discuss."

A cold chill raced down Brie's spine when she saw the flash of pain in his eyes. In a gruff voice, he confessed, "I suffered greatly when I was captured by the Koslov brothers."

Brie suddenly understood why he had wanted her to come this morning, and she felt goosebumps rise on her skin.

Rytsar took her hands in his, squeezing them tightly. "I understand the hopelessness and physical pain you endured at Holloway's hands better than anyone else can, because I experienced both during my captivity."

Squeezing her hands even tighter, his voice became low and harsh. "I have *not* allowed myself to think about what that maggot did to you because…" Rytsar glanced away, pausing for a moment before stating in a strained voice, "I knew it would drive me insane."

Shaking his head angrily, he looked at her again with tears welling up in his eyes. "Now that I am back…I must know, *radost moya*."

Brie nodded. She understood his driving need to know the details because she would be no different if their roles had been reversed. She also realized that after what happened with his first love, Tatianna, not knowing what happened could have the power to destroy him.

Thankfully, under Sir's loving care, along with the skillful guidance of the other Dominants she had trained with, Brie knew she could be open with Rytsar about her experience without compromising her own well-being.

Turning to face him, she looked deep into Rytsar's tortured blue eyes. "Only those who have suffered what we have can truly understand…"

Rytsar nodded, his gaze unwavering.

Swallowing hard, she warned him, "I don't want what I share to scar you any more than you have been."

"Do not concern yourself with me, *radost moya*," he

commanded, then let out a painful laugh. "I willingly accept the pain that will come, because it is the truth."

Brie accepted his answer. His courage was unquestioned, but she still felt concern for him. She knew that by sharing the brutal details of what she'd suffered as a captive at the compound, Rytsar's eyes would be opened to what Tatianna felt and endured all those years ago. She was afraid it might have the power to break his spirit.

"Rytsar, you need to know that you inspired me to fight hard to survive no matter how horrific things got at the compound. I never gave up because you never did— you came back to me, just like you promised."

He nodded but said nothing.

Brie glanced down at Little Sparrow with a sad smile. "Of course, I didn't have a sweet spirit like Little Sparrow caring for me."

Rytsar looked at the dog. "She was truly a blessing from God in my darkest hour." Looking back at Brie, he confessed, "But if I had been given the choice to sacrifice her help so that she could care for you in your time of need, I would have done so without a moment's hesitation."

Brie's heart ached knowing the depth of his love for her. She was deeply touched knowing that her well-being was the only thing that mattered to him. "While I may not have had Little Sparrow to watch over me, Tono's connection provided me comfort in the midst of my suffering."

"I want to understand," Rytsar stated gruffly, brushing her cheek with his calloused hand.

Brie was unsure how much Sir had shared with him about the extent of Tono's involvement during her captivity. Not only had the Kinbaku Master meditated the entire time she was held at the compound, but the unique connection they'd had helped aid Captain in pinpointing the general location of the compound.

Certain this was what Rytsar needed, Brie leaned forward and gave him a reassuring kiss. "I will tell you everything…"

Her Confession

R elating the details of her captivity took Brie hours, while Rytsar peppered her with questions that only someone who had been tortured to near-death would ever think to ask. When Brie finally came to the last night of her captivity and began sharing the specifics of the macabre scene Holloway had set up between her and Mary, Rytsar shot off the couch in a ball of rage.

Pacing the room, he shook his head violently as a low, ominous growl escaped his lips. Seeing his distress, Brie quickly brushed over the gory details to highlight the moment she was rescued. She wanted to spare Rytsar from dwelling on what would have happened to her if Sir hadn't stormed the compound when he did.

Brie felt pleasant goosebumps as she related the miraculous moment when Sir saved her life. She became even more animated sharing how the rescue party had risked their own lives to save every captive in the building when the compound became engulfed in flames during the intense lightning storm.

"It was surreal, Rytsar…" she murmured, remembering every detail of that night. Looking at him, she said in a voice full of satisfaction, "I can't tell you how good it felt watching that evil place burn to the ground. It was as if God Himself was exacting His judgment and punishment."

"He was, *radost moya!*" he snarled, his voice full of venom.

Brie jumped up from the couch and ran over to Rytsar, needing to wrap her arms around him. But when she hugged him, she felt his entire body shaking with rage.

He attempted to pull away from her, but Brie held onto him even tighter, pressing her head against his chest. She could hear the fierce Russian's heart thumping wildly.

Having shared her ordeal with Rytsar, she suddenly felt a sense of euphoria and freedom. It felt as if a weight had been lifted from her. Although Brie had been worried that talking about it might suck her back into the darkness, she felt as if the heavy burden of her experience had been partially released by sharing it with him.

It was proof that she was truly healing from the torture she'd suffered.

Wanting to relieve Rytsar of the burden she had passed to him by telling it, Brie said with conviction, "That place and the man behind it have been wiped from this Earth."

Rytsar pulled away from her, smashing his fist into his hand as he howled in anger. "I should have been the man to send him to Hell!"

"No, I would have lost you if you had. I could *not* have handled that!"

His eyes narrowed. "Instead of me, Marquis Gray had that privilege."

Still shaking with rage, he drew closer to her. "*Radost moya*, I must know what Gray shared with you about confronting that maggot."

Brie let out a nervous sigh. She understood he wanted to know what happened when Marquis Gray confronted Holloway, just as Sir had. However, unlike Sir, Rytsar was not a man to control his emotions and she knew she would have to proceed very carefully.

Rytsar's unrestrained passion was what made him so alluring—and dangerous.

"Tell me what Marquis told you, *radost moya*," he beseeched her. "I need to know exactly what he said."

Brie could tell it wounded Rytsar deeply to not have been the one to end the man's life. She understood his need for justice—not only for her, but for Tatianna and every slave who had suffered.

Wanting to provide him comfort, she explained what happened when she met with Marquis Gray, and how frightened she'd been when she saw how much the trainer had changed after his visit with Holloway at the maximum-security prison.

Rytsar frowned. "What do you mean?"

She shuddered when she thought back on it. "The moment I walked into his office, the entire room felt like a blackhole of pain. Then I met his gaze…"

He leaned forward, stating gently. "Tell me."

She whispered, "I saw a darkness in his eyes that

completely terrified me."

Growling in response, Rytsar stated, "Marquis has always been self-righteous and soft."

Brie shook her head, gazing at him somberly. "I respectfully disagree. I would never describe Marquis Gray in that way."

He countered, reminding her, "Marquis was the one who advised us to let the police handle Lilly. His misguided advice not only endangered your life, but *moye solntse's* as well!"

Brie paused for a moment, not wanting to upset Rytsar further. "But I agreed with Marquis, Rytsar. I could not have handled her blood on my hands." Lowering her head, she admitted, "I was actually grateful for his input."

"That is because both of you have no concept of the real world. You could not conceive of the depth of evil that exists."

Brie nodded, acknowledging he was right. Letting out a painful sigh, she admitted, "Neither of us understood that fact until we were confronted with the monstrous depravity Holloway was capable of."

The moment she uttered the man's name, she could sense Rytsar tensing up again.

Placing her hand on his, Brie continued, "When Marquis was faced with the truth of who Holloway truly was and the horrors that had been committed, he experienced what he called 'a dark night of the soul.' Have you ever heard of that before?"

Rytsar's expression became grave. "I have experienced it myself, *radost moya*."

She looked at him sadly. It pained her to learn he'd questioned his faith as deeply as Marquis had. "Marquis Gray confessed that he felt responsible for everything that happened to me because he was the one who introduced me to Holloway."

"Which is another reason for me not to trust the opinions of that man…" Rytsar snarled.

Tears pricked Brie's eyes when she explained, "Just like you, Marquis Gray envisioned every possible torture he wanted to inflict on Holloway, down to the most violent detail. He condemned himself for it, knowing that in his need for justice, he was as capable of committing the same violent audacities Holloway had." She whimpered when she added, "It almost broke him, Rytsar."

"The world will break you," he replied without sympathy. "It is inevitable."

She had experienced that herself and nodded sadly.

"Did Marquis tell you what happened when he confronted the maggot at the prison?"

Brie sucked in her breath, remembering the terrible truth Marquis Gray had shared with her when Holloway explained the reason he'd left Brie's collar on after he kidnapped her.

But rather than share that with Rytsar, Brie chose to keep that horrifying secret to herself—just as she had with Sir. Suddenly feeling anxious, she headed to the kitchen, telling Rytsar, "I'm going to make some tea."

He said nothing, but she could feel his eyes on her as she moved around in the kitchen.

By the time she returned, she had given herself

enough time to calm down and formulate what to say next. Handing him a cup, she blew on the hot tea before taking a sip.

"You were saying, *radost moya...*"

She nodded and took another sip before sharing what happened when Marquis Gray sat down to face Holloway at the prison. "It was powerful, Rytsar. Marquis Gray said he felt like he was channeling the wrath of God when he told Holloway there was no escape for what he'd done."

Brie then added with profound satisfaction, "Marquis even told me he saw the fear of God in Holloway's eyes."

Rytsar snorted angrily. "Good!"

Chills coursed down her spine when she said, "He also told Holloway that there is no redemption for an unrepentant heart and that retribution was coming."

The Russian's eyes narrowed. "Retribution is my middle name, and I would have gladly taken the maggot down to hell with me."

Brie was grateful that he had been forced to stay in Russia at the time. Seeing the state Rytsar was in now left no doubt in her mind that he would have destroyed himself to get at Holloway.

"Marquis Gray's final words to the man were..." Brie felt the chill in her heart grow stronger when she repeated them out loud, "'There are worse things than death.'"

Rytsar nodded, drinking the tea, as he mulled over those powerful words.

She sincerely hoped that what she said next would

bring Rytsar solace, "An hour after Marquis Gray left, Holloway was found dead in his cell."

"How did he die?" he demanded, setting his cup down on the table.

She shook her head. "Marquis doesn't know, Rytsar. The authorities have never said."

"I am not satisfied with that answer!" he growled, punching his fist into his palm.

Rytsar suddenly frowned and slowly turned his gaze back on her. "Something doesn't add up. I have never forgotten how soft Gray was, despite what the creature did to you and the baby, the day I confronted him with my desire to eliminate Lilly as a threat. What would spark such a dark and savage need from such a 'Godly' man to personally deliver justice to the maggot?"

Brie sipped her tea slowly, saying nothing.

Rytsar's eyes narrowed, his gaze penetrating her soul. "There is something you are keeping from me."

Her heart started to race, and she shook her head.

Leaning in close, Rytsar commanded, "Tell me."

She set her cup down as she hastily constructed an answer. "Marquis felt guilty about what happened to Mary and me. It must have pushed him over the edge…"

"*Nyet*. I have known the man for many years. He is always cool and collected. Something triggered that response from him."

Brie closed her eyes, unable to think clearly under his intense gaze.

"*Radost moya*, I will not ask again."

A whimper escaped from her lips, and she pleaded, "Please. I can't tell you, Rytsar. I haven't even shared it with Sir."

"Why would you lie to your Master?" he challenged.

Brie opened her eyes and boldly met his gaze. "It wasn't a lie!"

"Lies of omission are still lies."

Stating with a voice full of conviction, she said, "I would rather suffer the consequences of keeping silent than hurt Sir with what I know."

"Now you've piqued my curiosity even more…" Cocking his head to one side, he told her, "I will be the judge of whether or not you deserve to be punished for lying to your Master."

Tears filled her eyes. "Please…don't make me tell you."

"I'm waiting."

Brie took a deep breath. Afraid of how he would re-act, she knew he would never back down. With a troubled heart, she prefaced what she was about to say with an explanation. "It was a calculated strike to hurt both Marquis and Sir."

"So, the maggot wanted to provoke Marquis by wielding his power over the man?"

Brie lowered her head. "No, Rytsar. He wanted to poison their hearts and minds by sharing it."

Rytsar lifted her chin. She could tell his patience was nearing its end. "Tell me exactly what the maggot said to Gray."

With trepidation, Brie opened her mouth to speak, but her throat suddenly tightened up, making it difficult. Despite that, Rytsar's intense gaze seemed to pull the secret out of her.

"He told Marquis Gray that he kept my collar on because he wanted to send a message to both him and Sir. Holloway wanted them to find…" She felt her stomach twist in knots when she voiced the horrifying secret out loud. "…he wanted them to find my body broken and unrecognizable except for the collar around my neck."

Rytsar took a step back, his eyes widening as he balled his hands into fists. Brie could feel the burning heat of his rage and watched as the veins in his neck began to pulse. She instinctively reached out to touch him, but he backed away from her and headed to the other side of the room.

Little Sparrow whimpered, jumping to her feet and rushing over to him.

Rytsar opened and closed his fists repeatedly as he stared out of the window at the ocean, saying nothing to her for a long time. However, she could feel the building rage emanating from him—and it frightened her.

"This is why I wanted to keep it a secret!" she cried.

Rytsar didn't speak. Instead, the Russian let out a ferocious roar and slammed his fist into the wall, punching a hole into the plaster.

Little Sparrow yelped in distress.

"Don't hurt yourself!" Brie screamed. She ran to him, grabbing his bleeding hand and placing it over her heart. "Your rage has no purpose here. I'm okay…!"

His eyes flashed with anger and pain. She knew he was too wound up for her words to penetrate his all-consuming fury.

"Holloway is dead!" she shouted. "He can't hurt me anymore."

Rytsar stared at her, tears of rage rolling down his cheeks. In a low, gravelly voice, he told her, "I am angry at God." He ripped his bleeding hand from her grasp and looked toward the heavens, his booming voice filling the room. "I need vengeance!"

Brie could tell he was no longer with her. He was lost in a swirling cloud of darkness. She knew even without asking that he was consumed by a ravenous need for justice that was intertwined with the pain and heartbreak of his past.

Brie's heart broke when she realized, *This is what a berserker looks like…*

Little Sparrow started barking at him in alarm.

"Rytsar!" she shouted, joining Little Sparrow in a desperate attempt to bring him out of the painful trance he was locked in. When he failed to respond to her voice or her touch, she drew even nearer to him and cried, "Anton…come back to me."

She watched as he lowered his fist, his eyes blinking slowly. When she saw him unclench his jaw, she knew he was fighting to contain all of his violent emotions.

Little Sparrow started licking his bloodied fist, whining softly to him. He glanced down at her, saying nothing.

After several minutes had passed, Rytsar turned his head to Brie and stated in a hoarse voice, "It is good you did not tell my brother."

Brie's bottom lip trembled, and she nodded in answer.

"*Gospodin*, should I get the first aid kit?"

Brie looked back to see Maxim and several of

Rytsar's other men standing there on alert. She hadn't heard them enter the room.

Glancing down at his fist dripping blood onto the carpet, he shrugged. "*Nyet.*"

"I would like the first aid kit," Brie told Maxim.

Maxim looked to Rytsar, who gave a slight nod.

Rytsar then turned to Little Sparrow. She was staring up at him, wagging her tail slowly. With her ears down, she whined softly as she gently nudged him.

He patted her head, stating gruffly, "Do not concern yourself with me, *Vorobyshek.*"

Glancing at Brie, he stated, "The same goes for you, *radost moya.*"

Relief flooded through her now that he was himself again. Wrapping her arms around him, she shuddered when her fingers accidentally grazed the nasty scab on his back.

His wound was something he had yet to talk about…

Maxim returned with the first aid kit and handed it to Brie. He then turned to Rytsar and asked, "Is there anything you require, *Gospodin?*"

"Vodka."

His Confession

Maxim headed to the kitchen while Brie guided Rytsar back to the couch so she could tend to his bloody hand. By the time she had finished disinfecting and bandaging it, Maxim had returned and set a vodka bottle, two shot glasses, and a tray of pickles on the coffee table.

He nodded to Rytsar before heading down the hallway with the other men.

Rytsar huffed, waiting impatiently for Brie to finish wrapping his hand with gauze. As soon as she was done, he immediately poured two glasses and handed one to her.

"It's not even eight in the morning," she laughed in protest.

He raised an eyebrow. "It is evening in Russia."

"But I didn't even have a chance to finish my coffee yet…"

Raising his glass to her, he said, "Do you want to talk about the wound on my back?"

Pursing her lips, Brie picked up her glass and held it up to Rytsar. "Yes, I do."

Clinking his glass against hers, Rytsar downed the shot before she even had time to lift the shot glass to her lips. Shaking her head in disbelief, she swallowed hers, feeling the heat of the liquor as it traveled down her throat.

Although Brie couldn't believe she was drinking vodka this early in the morning, she knew that Rytsar needed the relaxing nature of the alcohol to calm the beast that she'd unintentionally awakened by her confession.

Setting her glass down, she asked him pointedly, "Tell me, Rytsar. How did you get that knife wound?"

Rytsar poured a second round of shots. "I've had a devil of a time trying to locate the creature after her violent attack on the Reverend Mother." He held up his shot glass. "Thankfully, the venerable Mother has a formidable constitution."

"Do you think she will fully recover?"

"*Da*," Rytsar assured her. "She appears to have recovered from her injuries."

"A toast to the Reverend Mother's health," Brie said, and they both downed the shot in her honor.

Rytsar frowned. "Unfortunately, she still insists on stepping down as the abbess, *radost moya*. As much as I tried to convince her otherwise, the venerable woman feels responsible for failing to help the creature and believes she is no longer fit to lead the convent."

She looked at him sadly. "That's such a shame...I hate the toll Lilly has taken on her life." Brie owed so much to the abbess who had helped protect her and her family from Thane's demented sister.

Rytsar looked at Brie somberly. "I told the Reverend Mother I wanted to permanently eliminate the threat but hadn't, and turned the creature over to her because of your insistence. She agreed with you and made me vow not to kill the creature."

Brie lowered her eyes in self-reflection, wondering if he may have been right about eliminating Lilly.

"But," Rytsar continued, "I respect the Reverend Mother, as I do you, so I willingly made that vow to you both."

Terror suddenly gripped her heart and she blurted, "Is that the reason for the wound on your back?"

Rytsar actually grinned in answer. "*Nyet.* While I admit that the creature is exceedingly intelligent like her half-brother, I am cunning like a Siberian tiger. Even though she eluded me at every turn, I came to recognize her greatest weakness."

Brie leaned forward, desperate to know. "What is it?"

His eyes flashed impishly when he told her, "Her great intelligence is also her downfall."

Brie tilted her head, confused. "How so?"

Before he answered, the Russian picked up the vodka bottle to fill her shot glass again, but she politely held her hand over the glass. "I'm sorry, I can't. I still have a full day ahead."

He smirked, filling his own glass to the top and downing it all in one gulp. Letting out a satisfied sigh, he handed her a pickle from the tray before chomping on his own.

"Unlike your Master, the creature has a grotesquely large ego to match her intellect. Once I tapped into that, I was able to set up a trap that could not fail…I orchestrated my own capture."

Brie's jaw dropped. She took a bite of the crunchy pickle, trying to calm her nerves as he continued.

Rytsar smiled when he said, "Having pinpointed the area where we suspected she was hiding, I let it 'slip' in an informal interview for a local news agency the location I would be visiting on a particular day."

Brie's eyes widened. "You set her up to capture you…"

He nodded with a glint in his eye. "I knew the only way I could draw her in was if I was alone. So, I ordered my men to remain outside of Moscow while I willingly walked into my own trap, fully aware that I would be isolated with the creature until my men could home in on my location."

Brie put down the pickle, her stomach churning with fear.

Rytsar laughed. "You should have seen the look of glee on the creature's face when she and I came face to face. She surrounded me with the four thugs she'd hired. To make my capture believable, I needed them to 'earn' it, so I put up a respectable fight. However, I purposely faltered to give her men control. Once they pounced on me, it took all four of them to hold me down so she could knock me out with chloroform."

"Oh, my God, Rytsar!" Brie cried in horror. She felt sick to her stomach knowing he'd put himself in such a vulnerable position.

He smirked. "I have a strong constitution, *radost mo-ya*, and quickly regained consciousness. I found myself in a room alone with the creature with my arms cuffed around a pole. She was ripping off the last of my clothes, so I took advantage of her proximity and surprised her with a solid kick to the face."

He smiled as if he was enjoying the memory of it.

"I'll never forget the creature's cackle when she gathered my clothes and burned them in front of me. Grinning like the Cheshire cat, she wiped the blood from her mouth, believing she'd outsmarted me. She was not aware that my tracker would be impossible to find for at least two to three days."

"Oh my," Brie murmured, putting her hand to her mouth. "You swallowed your tracker, didn't you?"

He nodded. "The creature may be intelligent, but she seriously lacks when it comes to inflicting torture. Instead of causing me physical pain, she used many of the same milquetoast tactics I'd used on her after her brutal attack on you."

Shaking his head, Rytsar snorted. "She even played the song 'You Are My Sunshine' when she left me alone." But his eyes darkened when he added, "The creature failed to realize that instead of the song driving me insane, it only served to bolster my resolve. I remembered clearly what she did to you and your unborn babe, and how we barely rescued you both from the slaver. My wrath only grew with each passing hour, and I belted out the song, drawing strength from it."

Looking at her gravely, Rytsar told her, "I know you can understand why my vow not to eliminate her was eating at my soul by this point."

Brie nodded. She was afraid if she ever found herself in the same room alone with Lilly, she would not be able to stop herself from wrapping her hands around the woman's neck in payment for trying to kill Hope.

Rytsar took his time pouring himself another shot. Glancing at his phone messages, he sent a short text before continuing. "I knew the narcissist would believe I could be broken just as she had been. To prove her right, I begged for mercy. But, in truth, I was struggling not to laugh."

His eyes suddenly became cold when he told Brie, "As a bare-knuckle fighter, I learned long ago that ego and over confidence can defeat the strongest opponent. In this case, it wasn't even a competition. The creature was so intent on revenge that she failed to pay close attention and didn't notice I had almost freed myself from my bonds. So, I teased her like a cat playing with a mouse for its own amusement."

"Why would you do that, when you know how dangerous she can be?" Brie cried.

"The creature has claws, it's true," he stated as he reached back to rub at the knife wound. "But she is no match for me."

"She almost killed you, Rytsar!"

"*Nyet*. She simply caught me by surprise with her neck knife."

"Neck knife?"

"A knife that hangs by a leather sheath around the neck," he explained. "She had it hidden under her shirt. When my men stormed the room, I broke from my bonds. As soon as she realized what was happening, she lunged at me with the blade. My reflexes are fast due to my fighting days, and I knocked her unconscious with my fist."

He added with a smirk, "It's a good thing it didn't kill her, or I fear the Reverend Mother would never have forgiven me."

"This is not a laughing matter," Brie insisted.

Rytsar's eyes twinkled as he pulled her into his embrace. "My plan worked out just as I had planned. You should have seen her face when she realized there was no escape for her."

Brie looked up at him gratefully, still digesting the fact that Lilly was safely confined in Russia and receiving the care she needed from Rytsar's friend, Dr. Volkov, who was a leading psychiatrist.

Rytsar leaned forward, grazing her cheek with his hand. "Imagine my relief knowing the chase was finally over, *radost moya*. After I delivered the creature to her new 'home' and verified for myself that she could not escape, I left her under the care of the good doctor." He kissed her on the lips. "I was finally free, knowing I would soon return to you…"

Brie traced the healing wound with her fingers, murmuring sadly, "But you have another scar that you must carry."

He wrapped his strong arms around her. "Scars gained in battle are sacred."

Brie stared deep into his piercing blue eyes. "I owe you my life, Anton."

He smiled as he glanced at her wrist, which bore the

scar from their blood bond. "*Nyet*. You only owe me your fidelity, protection, and comradeship, *radost moya*."

Wrapping her arms around the back of his neck, she pressed her lips against his, wanting to express the depth of her gratitude and love. When she pulled away, she murmured, "I may not be able to protect your body with my puny one…" She placed her hand on his muscular chest, "but I will protect your heart."

They both turned their heads when the doorbell rang. Rytsar released her slowly while Maxim went to answer the door.

Brie was thrilled to see Sir standing in the doorway holding both children. While Maxim stepped aside to let them in, Rytsar told Brie in a low voice, "As far as what the maggot confessed to Marquis, that secret shall go with me to the grave…"

Raising his arm in greeting, Rytsar smiled and shouted, "*Moy droog*, you're just in time to have a shot with me!"

Little Black Box

"This is a pleasant surprise, Sir!" Brie cried happily, taking Antony from him to snuggle with her son. She watched with delight as Hope ran to Rytsar with open arms, wrapping herself around his leg.

Sir told Brie, "I was finished with my earlier call and was feeding the children when Durov texted me with an invitation to join you."

Brie smiled at Rytsar. "So, that's who you were texting…"

"I felt it was necessary after our long talk, *radost moya*."

Rytsar picked up Hope to give her a big bear hug. It made Brie smile to see. "I'm glad you sent Little Sparrow to come get me this morning."

Rytsar walked over, taking Antony from her. "You and I needed this talk so all of us can live in harmony again."

Grinning, he told Antony. "*Moy gordost*, you grow more handsome each day. You have already surpassed your father."

Sir chuckled. "Good…"

Brie disagreed. "I love the way you look, Sir. You're perfect!"

He tweaked her nose. "It's not necessary to inflate my ego, babygirl."

"But it's true," she insisted. "I wouldn't change a thing about you."

When he wrapped his arms around her, Brie sighed happily, the synergy in the room filling her with contentment.

Rytsar told the children, "Your *dyadya* has gotten you both a new present. Would you like to see what they are?"

Hope's eyes lit up and she threw her hands in the air. "Yay!"

Seeing his sister's excitement, Antony clapped his hands. Rytsar's warm laughter rang through the house as he carried them down the hallway to the playroom with Maxim following close behind.

When Brie took a step to join them, Sir pulled her to him instead and said in a sultry voice, "Durov has a different kind of present in store for you, babygirl."

She turned to face him, laughing in surprise. "Really? Right now?"

"Yes," he murmured.

Responding to the lingering lust between them after their morning encounter, Brie stood on tiptoes to give him a kiss. Her body instantly reacted to his fiery embrace, and the kiss became more passionate.

Who would have thought a regular Monday morning could

turn out like this?

Rytsar returned wearing a huge grin on his face. "There is no better thrill than seeing their smiles whenever they receive my presents!"

Sir shook his head, chuckling, "It's amusing how you shamelessly spoil them despite being told not to."

Rytsar put his hand over his heart. "I am their *dyadya,* brother. It is my solemn duty to do so and I'm willing to suffer the consequences of my actions."

"I'll go warm up my bullwhip, then. It's been a while…"

"No, *moy droog,*" Rytsar stated in a serious voice, looking at Brie. "Although I experienced a sense of healing speaking with *radost moya* this morning, it has also reopened old wounds."

Glancing back at Sir, he said, "All three of us have suffered greatly, and it has left me with a need for deeper connection."

Sir looked at him thoughtfully. "How so?"

"I would like to propose a change of protocol for our scene."

"Go on," Sir encouraged him.

Looking at both of them, he stated, "I wish to call each other by our given names."

Brie's heart began to race. They had only done that once before and she'd never forgotten it. Calling each man by his given name changed the entire dynamic of the scene, adding an emotionally charged element to it.

"Intriguing request," Sir asserted.

Turning to Brie, he said, "If you are willing, answer with my given name."

Her heart beat faster as she bowed her head. "Yes, Thane."

Delicious goosebumps rose on her skin by just saying his given name out loud in this setting.

"Then Anton and I will do the same with you, Brie."

She blushed when she heard Sir say her vanilla name. It felt wickedly forbidden—but in the most sensual way.

Rytsar walked up and lifted her chin with his finger to meet his even gaze. "Say my name."

She bit her bottom lip. The sexual tension between them all was now off the charts.

"Anton." Just as with Sir, it felt wonderfully wicked when she said the name he'd been given at birth.

After a tender kiss, Rytsar took her hand and led her to the bedroom. When she turned her head in the direction of the children, he assured her, "No need to fret. Maxim is watching over them."

She squeezed his hand in thanks. The moment she entered the bedroom, Brie spotted a small black box tied with a gold ribbon sitting in the center of the bed.

Rytsar followed her gaze and smiled. "Yes, Brianna, that is for you."

She felt pleasant butterflies hearing him call her by her first name in that rich Russian accent. "May I open it, Anton?"

"Undress, and then you may get it and bring it back to me."

Since it was still morning, and she hadn't had a chance to get dressed yet, Brie was completely naked under her robe. Wanting to please both men, she was deeply grateful for her training at the Center. She'd learned the power of a well-executed striptease, with "tease" being the major component.

Although both men had seen her naked countless times, she knew there was something alluring about watching a person reveal themselves slowly and in small increments, while giving a teasing smile and flirtatious look as each piece of clothing was removed.

The two men stood beside each other watching as she gave them a teasing glance of her right breast by slowly—ever so slowly—dragging the material across her skin until her hard nipple was revealed. Covering it up again, she turned away from them and slowly inched up the hem of the robe until it showed the sexy curve of her ass. Wanting to give them an even bigger tease, she bent down so her ass was fully exposed along with her pussy.

"Damn…" Sir groaned.

Slowly standing back up, Brie turned to face them again and opened the bottom of her robe enough to expose her inner thigh. With a beguiling smile, she pulled back the satin material to expose her bare mound already wet with excitement.

Closing the robe back up, she untied the sash and pulled it out of the belt loops, letting the robe open fully. She shrugged her shoulders and the robe slipped off and fell gracefully to the floor.

Rytsar commanded seductively, "Turn around, Brianna."

Purposely slow in her movements, Brie reveled in the heated gaze of both Doms as she turned in place so they could see every part of her body.

Letting out a lustful growl, Rytsar stated, "I am

pleased. You may retrieve your gift now."

While she fetched the gift, Brie noticed Sir scooping her sash off the floor.

Hurrying back to Rytsar, Brie held up the small black box and smiled. "May I open it now?"

Rytsar smirked when he took it from her and set it on the side table. "*Nyet*. You must wait."

She let out a sad whimper as she glanced longingly at the unopened gift.

Holding up the sash, Sir said in a commanding tone, "Hold out your hands, Brie."

The moment he took hold of her wrists and began to tie them together with the sash, her pussy contracted in pleasure. Brie watched Sir's face as he was binding her, noting his focused attention. He made it seem as if the simple tie was the only thing that mattered. Once he was done, he glanced up and met her gaze. She trembled under the intensity of that gaze.

Being Sir's sole focus was always a humbling experience.

"Now that you are bound, where will I touch you?" he asked in a seductive voice, pulling the sash upward so her wrists were suspended above her head.

Brie held her breath as he ran one hand down her arm, lightly brushing the sensitive area of her armpit before continuing past the swell of her breast, the concave of her waist, down to the fullness of her hip. He stopped and reached behind her to give Brie a playful swat on the ass.

She purred, enjoying the sound of the contact echoing in the room.

"I like seeing you helpless like this," Rytsar growled, looking at her with a mixture of appreciation and primal lust. "But you are welcome to call your safeword, Brianna. I want you to feel safe even though we are about to ravage you…"

Brie didn't want her freedom. Being the center of attention with these two men was exactly where she longed to be.

Sir led Brie over to the pole in the center of Rytsar's bedroom and secured her bound wrists to a metal ring above her head. She stood there as their bound submissive, staring lustfully at the two men.

While Sir still wore the suit he'd worn for his earlier meeting, Rytsar only wore black sweats. He was completely bare-chested, showing off his muscular torso and the impressive red dragon tattoo that covered his left shoulder.

The look Rytsar gave her was impassioned but tender as he approached. Slowly falling to his knees, he grabbed her ass with both hands, burying his mouth in her pussy. Sir leaned forward and kissed her deeply while he played with her breasts, squeezing and tugging on her nipples.

Brie moaned, completely caught up in their sensual play. Rytsar spread her legs wider to admire her pussy before diving back in. He teased her clit with his tongue while slowly pressing his finger into her ass.

Sir cradled the back of her head as he plundered her mouth. Their intimate attention had Brie trembling all over, and soon her thighs began to shake uncontrollably in response to their sensual onslaught.

Rytsar stopped and stood up, untying her wrists as he explained to Sir, "Her legs are weak, *moy droog.*"

Holding out his hand to her, he stated huskily, "Come to bed, Brianna."

She shivered in pleasure responding to his command and readily took his hand. However, Rytsar wasn't kidding about her being weak in the knees and she relied on his support as he led her to it.

Sir headed to the opposite side of the bed, slid off his jacket, and undid his tie. He held her gaze as he slowly unbuttoned his shirt and took it off. He then removed his shoes and socks before undoing his belt and slipping off his dress pants.

Brie bit her lip when he removed the last article of clothing. She openly stared at his powerful thighs and handsome—very hard—cock.

"Open yourself to me," Sir commanded, his voice low and sultry.

Brie lay down on the bed and eagerly spread her legs so he could see how wet she was.

"Beautiful, isn't she, Anton?" he stated.

"*Da,*" he agreed thickly.

Brie turned her head and saw that Rytsar was fully undressed, staring hungrily at her. When she met his gaze, she was struck by the depth of love she saw in those blue eyes. "I am going to worship your breasts, *radost moya.*"

Her heart skipped a beat as he moved onto the bed and he descended on her. Brie closed her eyes to concentrate on the feel of his sensual lips encasing one nipple while he played with the other.

Brie felt Sir settle between her legs before he gave her wet pussy a long, slow lick. She moaned in ecstasy, her clit already sensitive from Rytsar's attention. While Sir drove her wild with need, Rytsar made love to her breasts with his lips, tongue, and the light pressure of his teeth.

The contrast between the intense stimulation Sir was creating between her legs and the Russian's gentle lovemaking made for a divine symphony of sensations.

Eventually, Rytsar moved down from her breasts, leaving a light trail of kisses down to her stomach.

When Sir was finished teasing her clit with his tongue, he began rubbing her G-spot vigorously with his finger, easily coaxing an orgasm out of her.

"Oh, God, Thane," she cried when her thighs began to shake again. She let out a passionate cry when her pussy suddenly gushed with watery come. To her surprise and delight, Sir spread her legs wider so both men could taste her.

"Who knew brie could taste so sweet?" Rytsar murmured as he licked her. Covering his finger in her excitement, he put it to her lips. Brie obediently sucked his finger, tasting the fresh sweetness of her own come.

"Delicious…" Sir agreed.

"I need more, comrade."

Chills of excitement flowed through Brie when the two men repositioned her. She eagerly settled on Rytsar's thick cock, grinding her sensitive pussy against him.

Sir took time coating his shaft in lubricant before positioning himself behind her. "I'm going to take you deeply, Brie."

"Yes, Thane. I long to feel all of you," she purred.

He grasped her buttocks and slowly pressed his cock into her tight ass, stretching and opening her body so it could better accommodate both men.

Brie reached down and felt their two cocks entering her. It was incredibly erotic and she moaned. Her body opened itself up, craving their dual attention. It wasn't long until the juicy wet sound of her excitement filled the room.

She cried out in pure ecstasy when both men suddenly began alternating their strokes. It seemed Rytsar and Sir were as connected to each other as they were to her, leaving Brie transfixed by the synergy between the three of them.

Rather than ramping up and fucking her harder, they made impassioned love to her. Each climax the men drew from Brie seemed to grow in intensity, carrying her into deeper and deeper subspace.

"Flying, are we?" Sir asked tenderly, sweeping her long hair to one side to get a better look at her face.

Flying so high, she was at a loss for words and turned her head back toward him to answer him with a smile.

Sir gave her ass a sexy smack. "Let's see if we can't get you even higher…"

She didn't think such a thing was possible until, as she began to come again, Rytsar whispered in her ear, "I love you, Brianna."

Brie's eyes rolled back as the powerful climax overtook her, causing her entire body to shudder from its intensity. While her inner muscles were still pulsing in ecstasy, she leaned forward to kiss Rytsar, and said breathlessly, "I love you, Anton."

It was truly otherworldly to feel the intense love of both men in physical and spiritual form. It felt as if the three of them were more deeply connected than before.

Brie believed it possible that her heart might burst from the sheer euphoria of it!

She then felt the heat of their climaxes as both men released, filling her with their seed. Riding on such an emotional high, tears of happiness fell unheeded down her cheeks and covered Rytsar's chest.

No one moved afterward as they slowly came down from the sensual encounter—one becoming three once more as they lay together in silence. While she was still flying in a state of rapture, Rytsar handed Brie the small black box tied with a gold bow.

Curious to find out what was inside, Brie undid the bow and placed the ribbon on the bed. She glanced at Rytsar before opening the lid.

The moment she saw what was nestled inside, Brie purred excitedly.

"Do you understand what it means?" Rytsar asked her.

Brie nodded as she gazed at it. "I certainly do!"

She then looked at Sir, who was smiling at her.

"Put it on," Rytsar commanded huskily.

Brie immediately slipped the small ring onto her second toe and admired it. She remembered the silver toe ring with the white flower that Rytsar had given her for Christmas several years ago. Unlike that band, this one was made of gold and had a pink flower with a yellow center and a tiny citrine gemstone set in the heart of the blossom.

She turned to Rytsar and threw her arms around him. "I love it!"

The sexy sadist held her tight as he leaned in to bite the delicate skin on her throat. She let out a soft moan when she felt the pressure of his teeth. After he broke the intimate embrace, Rytsar leaned back against the headboard and informed her with a smile, "This is your warning, *radost moya*. At any moment, I may steal you away to the Isle. You won't know where or when I will come for you."

Rytsar then gave her the gentlest of kisses, his lips lightly brushing against hers. "You will become the object of my obsession for the duration of the trip."

"Oh, my…" she murmured. "I love the sound of that."

He raised an eyebrow. "But, you should know, I have already planned our first scene there."

"Any hints?" she asked him playfully.

He only smirked.

"Why must you be so cruel?" she cried, pouting.

He nipped her bottom lip in answer.

Brie pulled away from him, giggling, then turned to Sir and asked, "What do you know about this trip, Sir?"

He reached out to gently tuck a lock of hair behind her ear. "Durov and I have had quite a lengthy discussion about it."

"And…?"

"We both agree that you would greatly benefit from another lesson in patience."

Brie flopped down, her head on the pillow, and whimpered as she stared up at the ceiling.

Both men chuckled as they left the bed and began to dress.

Staring at the toe ring, Brie's heart started to race when she thought about returning to the Isle with Rytsar and Sir.

That small island held a very special place in her heart...and her loins.

Two Voices

E diting on her second documentary had begun, and Brie was packing up everything she would need for her meeting in downtown LA when she got a text from Marquis Gray.

Brianna, I would like you to come as soon as possible.

Brie felt a chill as she reread the text from Marquis Gray. She knew he would never make such a request unless it was urgent.

She quickly texted him back.

Is everything okay, Marquis Gray?

His text was immediate.

No, it's not.

Brie frowned. Before she could text him back, he typed.

It involves Wallace.

Goosebumps immediately rose on her skin knowing Faelan was involved.

I have an important meeting today. I need time to reschedule before I can come.
Please hurry.

His simple response concerned her even more.

Should Sir come as well?
No need.

Although it made things easier for her as far as childcare, his short answers worried Brie. What could have happened for Marquis Gray to request her presence out of the blue? Before she had a chance to question him, he added.

I must go. Let yourself in.

Brie stared at her phone, a feeling of apprehension washing over her. Shaking her head to clear her mind, she headed downstairs to tell Sir what was happening.

Brie had to slam on her brakes when a careless idiot cut into her lane, nearly hitting her car. He swerved into the outer lane, hit his gas pedal, and then sped off well over the speed limit.

"Asshole!" she screamed even though he couldn't hear her. She then blushed, remembering what Mr. Gallant said when she'd cursed in front of him. "I am offended by your words, Miss Bennett. I should never hear curse words come from your lips unless I ask for them…"

She chuckled at the memory and murmured sheepishly, "Sorry, Mr. Gallant."

Worried she might get into an accident, Brie focused on the road even though her mind was going a mile a minute. It had been difficult to postpone the meeting because many items on the agenda revolved around the documentary and were time-sensitive. But it wasn't even a question for Brie. She'd do anything to help Faelan after everything he had done for her.

Her mind buzzed with concern, wondering what had happened to him. Was this about that damn letter? Or did something happen to his little girl, Kaylee? Brie couldn't bear the thought of anything happening to the little girl!

Faelan had been through far too much in his life—more than any person should ever have to endure.

When she eventually pulled up to Marquis Gray's house, Brie noticed Faelan's blue Mustang in the driveway. She breathed a sigh of relief.

Whatever had happened, at least he was here now and she could talk to him.

After walking up to the door, she hesitated for a moment. Although she felt uneasy letting herself in without knocking first, she dutifully followed Marquis's instructions. The moment she opened the front door, she could hear Faelan's enraged roar.

"I need justice!"

Her heart raced hearing the anger in his voice. She quickly shut the door and hurried to join them. Goosebumps rose on her skin as a feeling of déjà vu washed over her, bringing back memories of the time she had walked into this very house and heard Kaylee's grandparents screaming at Marquis Gray. They had demanded that he allow them to take Kaylee from Faelan so they could raise the baby on their own.

The instant Brie entered the room, both men turned to stare at her. Marquis Gray looked relieved, but Faelan narrowed his eyes when he saw her.

He turned on Marquis Gray. "What is she doing here?"

"I asked Brianna to join us for this discussion," Marquis replied calmly.

Faelan shook his head, telling Brie, "Go back home to your Master."

"Stay, Brianna," Marquis Gray insisted.

Faelan growled at him, then told Brie more forcefully, "Go now."

When Brie refused to budge, he snarled at Marquis Gray. "How dare you treat me like a child!"

"In what way am I treating you like a child?" Marquis asked, his voice cool and collected.

Faelan pointed at Brie. "By bringing her here to act as my babysitter."

Replying in an even tone, Marquis Gray stated, "Brianna is not here as a babysitter, but as your long-time friend."

Faelan looked upward, howling in frustration. "I don't need anyone to placate me, Asher!" Glowering at Marquis Gray, he cried, "I just need some fucking justice for the wrongs that have been done to me, goddamn it."

"Sit down and we can discuss this."

Balling his hands into fists, Faelan shouted, "I don't want to *discuss* it, motherfucker!"

Marquis stared hard at him, the tension in the room increasing with each passing second.

Faelan's face reddened, and it looked to Brie as if he were about to explode. But, after several more tense moments, he took a deep breath and said through clenched teeth, "I didn't mean that last bit. It was said out of anger."

Not one to lose his composure, Marquis simply raised an eyebrow. "I will forgive you for the insult if you sit down." He gestured to the couch and directed Brie to sit beside Faelan.

The waves of fury rolling off the man unsettled Brie even though she knew they were not directed at her. In a heightened state of discomfort, she lowered her head, silently waiting for one of them to speak.

The men said nothing as the three of them sat there enduring the excruciating silence. Soon, it became too much and Brie looked up. She became keenly aware of Celestia's absence and was alarmed by it. "Where is Celestia?"

Marquis Gray did not take his eyes off Faelan when he answered, "She went to the park with the chil-dren…so we could talk." Brie noticed he emphasized the word "talk" for Faelan's benefit.

Snorting in disgust, Faelan continued to seethe in silence beside Brie. The unpleasant standoff continued until Marquis broke it with a direct question. "Are you seeking justice or revenge, Todd?"

Faelan's nostrils flared. "I need that woman to pay for what she and her husband did to me and my family, Asher!"

Brie was certain he was talking about Mrs. Fisher, the woman who had kept a terrible secret from Faelan for years—a truth that hadn't been revealed to him until only a short time ago, when he received her letter in the mail.

"Pay how?" Marquis Gray pressed.

Faelan's lips twitched before transforming into a cold sneer. "I want her to feel the pain she caused my family—especially my kid sister, Lisa."

Marquis followed up his statement by asking pointedly, "Did the woman personally attack you?"

"No," he snapped. "But her husband sure in the hell did, and she never did a damn thing to stop it, Asher. She was right there the whole time!"

Faelan let out a furious growl. "After that woman discovered her son not only planned to kill her and her husband, but countless students at that school, she should have fessed up. But no! She let my family take the brunt of her husband's unwarranted wrath while she kept that vital truth from us."

His voice grew fiercer when he added, "In my book, *inaction* can be just as destructive."

The trainer nodded, digesting what Faelan said. "So,

if you can cause her an equal amount of pain, it will ease your own suffering?"

Snarling, Faelan shot back, "At least justice will finally have been served!"

Marquis Gray met his gaze directly. "And that will bring you and your family peace?"

"Why the hell are you asking me that?" Faelan demanded.

Faelan then turned from him, appealing to Brie. "That woman knew the debilitating guilt I've suffered ever since the accident, but she *still* kept silent."

"It was horribly unfair," Brie agreed.

Faelan threw up his hands in vindication. "See? Even Brie agrees!"

Brie stared at him openly, her concern for him growing, seeing how agitated he'd become. "Faelan… I'm worried about you. Something has changed since you read that letter." When she tried to reach out to him, he immediately pulled away and glowered at her.

In a quiet voice, she added, "It seems like this is tearing you apart."

"What do you expect? You know what was in that letter, Brie. I haven't been able to think about anything else."

"Are you planning to visit the woman so you can confront her in person?" Marquis Gray asked.

"I am! And there is nothing you can say to convince me otherwise. I already have childcare lined up for Kaylee, and I'm flying out this weekend."

Marquis Gray nodded, saying nothing.

But Brie pleaded. "Don't…"

Faelan narrowed his eyes. "Don't *what*, Brie?"

Swallowing hard, she forced herself to state her concern. "Don't do anything that Kylie would be ashamed of."

Pain flashed across his face, and he suddenly looked hurt. "Why would you say that to me?"

Her bottom lip trembled. She was afraid her words might trigger him, but she felt just as strongly that he needed to hear it. "I know Kylie helped you make peace with Trevor's death. You've come so far, Faelan. I would hate for the contents of that letter to unravel all of the progress you've made."

She lowered her eyes, saying in a softer voice, "Don't let this compromise who you are as a man…and as a father."

He looked at her in disbelief. "My family *deserves* justice! Those two people ruined our lives—"

Marquis Gray interjected, "Todd, Brianna only has your best interests at heart."

Directing Faelan's attention back to him, Marquis shared, "I recently struggled with my own violent need for justice. As you know, it led me down a dark path I almost didn't return from. I have always lived by the belief that God causes all things to work together for good. It brings me great comfort to know that what I learned from my own suffering, I can now pass on to you. Because nothing we experience in life is wasted, no matter how painful, if we can ease someone else's journey by imparting what we have learned."

Marquis leaned forward, stating in a solemn tone, "There are two different voices in our heads, Todd. One that brings life and the other that only brings death."

Faelan furrowed his brow. "I have no idea what you mean by that."

Marquis Gray's expression softened as he explained, "The voice of light leads you forward, but the other voice will push you back. One voice quiets your soul, while the other forces you to rush heedlessly into a situation. One voice will reassure you, while the other seeks only to frighten." The trainer's eyes flashed with greater intensity. "There were many times when my thoughts completely terrified me."

Brie nodded, remembering the personal battle Marquis Gray suffered after learning of the many atrocities Holloway committed at the compound.

"Listen to the voice that enlightens you, not the one that confuses you," Marquis Gray encouraged Faelan. "The greatest test that I've found is if the voice you are listening to fills you with conviction or condemns you."

Marquis looked at Faelan thoughtfully. "I can sense the conflict inside you, but do not allow it to torment you. Once I recognized the difference between the two voices, it became much easier to navigate which one I should follow."

Faelan let out a ragged sigh but said nothing. Getting up from the couch, he walked to the window and stared out, looking as if he was deep in thought.

Brie met Marquis Gray's gaze. The warmth and compassion in his eyes filled her with a sense of hope.

Faelan cleared his throat and turned to address Marquis. "I'll take what you said under consideration, but I am still going to confront her this weekend."

Marquis Gray nodded. "You need resolution on this matter, and I'm fully confident you will follow this through to its natural conclusion."

Faelan sighed painfully. "This thing with Mrs. Fisher…it's not just about me. It's about my parents who were forced to isolate themselves in the mountains of Colorado to stop the constant harassment." His gaze darkened. "And it's about Lisa. She was innocent in all of this, yet she was the one who suffered the most. That's why I have to confront that woman, so she can face the damage she's caused by her silence. My family deserves justice! I was the one who caused the accident, and it's *my* duty to see that they get it."

Brie could feel his fury returning when he spoke about his family.

"They deserve some kind of restitution for having their lives ripped apart!"

"What kind of restitution do you have in mind?" Marquis Gray asked.

"I'm not sure yet," he grumbled, "but the Fishers were the richest people in the town, so I'm sure we can come to some kind of mutual agreement."

"Do you believe money is the answer?" Marquis Gray asked, eyebrows raised.

"Sure! My sister is raising a family and could use it. Besides, my parents should be compensated for having to move to another state to protect their children from the Fishers' harassment."

Marquis Gray asked him pointedly, "And you?"

Faelan huffed. "I don't want a damn thing for myself. This is about my family and the cruel treatment they've endured. Nothing else."

Marquis Gray looked at him with compassion. "I understand your need for closure, Todd. I believe, if you can gain anything from the lessons I've learned and apply them to your current situation, you will be able to discern what steps you need to take."

He paused for a moment, then glanced at Brie. "And, I agree with Brianna. You have built a strong foundation upon the ruins of your past. I will pray for you as you confront this woman who wronged you."

Brie could tell Faelan was still seething underneath by his clenched fists and the unnaturally tight expression on his face. Even so, he nodded curtly. "I appreciate that, Asher."

Despite Faelan's forced calm, Brie was still concerned about him. The Fishers' cruel lie altered the life of his family and only added to the debilitating guilt he'd already suffered because of the car accident. Although he had just recently learned that Trevor planned to end the lives of his schoolmates, Faelan had confessed to her that he could not accept the fact that he'd taken another person's life—even if the cause of it had been his inattention at the wheel rather than a desire to kill anyone.

Like Marquis, she understood Faelan's need for restitution when it came to his family. He was responsible for the accident, but it was the Fishers' actions that damaged his family's reputation in their hometown. Still, Brie was afraid that the fury and guilt he continued to carry might cause Faelan to act irrationally when he finally met the woman face to face.

When Faelan stood up, Marquis Gray rose from his chair and held out his hand. Shaking his hand firmly, Marquis said, "May you find the justice you seek and a peace you haven't known before."

Faelan's sarcastic laughter filled the air. "That would take a fucking miracle."

Before he left, Brie told him, "Sir wanted you to know that you are free to call either of us if you need anything."

He stared at her for a moment, before replying, "I'm certain that won't be necessary, but tell him thank you."

Even after Faelan left, his seething fury seemed to remain in the room like a ghost. "Do you think he is safe to go alone?" she asked Marquis Gray pensively.

Placing his hand on the small of her back, Marquis guided her down the hallway to the front door. "I trust that the things we shared will resonate with him." He stopped for a moment and turned to face her. "I want to thank you for coming on such short notice, Brianna. I was getting nowhere with Todd, but your presence seemed to have a calming effect on him."

She laughed. "It didn't seem that way to me."

Marquis Gray resumed walking her down the hallway. "It is easy as individuals not to see the profound difference we make."

Beautiful Condor

S ir was sitting on the couch with Brie, waiting for her parents to arrive so they could babysit the children. Tonight, they planned to meet with Master Anderson at a bar near his place. He'd shared that he had something important to discuss with them.

Brie had no idea at first that something miraculous was about to happen. While the two of them were watching the children play on the floor with Shadow, Brie happened to glance out the window.

She immediately stood up, astonished to see a huge condor flying low to the ground as it followed the shoreline.

"Sir!" she cried, pointing at the condor.

He stood up and quickly joined her at the window. Together they watched the giant bird until it finally flew out of view.

Sir smiled, clearly moved by the sighting. "There is an important aspect to condors that many people in America tend to dismiss."

Red Phoenix

Intrigued, she asked, "What's that, Sir?"

"In other parts of the world, the condor is revered above other animals because it only cleans up what has already passed from this world."

Brie crinkled her brow, unsure what he meant.

Walking back, he sat down on the couch beside her and explained, "While Americans tend to think that eating dead carcasses is disgusting, the simple fact is, a condor never needs to take another life to survive."

Brie stared at him with a sense of awe. "That's profound, Sir. I've never thought about it like that."

Taking her hand, he said, "After living through hell with my mother and seeing the destruction she caused, I was determined not to cause harm to anyone in my path. Not as a Trainer, and not as a partner."

She squeezed his hand and snuggled against him. "That's the reason you turned me down when I bowed before you at the Collaring Ceremony. You were so determined not to hurt me that you almost lost the chance at this life we have now."

Brie glanced at the children, feeling extremely grateful.

Sir kissed her hand tenderly. "It was a decision based on concern for you but, thankfully, it turned out that I'm a selfish bastard and claimed you anyway."

She grinned, giving him a kiss. "I will forever be happy you did, Sir."

Brie turned back to watch their children, thinking about the past. She hadn't forgotten the struggles they'd faced in the beginning after she was first collared. The wounds Sir carried were deep, and she suffered initially when they were forced to confront the demons he'd buried.

But their love for each other was powerful. So strong, in fact, that they had been able to overcome that difficult period in their lives and grow closer as a couple because of it.

Brie glanced at Sir, studying him covertly.

Although he had mastery over them now, she realized that under the right circumstances, those demons could easily appear again. Based on what he'd shared with her, they had resurfaced the moment she'd been kidnapped by Holloway.

His demons were not only destructive but exceedingly powerful. One had only to look at his mother and Lilly. Brie felt a deep sense of respect for Sir because he carried that burden with the unwavering intent not to destroy others.

He was very much a condor.

Snuggling up to him, she purred, "I love that your first instinct was to protect me."

Sir squeezed her tight, kissing the top of her head. "Always."

When Sir escorted Brie into Master Anderson's favorite bar, she squeaked when she caught sight of the handsome cowboy. "There he is!" she told Sir, pointing him out.

Sir chuckled. "Certainly can't miss Anderson in a

crowd..."

Master Anderson stood up and took off his black hat, waving it in the air. "Over here, you two!"

Brie smiled as she walked up to him. Master Anderson was impossible to miss in LA whenever he wore his leather boots and a stylish shirt with several buttons undone to show off his muscular chest.

She noticed the other women staring at him as the two of them joined him at the bar. It struck Brie that Master Anderson carried himself with an even higher level of confidence now that he was an engaged man. And it seemed to make him more attractive to other women, even if he was very much taken.

He shook Sir's hand enthusiastically. "Great to see you, buddy. Really appreciate you coming on such short notice."

Sir smiled. "Anything for a friend."

Master Anderson turned to Brie. "Glad you could join us, young Brie."

She giggled. "I think I'm way past being called 'young', Master Anderson."

"I respectfully disagree," he told her. "You will always be young to me."

She threw back her head and laughed. "I can just imagine it. You're eighty-four and I'm seventy-two but you will still insist on calling me 'young Brie'."

"That's right," he chuckled.

"So, what's the reason for this meeting?" Sir asked, gesturing for Brie to sit down beside him.

Master Anderson set his hat down on the bar and grinned at Sir. "I can't believe it, man! You are seriously glowing with happiness right now."

Sir nodded, glancing at Brie. "Things are going well." He paused for a moment, his smile widening. "Extremely well for us, in fact."

Slamming his fist on the bar, Master Anderson exclaimed, "That's awesome, buddy. When I first met you, I never thought this day would come."

Sir smirked. "Neither did I, actually." Looking Master Anderson over, he stated, "You appear to be 'glowing' as well."

"That I am!" he grinned.

Brie was certain she knew the reason why. "So, that must mean the wedding plans are going well."

Still grinning, he shook his head. "Not in the slightest."

Her mouth popped open, surprised by his answer. "Oh no! What's wrong?"

"Shey is insisting on doing everything on the cheap. From the venue down to her dress, and she's not giving an inch no matter what I say."

Sir furrowed his brow. "I wonder why she is being so insistent."

Master Anderson leaned in close, telling the two in a low voice, "She refuses to go into debt for our wedding and doesn't believe that I can afford it."

Brie brought her hand to her mouth, laughing. "It seems your 'little secret' is biting you in the behind, Master Anderson."

He chuckled good-naturedly, nodding. "That it does, young Brie… And it doesn't help that my parents are enthusiastically supporting her and offering different ways they can help."

Sir leaned back in his chair, snorting in amusement. "Let me get this straight. You want to spoil her, and she's refusing to let you."

"Pretty much," he huffed, sweeping his hair back in exasperation.

Sir shrugged. "Well, I happen to agree with her."

Master Anderson stared at him in disbelief. "*What?*"

"You can't fault Shey's reasoning. It makes sense to start your relationship on firm financial ground. An elaborate wedding isn't going to affect the quality of your marriage."

Master Anderson crossed his arms, stating sarcastically, "This from the man who had his wedding in Italy—in a castle, no less."

Sir chuckled. "I assure you everything was paid for in full."

Master Anderson threw up his arms. "My wedding would be, too!"

Sir shook his head while motioning the bartender over. "But Shey doesn't know that. As far as she is concerned, she's acting in your best interest by honoring you and your future together with a simple wedding."

Master Anderson leaned in even closer and whispered, "But I'm a freaking millionaire."

Brie grinned, finding the situation hilarious. "This reminds me of your proposal dinner when both your family and hers insisted on getting the cheapest item on the menu. It was such an adorable show of love and concern for you."

Master Anderson shook his head and laughed. "I had

to fight tooth and nail to get them to order the food they wanted."

Turning to Brie, he said in exasperation, "But Shey's not bending on this wedding thing. We're butting heads something fierce."

Brie felt a swell of compassion for him, understanding how deeply he loved Shey. "I know you want to spoil her rotten, Master Anderson. However, in this case, I think you should see this as the beautiful act of love it is." She reached out and patted his hand. "Shey *really* loves you."

"True enough," he confessed. "I'm one hell of a lucky dude and I am well aware of that."

Sir slapped Master Anderson on the back. "Then it seems prudent for her sake and yours to fully embrace the wedding of her dreams, even if it isn't what you had planned."

Master Anderson stared at Sir for a long time before letting out a long sigh. "I suppose you're right…"

"I know I am," Sir stated confidently.

"I do have a suggestion," Brie offered humbly.

Master Anderson smiled. "What's that, young Brie?"

"Let Shey plan the wedding of her dreams, while you secretly plan the honeymoon of yours. That way you both get what you want."

He sat back with a huge grin on his face. "That is a mighty fine idea."

"Do you have any idea where you will go for the honeymoon?" she asked him.

Master Anderson nodded confidently. "I'm aiming to give her an animal lover's dream and have been thinking of taking her on a luxurious safari for our honeymoon. I would spare no expense to show just how much I love that gorgeous woman of mine."

"I think that's a lovely idea!" Brie exclaimed.

He laughed at himself. "It's hard as a Dom to take a back seat on this wedding when it's something extremely important to both of us. However, knowing I can surprise her with a lavish honeymoon suits me just fine."

Looking at them both, he stated, "I'm grateful to you. Sometimes a guy just needs the perspective of people who know him well to clearly see the path ahead."

Sir clasped his shoulder. "It's an honor to be asked."

"On that note, I want to confirm that you're still on board for acting as my best man."

"Of course," Sir replied. "Have you finally decided on a date?"

Master Anderson grinned. "Shey has always wanted to be a June bride."

"Aww…that's so sweet," Brie cooed.

Winking at her, he said, "Naturally, I was tickled to learn that the ninth of June just happens to fall on a Saturday this year."

"Why so?" she asked, feeling as if she was missing something.

His eyes twinkled when he answered, "The wedding will be on the sixth month on the ninth day…"

Envisioning the numbers in her head, Brie suddenly burst out laughing. "You're so naughty! What does Shey think about the date?"

His grin grew wider. "She says it's perfect since she

plans to indulge in plenty of it on the night of our wedding."

Brie laughed. "No doubt about it—you two are perfect for each other."

Master Anderson suddenly got a serious look on his face. "As you know, Shey doesn't have any siblings, and she wanted to ask you to be part of her bridal party, but she's been too shy, knowing you are busy working on the film."

"I'd love to be part of the wedding!" Brie assured him. "Now that I know the date, I can work my schedule around it. Are you planning on a Vegas wedding since that's where the two of you met?"

"Nah…Shey's been dreaming of having a traditional country wedding. Naturally, my parents were enthusiastic about the idea and offered the ranch as our "venue"."

Sir nodded in approval. "That would be a scenic spot to have a wedding."

"And will cost us exactly zero, which makes Shey happy."

"I bet it does," Brie giggled. "I can't think of anything more romantic than to be married at the home where you grew up."

Master Anderson smirked at Sir. "Shey wants to hold the wedding reception in the barn. So, you know what that means, buddy…"

"I'm certain I don't."

"As best man, I'll need you to help muck the stalls."

Brie was amazed when she saw a blush form on Sir's cheeks.

"I have to know. What the heck happened at the

barn?" she implored, looking at them both. "You always rib each other about it, but I have no idea what could possibly be so funny."

Raising an eyebrow, Master Anderson glanced at Sir. "Perhaps young Brie, here, could help?"

Sir shook his head, chuckling.

"Oh, I'd be more than happy to help!" she insisted. "Whatever you need."

Master Anderson sat back in his chair and said with a twinkle in his eye, "I just may take you up on that…"

While the men finished their drinks, Brie stared at the two of them, feeling a sense of excitement. She loved the idea of being a part of a traditional country wedding on the very ranch Master Anderson grew up on. But even better than that…she might finally discover their inside joke after all these years.

The Girls Gather

B rie called Lea and then Mary, inviting her in a three-way call. "Hey, working on this documentary is getting pretty intense and I'm in serious need of a little girl time before I go nuts. Do you think the three of us could meet up?"

"I'm free," Lea answered immediately.

"Great! What days work for you?"

"Oh…I meant I'm free today. The rest of the week is devoted to Hunter's family. They're coming to visit, and this'll be my first time as 'official hostess'."

"Do they know he collared you?" Mary asked her.

"Of course! Hunter is very open with his family, even though none of them are interested in the lifestyle themselves."

"That's open-minded of them," Brie said, feeling a little jealous remembering her own father's reaction.

"Yep, his family is really cool, and I like them a lot." Then she whimpered, "But there's only one problem."

Brie frowned. "What's that?"

"They don't laugh."

Mary snickered. "Oh, my God! That's perfect!"

Brie thought it was funny too, but stifled her laughter, and asked, "What do you mean they don't laugh?"

"I'll crack a killer joke and they just smile at me. That's it. Total silence."

"Newsflash…they don't think your jokes are funny," Mary laughed.

"Oh, they compliment me on my jokes, woman! They just never…laugh."

"I can see how that would make things awkward for you," Brie stated, struggling hard not to giggle.

"I know, right?" she exclaimed. "Anyway, I'm free today. When do you want to meet?"

"I'm open in the afternoon," Brie told her. "How about you, Mary?"

"No can do. I already agreed to watch the baby while Marquis and Celestia take scuba diving lessons."

"That's really cool they're learning to scuba dive," Brie said, impressed.

"Yeah, I like that Marquis Gray and Celestia are adventurous for older people," Lea piped up. "Hey, I've got an idea! Why don't we help you babysit? It doesn't matter where we meet. We'll just spend the whole time gabbing anyway."

"I'm game," Brie agreed, eager to see her besties. "How about you, Mary?"

"If I can get someone else to change his diapers, I'm all over that shit."

When Brie arrived at the house, Celestia greeted her at the door dressed in a one-piece swimsuit and beach shorts. "How wonderful to see you again, Brie!"

Brie grinned, giving her a big hug. "I always love your hugs."

Celestia returned her smile. "I feel the same, Brianna. Do come in! The other girls are already here."

Brie walked into the living room to find Marquis dressed in swim trunks and a t-shirt. It was a little disconcerting to see the esteemed trainer dressed so casually, and it only highlighted how extremely pale his skin was.

Instinctually bowing her head in greeting, she said, "Good afternoon, Marquis Gray."

"A pleasure to see you, Mrs. Davis," he replied in a formal tone.

Brie gave Lea a quick hug and then walked over to Mary, who was holding the baby. Seeing how healthy the little boy looked, she said in surprise, "I can't believe this is the same child. Caden has grown like a weed since leaving the hospital."

Celestia stated proudly, "He's gained three pounds already. The pediatrician said he's now in the normal weight range."

"That's amazing, considering how tiny he was when you adopted him."

Marquis Gray looked tenderly at the infant. "He simply needed a secure environment and an abundance of love to flourish."

Glancing at Celestia, he added, "When we were younger, the two of us talked about wanting a family, but when we found out that we were unable to conceive, we chose to invest our efforts in the Submissive Training Center." He held out his hand to his submissive. "It's something neither of us regrets."

Celestia gazed at her Master lovingly. "Assisting the submissives at the Center has brought us both great joy." She then glanced at the small child sleeping in Mary's arms. "But this little boy has truly been an unexpected miracle in our lives."

Looking at Mary, her smile grew wider. "As is having your love and support in helping to raise him, Mary."

Mary looked as if she was struggling to hold back her tears. "I'm grateful to you both for saving him…" Looking down at the baby, her voice caught when she added, "No child should grow up unloved."

She met Celestia's gaze again, stating, "But I know I will never be fit as a mother because I'm too damaged to be good for anyone."

"Not so, Miss Wilson," Marquis Gray stated firmly. "Do not accept the label of 'victim' others have tried to place on you, because it strips you of your power. Yes, you have indeed suffered unspeakable ordeals, but you are not only a survivor but a conqueror. Your body and mind may carry the scars of a seasoned tigress, but you have learned from each and every battle and have become wise beyond your years."

He said with pride, "Because of your tenacious spirit, what was meant to tear down and destroy you has honed you into a woman of immense power. Do not allow *anyone* to strip you of that truth."

Mary stared at him for several moments. Looking down at the sleeping boy, she vowed, "Caden, I will teach you what I've learned so you won't have to suffer like I did."

Marquis Gray placed his hand on her shoulder. "That is what every good parent does."

She continued to stare at the child, her lips trembling as she nodded.

Marquis Gray then picked up a duffle bag lying on the floor beside him and held out his arm to Celestia. "Let's leave the women to run the ship while we go on our own adventure."

She flashed him a radiant smile. "I would love that, Master."

As they were leaving, Celestia turned around to tell them, "I left some treats for you in the fridge. Enjoy!"

Brie shook her head as she watched them leave. "I don't know how Celestia does it. Caring for a baby and still finding time to make us treats on such short notice? She puts me to shame."

Mary snorted. "Well, for one thing, the woman can cook."

"I'm not that bad…anymore."

Mary waved off her protest as if Brie's improvement didn't count.

She then shared, "I've had the privilege of watching those two in action. It's like they were made for this parenting stuff. I suspect it must be because they've been together for so long. I saw the same exact thing while they were taking care of Kaylee."

"What do they do?" Lea asked her.

"Marquis and Celestia have this silent language all their own. It's as if they can read each other's minds. They finish whatever the other is doing when they take care of a baby. It's like how some couples finish each other's sentences. They work in tandem without ever needing to say a word."

"That's interesting…" Lea murmured as she headed to the kitchen. "I guess I never saw Marquis Gray as a family man, getting all spit up on and changing poopy diapers."

Mary looked thoughtful for a moment before telling Brie, "He was made to be a parent. They both were. It's like they've just been waiting all this time for an opportunity to shine."

Brie noticed the baby was stirring in Mary's arms, and nodded. "It certainly seemed that way when they were caring for Kaylee."

Lea came back holding Celestia's tray of goodies. "I know Hunter had his heart set on a passel of kids, but I'm still trying to figure out if I can handle all the disgusting things they do."

"Oh, like diapers?" Mary asked.

Lea nodded vigorously. "Exactly!"

"Well, the only way to address fears is to face them," Mary stated, holding out Caden to her. "And you happen to be in luck because he needs to be changed."

Lea's eyes widened as she stared at the infant. "No…!"

Brie took the tray from her and set it down. "Don't

worry, girlfriend. I'll walk you through it."

Lea crinkled her nose as she took the baby from Mary. "But I can't handle the smell!"

"Look, I know you've eaten ass before," Mary told her as the three of them headed to the nursery. "This doesn't even compare."

Lea whimpered back at her, "But I do that for fun…!"

After washing her hands multiple times, Lea rejoined them in the living room.

Brie took advantage of that time to hold Caden. She rocked him gently as he fell back to sleep in her arms.

"Hey, Lea, you might want to warn that Hunter fellow of yours that he'll need to collar another sub if he wants any kiddos," Mary teased her.

Lea stuck her tongue out and turned to Brie. "Did you know that Mary has the hots for a Dom with a diaper fetish?"

She looked back at Mary gleefully as she delivered the punchline to her joke, "Although Mary doesn't like it, she thinks she can change him."

Mary sucked in a deep breath, holding back her immediate response.

Brie quickly grabbed a cream cheese pinwheel from the tray and sat back to enjoy their snarky banter.

Mary planted a fake smile on her face and stared at Lea in silence for several moments. "Tell me, Lea the

Lame, when Hunter's family smiles at you, is this what it looks like?"

Lea pursed her lips and then suddenly picked up a throw pillow from the couch and whipped it at Mary's head.

"I swear," Brie laughed. "If Marquis Gray saw the way you two behave, he would send you both straight back to the Training Center."

Both girls turned on Brie with pillows raised.

"Hey, you can't hit me. I'm holding the baby!"

Lea snatched the baby from her while Mary pummeled her with a pillow.

Brie couldn't breathe, she was laughing so hard. "How juvenile can you get?"

Mary stopped for a moment and challenged her with a gleam in her eye, "Do you really want to find out?"

Brie shook her head "Nope! Absolutely not."

After several more whacks with the pillow, Mary tossed it onto the couch and grabbed two pinwheels from the tray before sitting down.

Still out of breath, Brie laughed, "Who would believe the top graduating class of the Submissive Training Center is composed of a bunch of idiots?"

"All but one…that would be me," Lea stated in a singsong voice, cooing at the baby. "Isn't that right, little Caden?"

Brie sighed with contentment. "This is exactly what my heart needed."

"So, what's happening with the film, Stinks?" Mary asked in a serious tone, popping another pinwheel in her mouth.

She let out a long sigh before answering. "I thought finishing this film would be super easy, but Michael Schmidt keeps making suggestions on how to improve it."

"That's the cinematographer, right?" Lea asked her, grabbing a pinwheel for herself. "What kind of suggestions?"

"Originally, he said he was fine with Marquis's flogging scene. But now he's insisting on including different angles."

"What's the problem with that?" Lea questioned.

Brie frowned. "Lea, I shot that with a stationary camera because I was a part of the scene. How can I seamlessly replicate something that took place years ago?"

"You'll have to scrap the original," Mary stated emphatically.

Hearing those words cut Brie like a knife. "That's what Mr. Schmidt told me, but the reason that scene is so powerful has everything to do with what was happening between Sir and me at the time."

Mary rolled her eyes. "You're going to have to remind me, Stinks. I don't keep track of your love life."

Brie gave her a sideways look but explained, "Sir was struggling with the decision of what to do with his mother after she was put on life support and was pronounced brain dead."

Lea looked at Brie compassionately. "Oh, yeah...I remember how bad it got between you."

Brie nodded sadly. "It almost tore us apart, so Marquis Gray confronted Sir on it." She shivered, remembering that night. "I'll never forget the verbal fight they had."

"But what has that to do with the film?" Mary pressed.

"Marquis Gray insisted on doing a flogging scene with me during that time. Sir wouldn't allow it unless he was present." Tears brimmed in Brie's eyes remembering how the scene played out. "The eighty-tail flogger felt incredible and made for a stunning visual on film."

"What was that like?" Lea asked with interest.

Brie laughed. "I was intimidated by how huge the flogger was, but just before the scene started, Marquis Gray whispered in my ear, 'Remember who you are.' I'm telling you, that simple statement set the tone for the entire scene…"

Smiling to herself, she shared, "The sound of Mozart filled the room, and then I heard the massive flogger when it started cutting the air…" She shivered again. "The impact of it covered my entire back, all eighty tails striking at once. It was like nothing I'd ever experienced before. Every lash was perfect and all-encompassing."

Brie looked at her friends. "I was flying on an incredible subhigh by the time he was done, and then do you know what Marquis did?"

Both of them shook their heads.

"He told Sir he didn't have time for aftercare and left the room."

Mary and Lea looked as shocked as she'd felt at the time.

"Somehow, Marquis knew that having Sir watch the scene and then forcing him to take care of me afterward would break down the wall between us." A single tear rolled down Brie's cheek when she confessed, "That moment changed everything for us."

"Marquis likes to throw those curveballs, doesn't he?" Mary stated.

Lea's eyes suddenly lit up. "Hey, Brie! I have an idea."

"Let me have it, girlfriend."

"If I recall correctly, in your original version, Marquis talked about the importance of trust."

"That's right!" Brie sat up straighter, impressed that she remembered.

"Well, what if you film it again, but from the opposite side of the room to represent two perspectives, then you can each talk about the scene from a Dominant's and a submissive's point of view. That way, you won't have to lose the intensity of the original scene, but you can supplement it with the new angle and perspective."

Brie stared at her in amazement. "Lea, that's brilliant!"

Mary glanced at Lea, pretending not to be impressed. "Eh...it's not bad."

Lea laughed at her. "You're just jealous I'm smarter than you and thought of it first."

"Nope, not jealous of you in the least. But I *am* jealous of Stinks, here. Getting the opportunity to experience that eighty-tale flogger with Marquis Gray a second time? You're one lucky bitch, that's all I can say."

Her brain hadn't registered the reality that she'd be scening with Marquis again until Mary mentioned it. It had been years since she'd felt the invigorating thud of his flogger....

"I'll ask Sir first before I present the idea to Mr. Schmidt of course. But thank you, Lea!" She grinned. "I feel like a huge weight has been lifted off."

Lea beamed. "Anytime, girlfriend!"

"Well, we're curing Lea's distaste for disgusting babies, and you just got the answer you needed for your documentary. So let's concentrate all that energy on me," Mary insisted, pointing to herself with both hands.

Brie readjusted her position on the couch, so she was completely facing Mary and giving her all of her attention. "Okay, shoot. What do you need, woman?"

"As you know, I've been seriously creeped out about inheriting Holloway's blood money. And the only thing I can think to do with all that cash is to divide it between every person rescued from the compound."

"That's a great idea!" Lea agreed with enthusiasm. "That asshole was going to use it for his own evil purpose, but you can make something good come from it."

Mary looked at Brie. "What do you think, Stinks?"

Although Brie liked the idea, she had reservations about it. "I'm just worried, knowing how badly they were traumatized. We're all still recovering from the physical and psychological damage he caused."

Mary frowned deeply, informing her, "We lost another one to suicide two weeks ago. What if that money could have saved her?"

"Or, what if it sends them over the edge, Mary?" Brie countered. "Such a huge lump of money might end up ruining their lives. I worry about people swindling them out of the money or worse…in their current mental state, they might end up dying of an overdose just to escape the pain." Thoughts of Tatianna suddenly came to Brie's mind, knowing the pain had become too much for her even though Rytsar rescued her.

Mary nodded solemnly. "I've thought about that, too."

Brie sighed heavily, and the three sat in silence thinking about it for the next few minutes.

"You know, I remember Rytsar telling me about his brothers once. How he had to be creative in the ways he helped them financially so it wouldn't become a curse for them. I highly recommend you call him, Mary. I'm certain he could help you figure out a workable solution to distribute the money in a way that would truly benefit them."

Mary looked at her gratefully. "Thanks, Stinks."

Brie noticed that Lea was distracted, tickling the baby's tummy to make him smile.

"You know why they named him Caden?" Mary asked them.

Brie took the bait. "Why?"

"Marquis and Celestia asked me to name the boy."

Lea looked up. "That's such an amazing honor."

Brie smiled at Mary. "Why Caden?"

"It means 'spirit in battle'. Since the kid already survived the loss of his mother, I wanted him to have a name to reflect his warrior spirit."

"It's a beautiful name," Lea told her, looking down at the baby and smiling.

Brie was surprised when Lea's face suddenly twisted

into an unreadable expression.

"Don't tell me," Mary said, laughing. "The little warrior needs his diaper changed again."

Lea looked at them both, her eyes watering as she tried desperately not to gag.

"Let me give you some sage advice when you change him this time," Mary instructed her. "If the baby's legs turn blue, it's too tight. If they turn brown, it's too loose."

"How can you joke at a time like this?" Lea cried, rushing back to the nursery.

Mary smirked at Brie. "You heard it here, Stinks. The self-proclaimed 'Queen of Jokes' just admitted there are times when jokes are *not* appreciated."

Mary then called out. "Hey, Lea. I got another one for ya! Knock, knock…"

Quiet Heroes

Brie was headed home after an exhausting day of back-to-back meetings. She hadn't been able to convince Michael Schmidt to embrace Lea's unconventional idea of the dual Dom/sub perspective to enhance Marquis's flogging scene. However, Brie still held out hope that his resistance was starting to crumble.

The only thing on her mind as she drove through the stop-and-go traffic was getting back to the house so she could jump into a hot, relaxing bath and unwind.

When her cell phone rang, she casually glanced over and was surprised to see that Faelan was trying to video chat with her. She hadn't heard a peep from him ever since he flew across the country to confront Mrs. Fisher.

When she didn't respond, he killed the chat request.

With her curiosity piqued, Brie decided to take the very next exit off the highway and headed to the nearest convenience store parking lot. She parked her car under the shade of a tree, wanting to fully concentrate on her conversation with Faelan without endangering anyone on the road.

Hitting the video chat button, she waited nervously for him to answer, concerned it might be bad news.

"I was wondering if you would pick up." Faelan looked and sounded agitated, which did not bode well.

"Is everything okay?" she asked.

"No! And I really can't take it anymore…"

"Oh no!" Brie cried, clutching her phone anxiously. "What happened?"

"Mary happened!"

Brie frowned, unprepared for his answer. "I thought you were talking about Mrs. Fisher."

"I am…" he growled.

"Wait. What do you mean?"

"I told Mary what happened, and she refuses to let it go!"

"Let what go?" she asked fearfully.

He just shook his head, looking more agitated than before.

"Faelan, you're going to have to calm down and explain yourself. I have no clue what you're talking about."

"I swear, Brie, if you react like she did, I'm going to lose it."

She could see he was teetering on the emotional edge and did her best to calm him. "Look, there's no way for me to know how I'm going to react unless you tell me what happened."

He had a pained look on his face when he said, "Things did not go the way I expected with Mrs. Fisher."

"Okay…is that good or bad?"

He laughed ruefully. "That's a question I don't really

know how to answer."

"You're killing me with the cryptic answers."

"Fine," he said, frowning. "So, I pulled up to her house, and I was ready to go all apeshit on the woman. After everything my family went through…knowing the part the Fishers played in the destruction of our lives *after* they learned the truth about their own son…" He glanced away, his eyes dark and moody.

Brie groaned, already envisioning the yelling match.

"I should have been surprised that she was living in such a rundown part of town, but I really didn't give a rat's ass at the time because I was too revved up on adrenaline. In fact, I couldn't stop my hand from shaking when I rang the doorbell."

"This isn't sounding good…"

"It wasn't," he said, rolling his eyes. "It took that woman ages to get to the door, and each passing second only gave me more time to brood over the injustices my family has suffered because of her silence."

Brie's stomach twisted in knots. "Faelan, just tell me what happened when she answered the door."

He snarled in irritation as he retold that moment, "I stood there and watched the doorknob turn so damn slow I was ready to grab it and wrench the door open myself." His voice suddenly dropped when he said, "And then I saw her…"

When Faelan didn't say anything more, her fears grew. "Oh God, Faelan, what did you do?"

"Mrs. Fisher was so bony and frail, Brie…I don't think I've ever seen a woman as fragile as that." He looked at her, letting out a ragged sigh. "I swear the moment we were face to face, all the fight completely drained out of me."

Brie was surprised, remembering the heated conversation he'd had at Marquis Gray's house recently. "What did you tell her?"

"Nothing…at first. I just stared at her in shock. It was obvious the old woman had no clue who I was, and you won't believe what she said next."

"I can't imagine."

He had a devastated look on his face when he mimicked the old woman's voice, "'You look like such a fine young man…'" Faelan shook his head and said in a broken voice, "Mrs. Fisher even invited me to come in and offered to make me a sandwich, Brie."

Faelan covered his face and groaned. "Fuck…I wasn't prepared for that. Not for how frail she was or for the way she greeted me, thinking I was a complete stranger. Hell, I could have had bad intentions toward her…"

He looked at Brie, laughing ruefully. "Actually, I did."

"What did you do after that, Faelan?" she asked breathlessly.

"I told her who I was."

She gripped the phone more tightly. "How did she react?"

"The old woman just tilted her head and smiled." Mimicking her voice again, he repeated her words, "'Your parents must be so proud to have such a respectable young man for a son. I don't get many visitors. Please come in and let me fix you something to eat, dear.'"

Brie gaped before saying, "She really had no idea who you were, then?"

"There wasn't even a spark of recognition in Mrs. Fisher's eyes."

"Oh, wow." Brie couldn't imagine how difficult it must have been for Faelan to finally confront the person who had wronged him and then to have that happen…

Faelan gritted his teeth when he told her, "I was caught completely off guard and had no clue what to do. So…I followed her inside."

Her heart started to race. "Please don't tell me you did something foolish."

Snarling irritably, he said, "According to Mary, I did."

"Why? What happened?" Brie asked, hardly able to breathe.

"Her place was tiny but looked like a perfectly pre-served museum from fifty years ago. Even though this woman could barely walk, the few possessions she had were dusted and in their place…including portraits of her husband and Trevor, sitting on a small bookshelf."

Brie's stomach sank as she imagined the scene play-ing out in her head. "How did you feel when you saw those pictures?"

"God…" He stared at her, looking bereft. "Seeing their smiling faces staring back at me was fucking surreal. I mean, as much as I hated what Mr. Fisher did to my family, I killed that kid staring back at me from the bookshelf. When Mrs. Fisher caught me looking at their photos, she smiled at me and told me their names, saying that they were waiting for her in heaven."

Faelan paused for a moment, then growled in disgust. "I just sat there in her tiny kitchen like an idiot, Brie. I felt completely numb inside as I watched the tiny woman take food from a sparse pantry and make me a baloney sandwich."

Brie's heart broke hearing that. "Did you end up confronting her, Faelan?" she asked softly.

"No," he muttered. "I didn't see any point. The woman in front of me was lost in her own little world. Sure, I could have laid into her. Heck, if I had wanted to, I could have beaten her to a pulp and no one would have been the wiser. But what good would it have done? I know my family would have been horrified, and it wouldn't have changed what happened in the past."

Brie was relieved to hear that and told him, "You did the right thing."

"Oh, yeah?" he snorted angrily. "Well, Mary sure doesn't think so. She's been calling me every day since, insisting that she fly back with me so she can confront the woman if I won't."

Brie took a moment to reply. "Mary has been wronged so many times in her life without gaining any resolution. Although I believe she has your best interests at heart, I think her reaction may be more about her needing a resolution that she can never have."

"Huh…I never thought about it like that." Faelan looked away from the camera, lost in thought.

"Honestly, most people would agree with Mary. Mrs. Fisher should be held accountable and made to pay for your family's suffering. However, the only people that matter in this are you and your family. You are the only ones who should have any say in what that restitution looks like."

He smiled sadly. "Funny you mention that. I talked to my parents and Lisa before I left to see her. Not one of them wanted me to confront her, afraid that I would only be stirring a hornet's nest. All three insisted they didn't want her money. But I didn't give a fuck what they said. I thought I knew what was best for them and I was certain of that right up until that frail, wisp of a woman, opened the door."

"It sounds like you followed the right voice just like Marquis Gray advised."

Faelan huffed, shaking his head slowly. "Maybe…but I'm feeling like a real chump now. Hell, before I left her house, I even offered to take the trash out for Mrs. Fisher. I mean, a real man wouldn't do that shit," he snarled in disgust.

Brie laughed at his statement. "It sounds to me like that's exactly what Kylie would have wanted you to do. She didn't have a mean bone in her body. I bet she'd be extremely proud of how you handled yourself with Mrs. Fisher."

"Fuck you, Brie…" he muttered darkly, glancing away. "You always insist on bringing up Kylie when you know how much it hurts me."

Brie said in a quiet voice, "I never mean to hurt you, Faelan."

He shook his head in disbelief. "Mary slams me for being a pussy and you fucking stab me in the heart by bringing up Kylie."

Brie frowned. "Do you really want me to stop talking about her?"

"No," he groaned miserably, then met her gaze. "But it still rips my heart."

Brie looked at him in compassion. "Since my intention is not to hurt you, let me change the perspective. When you think of your little girl, how does that make you feel?"

She could hear the difference in his tone when he said, "I love Kaylee more than life itself. That's not some fucking platitude. I seriously mean it. I would die to protect her."

"I know you would, Faelan. So, when you think of your daughter, what would she be prouder of? That her daddy beat up an old woman and sued her for whatever pennies she had left, or that her daddy showed mercy to a frail elderly woman who can't remember her past?"

Faelan rolled his eyes, growling under his breath, "I still feel like a wuss."

"A wuss would have thrown a punch and then justified it," Brie insisted. "It takes a real man to recognize the truth and not act."

When he didn't respond, she added, "Seriously, Faelan. You know she's proud of you."

A text from Sir suddenly popped up on her phone.

After reading it, she apologized to Faelan. "I'm sorry, but I have to go. I've been sitting in a parking lot talking to you, and now Sir's worried because I'm late coming home."

"Pass on my apologies to him," he said.

Before she hung up, she asked hesitantly, "Faelan…?"

"What?"

"If you never get the restitution you deserve, what will you do?"

He grunted, looking as if she'd socked him in the gut. "That's exactly what I'm facing, Brie. And, to be honest, I don't have a fucking clue."

When Brie finally arrived home, she dropped her purse just inside the entrance, tossed her keys in the candy dish, and leaned against the door. "Oh, man…what a long day."

"Mommy!" Hope cried.

Brie couldn't see her just then, but smiled when she heard her daughter's little footsteps running to greet her. When Hope rounded the corner, Brie bent down with her arms spread wide and swooped her up in her arms. "How are you, sweet pea?"

Sir walked up to her, looking at Brie with sympathy. "I can tell you've had a rough day by the expression on your face."

She gave him a weary smile. "It was certainly tough to get through."

"Any progress with Gray's scene?"

"No, but I'm beginning to wear Michael down…" She moved Hope to her hip and raised one fist in the air, stating comically. "I believe in me!"

"That's my girl," Sir chuckled, leaning in to kiss her

on the lips.

When Hope started making kissing noises, Brie giggled in the middle of their kiss.

Sir pulled away with a grin. "Why don't you change into something comfortable and join me on the couch? We can watch *Totoro* with the children while I rub your back."

"That sounds divine, Sir…thank you. But what about dinner?"

"Actually, Baron invited us to his place tonight. He mentioned that he has a submissive he'd like you to meet. I've arranged for your parents to watch the kids, but if you're too exhausted, I'll call to reschedule while you change. I know Baron will understand."

Brie perked up the moment she heard Baron's name. She hadn't seen him since their touching session together at his place, when he'd helped her embrace the feeling of freedom again while under the safety of his care. She remembered how powerful that night had been for her emotional recovery.

Smiling at Sir, she said, "I'm familiar with the power of your touch, so I'm certain I'll be fine to attend dinner after a backrub."

He winked at her, taking Hope from her arms. "If you're sure…"

"I am," she stated confidently, turning to head down the hallway. She thought it was humorous how she'd gone from being completely exhausted to suddenly excited about the evening ahead.

It just went to show how life was all about perspective.

On the drive over to Baron's house, Sir explained that Baron was concerned about the particular sub that he was asking Brie to meet. Sir then shared that Baron had originally found the woman living on the streets. It had taken him weeks to gain her trust enough for her to attend one of their weekly classes. However, she still remained aloof and distrustful.

"Baron believes you may be able to bridge the gap."

"Why me, Sir?"

He furrowed his brow. "Baron suspects she may have been subjected to extreme punishment and abuse based on her reactions to him, as well as her interactions with the other submissives. However, she has shared little of her past with him, so he is basing that purely on his own observation and instincts."

Brie completely trusted Baron's instincts and told Sir, "I've never forgotten how he saved me at the Kinky Goat. He has always had a heart to help those who are being abused or mistreated."

Sir nodded and stated solemnly, "I will always be grateful to Baron for protecting you that night."

Brie reached over and squeezed his hand.

When they arrived, Brie noticed there were several cars parked in the driveway. "Wait. I thought this was a private dinner."

Sir smiled. "Candy and Captain were also invited."

She squeaked in excitement. "Oh, my goodness! I get to see them, too?"

Chuckling, he explained, "Baron wanted to bring us all together."

As soon as Brie got out of the car, she rushed up to the door and rang the doorbell. Stepping back, she waited anxiously with Sir.

Opening the door, Baron stated with a welcoming smile, "Well, hello, Sir Davis," then turned to Brie, "…and Mrs. Davis."

Brie grinned at him. "It's wonderful to see you again, Baron."

"Likewise," he replied, gesturing for them to enter. As she walked inside, he told her, "You look well."

"I am," she responded. "And I continue to face each day with courage."

He nodded in approval. "You wear that bravery well."

"I owe part of that to you, Baron."

He shook his head. "I only acted as a catalyst. You alone are the source of your power."

She bowed to him. "Thank you for helping me to see that."

Gracing her with a warm smile, he said, "Anytime, Mrs. Davis."

Brie followed him to the kitchen, where she saw Captain and Candy were busy preparing a Caesar salad from scratch. She noticed a young woman standing in the far corner, watching the two silently.

The woman's face was strikingly beautiful and framed by long box braids. But the instant Brie entered the room, she could feel fear radiating off the woman. When Baron walked up to introduce them, the woman immediately gazed down at the floor.

"Mrs. Davis, this is Shanice," Baron began. "Shanice, this is the lady I spoke to you about earlier. She is a good friend and someone I admire."

Brie blushed on hearing his praise and held out her hand to Shanice. "It's nice to meet—" Feeling the woman's fear increase, she stopped midsentence and immediately put her hand down by her side.

Rather than make Shanice any more uncomfortable, Brie took a step back. "I look forward to eating dinner with you tonight." Brie purposely worded her simple greeting so it required no response. She didn't want Shanice to feel any pressure to speak when it was obvious that she was struggling with tonight's social interaction.

Brie agreed with Baron's assessment that Shanice had experienced severe trauma. Based on her reaction just now, Brie feared she'd endured unspeakable suffering and her heart immediately went out to Shanice.

Understanding that she needed space and time to adjust to having strangers present, Brie smiled at her before walking over to Captain and Candy.

Giving Candy a big hug, she gushed, "I didn't know you were coming. This is a wonderful surprise."

"I was excited when Baron invited us to join you tonight," Candy said, hugging her back.

Captain put down the chef knife he was using and turned to Brie. "You are certainly looking well, Mrs. Davis."

"Thank you, Captain," she said, smiling at the kind man. "I have so much to be grateful for." She reached out to touch his arm. "I'll never be able to repay you for helping to rescue all of us at the compound."

Brie noticed that Shanice briefly glanced up and stared at Captain, her expression unreadable.

"You owe me nothing," he stated gruffly. "I simply aided Sir Davis where I could."

"You risked your life for us," Brie reminded him.

He shook his head and said gravely, "I witnessed firsthand the suffering you and the survivors endured at that godforsaken place. I would have considered it an honor to die trying to protect each and every one of you."

"You're a true hero, Captain," Brie stated softly.

He shook his head curtly. "No. I am just an ordinary man."

"A *good* man," she insisted, suddenly overcome with emotion.

Candy wrapped her arms around him. "The best!"

Captain shook his head. "No reason to get sappy, ladies." Picking up the knife, he went back to chopping.

During dinner, Brie purposely shared some of her experiences as a captive, as well as the steps she'd taken after the rescue to heal from the trauma. She emphasized how vital Sir and her friends had been in aiding in her recovery. Brie hoped that in some small way, it might help Shanice understand that she was not alone and there was hope for a better future.

As they were readying to leave, Shanice walked up to her. Without making eye contact, she said in a whisper almost too faint to hear, "Can we talk?"

Brie set her purse down. "Of course."

Baron suggested they go to his office for privacy. After Brie shut the door, she asked Shanice, "Would you like to sit?"

"No," the woman blurted, then lowered her eyes. "I will stand."

"Okay," Brie replied in a gentle voice as she sat down on a nearby chair. She wondered if sitting made Shanice feel trapped. If a person were standing, it gave them the option to escape at any moment.

"I heard what you said at the table," she began, her gaze still lowered. "I…"

Brie said nothing, waiting for her to speak again.

"I don't feel safe."

"With me?"

She shook her head.

"With Baron?"

Again, she shook her head. "Ever."

Brie took in the immensity of that statement and nodded. "I felt that way, too—once."

Shanice looked up, her eyes pleading for help. But then she glanced away and frowned.

Realizing that eye contact felt threatening to Shanice, she suggested, "What if I turn away from you so you can say whatever you want? I won't ask questions. I'll just listen." She paused for a moment. "After I was rescued, I found it therapeutic to simply voice the nightmare I'd experienced out loud."

Understanding how vulnerable she must feel, Brie added, "Anything you say will be kept in the strictest confidence. I won't tell anyone. Your experience is only yours to share."

When Shanice didn't respond, Brie looked at her with compassion. "Would you like to try that?"

She nodded slowly.

Brie turned away from her and waited.

It crushed her heart to hear the extent of Shanice's abuse, and she let the silent tears roll down her cheeks as Shanice voiced out loud the torment and agony she'd suffered. When the woman finally fell silent, Brie wiped away her tears before turning around to face her again.

Shanice stared at Brie, her eyes wide open like a frightened deer caught in headlights.

Brie simply nodded, acknowledging every word she had spoken, and looked at her compassionately. She then stood up slowly, careful not to startle Shanice by moving too fast.

Although the horrors Shanice experienced were much different from her own, Brie understood the destruction they had wreaked on her soul.

Realizing the importance of this moment for Shanice, Brie told her, "Today, by sharing what happened, you reclaimed a part of yourself."

Boldly meeting her gaze, Shanice nodded.

Butterflies

"I have a special evening planned for us tonight."

Brie swung around in her computer chair and smiled up at Sir. "Oh, I love the sound of that, Sir. Where are we going?"

He pulled two tickets out of his shirt pocket and handed them to her. Brie's eyes widened when she saw they were tickets to his favorite opera, *Madame Butterfly*.

Popping out of her chair, Brie threw her arms around him. "Thank you, Sir!"

Drawing back, Brie smiled as she stared at the tickets while heated memories of her first night at the opera with Sir flooded her mind. "I can't believe how long it's been. I was just a student at the Submissive Training Center back then…"

"I thought we could enjoy a trip down memory lane together." He cupped her cheek. "However, tonight will end very differently for you."

She gazed up into his eyes, remembering the thrill—and the heartbreak—of that evening when he'd played the role of her Khan. Tracing his sexy bottom lip with her finger, she asked teasingly, "Will a 'priest' be joining us tonight?" referring to her journal fantasy that had inspired that memorable night.

"No priests will be present," he replied with a smirk. "I want you to watch the entirety of the performance."

Brie sighed, pretending to be disappointed. "No extra-curricular activities in the theater box, then?"

"I didn't say that, babygirl," he answered with a seductive grin, leaning down to kiss her on the neck. "But tonight, it will just be the two of us."

Brie's pussy contracted in pleasure the moment she felt the erotic pressure of his lips on her throat. He already had her panties wet by the time he broke his embrace.

She looked at him and whimpered, "How can I possibly concentrate on my work now?"

Sir winked at her as he headed back downstairs to his office.

Wanting to replicate what she privately considered their first official "date," Brie chose an elegant gown of gold and slipped on six-inch heels. Underneath her gown, she wore a black lace lingerie set.

Sir followed her lead and wore a dark gray suit similar to the one he had worn on that night years ago.

Brie smiled as she watched him adjust his tie. "I feel nervous butterflies already, just like I did that night."

"Good," he answered.

When there was a knock on the door, Sir insisted on answering it. Brie was surprised to see Rytsar walk in carrying a fur coat, which he promptly handed to Sir. He then gave Brie a private grin before turning to the children.

"Watch out for your *dyadya*. He's a big, bad Kodiak, and he is about to gobble you up for a snack."

Hope let out a high-pitched squeal and started racing around the house. Antony crawled away as fast as he could when Rytsar started taking slow-motion steps toward him. After chasing the kids for several minutes amid squeals of laughter, Rytsar swooped both of them into his arms.

He glanced at Sir as he headed for the front door to leave with the children. "Have fun, *moy droog*. I expect a full accounting in the morning."

Sir chuckled. "A gentleman never kisses and tells, old friend."

"Sir, you are no gentleman," Rytsar countered as he left.

Brie covered her giggles.

Sir turned to Brie. He set the fur down and motioned her to come to him. When she did, he wrapped his arms around her waist and slowly hiked her dress up inch by inch. Finally, he grasped her buttocks with both hands and murmured, "Such a fine ass, babygirl…"

He then peeled off her black lace panties and tossed them to the floor. "You won't be needing these tonight."

"Yes, Sir," she agreed excitedly.

"Turn away from me," he commanded in a sultry

tone.

Brie purred as she turned, knowing what was coming next...

Sir took her wrists and bound them together behind her back with a length of black satin. She then felt the soft caress of the fur on her shoulders as he hid her bound wrists from view with the long coat.

"My elegant property," Sir whispered, causing goosebumps to rise on her skin. Placing his arm around her, Sir guided her out the front door, where she found a limousine waiting for them at the curb.

Once in the limo, Sir sat beside Brie, keeping his arm wrapped around her possessively as they rode in silence to the theater. She basked in the feeling of intimacy his presence inspired. Her excitement only increased when the limousine pulled up to the theater entrance.

Brie felt a familiar thrill the moment Sir helped her out of the vehicle. She knew no one around them suspected that she was bound underneath the luxurious fur she was wearing. Holding her head up proudly but at a respectful angle, Brie followed Sir as he led her into the opulent theater.

She was surprised and touched when the attendant took them to the same private box they'd watched the performance from before. "You thought of everything, Sir!"

He smiled as he sat down beside her and gently slid the fur off her shoulders, setting it aside. After untying her wrists, Sir gave her a tender kiss on the lips.

Brie sat beside him, scanning the large auditorium as she looked at all the elegant people dressed up for the evening. The constant din of hundreds of people talking all at once suddenly quieted the moment the lights dimmed.

Sir leaned in and asked, "Are you ready to have your heart broken?"

Brie's heart raced as the curtains went up and the first scene began with Lieutenant Pinkerton of the U.S. Navy. He was inspecting a house overlooking Nagasaki harbor, which he was leasing from Goro, the marriage broker…

While Brie loved the lavish costumes and elaborate sets, she was utterly transfixed by the soulful voice of the heroine as she expressed her love for her husband. The fact that he was indifferent to her made it utterly heart-breaking.

Brie was pleasantly surprised when, during the second act, Sir reached into his jacket and pulled out a velvet box. She smiled when she recognized the long strand of pearls he held in his hand. They were the very same pearls he'd given her that night as her Khan.

"Hold these," he murmured seductively, placing the pearls in her hands. Sir then moved the chairs to the side and commanded Brie to lie down on her back.

Brie eagerly complied, loving the naughty thrill of a public scene. Clutching the pearls against her chest, she waited breathlessly while she watched Sir unbutton his jacket. The darkness of the theater gave the illusion of privacy even though anyone sitting in the adjacent boxes could observe them if they were to stand up during the performance.

Sir lay down beside Brie before taking the pearls

from her. "Hike up your dress so your pussy is fully exposed to your Master, téa."

Hearing her pet name sent exhilarating shivers through Brie. Anxious to obey, she lifted her hips and sensually inched the hem of the dress up to bare herself to him.

Sir watched in rapt attention, his eyes burning with desire in the faint light. Taking the strand of pearls, he placed them on either side of her clit and then pulled the necklace taut so that the pearls caressed both sides of her sensitive clit.

Slowly pulling the strand downward, Sir caused each individual pearl to rub against her clit as it passed. It was incredibly erotic, and she squirmed in pleasure. When Sir reached the end of the strand, he repositioned the necklace again and slowly dragged it down a second time. Brie moaned in ecstasy, momentarily forgetting where she was.

"Shh…" he cautioned.

Brie bit her lip, not wanting his sensuous torture to end. Sir indulged her, making several more passes before he held up the strand of pearls and twisted them once. "Lift your head, téa," he ordered, then carefully placed the pearls around her neck.

She could smell a trace of her excitement lingering on the jewelry, which turned her on. Then she heard Sir undoing his belt and unzipping his pants, and her pussy became dripping wet. She just knew he was about to claim her to the sound of the opera singer's beautiful voice.

Brie held her breath as Sir positioned himself above

her. Spreading her legs wide, he slowly pushed the length of his cock inside her. It was so decadent and daring to be making love when there were so many people around them.

But Brie forgot about the rest of the world when Sir pressed his lips against hers. She returned his ardent kiss, wrapping her arms around his neck, as she freely gave in to his carnal passion.

Her Master explored her body with his hands while taking her deep with his cock. Brie reveled in every thrust of his shaft, not wanting him to stop. But, the moment she heard his low masculine groan, she completely lost control. With no way to prevent it, she embraced her orgasm, squeezing his shaft with each pulse of her climax.

Rather than reprimanding her for coming without permission, Sir responded by pumping into her harder and faster, as he joined her with his own release.

The two lay there afterward, breathing heavily as they listened to the singer's exquisite voice ringing through the theater as she finished another song.

"Hurry," Sir suddenly warned. "We don't have much time."

Brie rushed to pull down her dress while Sir stood up and zipped his pants. Holding out his hand to her, Brie took it, and he quickly hoisted her to her feet at the same time the lights turned back on, announcing the final intermission.

Sir smirked as he nonchalantly buckled his belt. After putting the chairs back, he gestured for Brie to sit with him again.

Chuckling lightly, he told her, "That was a little too close for comfort."

Brie giggled when an attendant pulled back the curtain just seconds later, asking if he could fetch them a drink during the intermission.

Sir held up two fingers. "We'd like two martinis."

"Certainly, sir," the man replied, closing the curtain again.

Brie felt sensual butterflies fluttering in her stomach, still flying high from the sexy encounter and the thrill of almost being caught.

Before the lights dimmed for the final act, Sir sat back in his seat, sipping his martini, and told her, "The end of *Madame Butterfly* is exceedingly tragic, babygirl."

She sighed nervously, never having seen the opera in its entirety before. "I've heard that before and I'm a little scared. I hate sad endings."

"Remember, babygirl, even in pain there is beauty."

"I'll keep that in mind," she promised.

As she waited for the lights to dim, Brie was overcome with a sense of wonder as she stared at Sir. That first night when she sat next to him in this very booth, she'd fought her intense feelings for him.

It seemed impossible that she was sitting here now as his wife and submissive. It was a beautiful miracle.

Admiring him in the dark, Brie was gripped by the immense love she felt for the man, deeply impressed that he had faithfully kept his vow to her at the Collaring Ceremony. Sir had guided her with thoughtfulness and understanding, encouraging her to grow as both a person and as a submissive.

Over the years, he'd constantly kept her on her toes, providing her with a myriad of experiences that most submissives could only ever dream of. That alone was reason enough to be madly in love with the man. But Sir hadn't stopped there.

Oh, no.

Thane Davis was a condor. When he'd claimed her heart, he had simultaneously surrendered his—fully committing to her emotionally until the end of time. Brie was secure in his love for her and knew without question that he would do everything in his power to keep her and their children safe from all harm.

That night many years ago had ended badly because she had mistakenly blurted out the word "love" in front of him. As a result, he'd cut the evening short, and she believed all was lost.

Brie now knew that Sir had been fighting the same feelings for her but had denied them out of a need to protect her. Knowing that only made her love him that much more.

Brie turned her attention back to the opera, readying herself for a tragic ending. When it finally came, and she watched Butterfly commit *jisatsu* from behind a screen, Brie burst into tears, feeling the immense pain of her loss.

When Sir noticed Brie crying, he reached out to wipe the tears from her face. Pulling her to him, he let her curl up in his lap while he held her tight. Brie gratefully laid her head against his chest, cherishing this sad but beautiful moment with him.

At the end of the performance, Brie stood up with

Sir and clapped enthusiastically. The entire theater filled with a round of applause, and it continued even after the performers made their final bow.

While everyone began to file out of their boxes, Sir turned her around and bound her wrists once again—the act a beautiful reminder that she was his beloved submissive. Draping the fur over her shoulders, he led her out of the private box and into the throngs of patrons.

Brie blinked in response to the brightness of the lights, the transition from the opera's tragic story to real life taking her a moment to adjust to. Sir deftly guided her outside to the limousine, which was dutifully waiting for them at the curb. Sir spoiled Brie on the ride home by playing with her hair the entire trip. Feeling his fingers comb through her hair was almost orgasmic, and she never wanted it to end...

Once they arrived home, Sir walked her inside and immediately removed the fur coat. He then unbound her wrists in silence. After helping Brie out of her six-inch heels, he rubbed her feet for several moments before unzipping her dress and removing her bra. After he had her completely naked, Sir picked Brie up and carried her to the bedroom.

Laying her on the bed, he stripped down and joined her there.

That night, Sir made slow, passionate love to her, covering her body with soulful kisses and gentle caresses. Their connection went far beyond the bonds of Master and submissive or husband and wife. The two soared as condors, intimately uniting on an emotional level they had never experienced before.

Asher's Gift

B rie was thrilled when Michael Schmidt finally broke down and gave her the go-ahead to film the second perspective of Marquis Gray's flogging scene. She immediately called the trainer and was grateful when he was quick to schedule the session with her.

When Brie spoke to Sir about filming the scene, she assured him, "There is no need for you to attend this one, Sir. I know how demanding your work schedule is right now."

He stopped typing on his computer and turned to face her. "This is the same scene you filmed with Gray, shot from your perspective, correct?"

"Yes, Sir."

"It stands to reason that you will need to create the same environment if you wish to produce a believable reproduction of the original scene."

"Absolutely," she agreed. "I've been studying the scene for weeks and know every detail, down to the minuscule expressions on my face," she said with a laugh.

"Authenticity will be the key to reenacting this scene. I understand that. Therefore, I will join you as an observer, just as I did on that day."

She looked at him, stunned.

"Why the surprised look, babygirl?" he said with a chuckle. "I support you and want nothing to impede the success of your work."

"I didn't want to impose…" she began, then stopped herself and smiled at him. Accepting his heartfelt support of her film, she simply said, "Thank you, Sir."

His warm smile was her reward. "So, tell me, Mrs. Davis. What time are you meeting with Gray so I can pencil you in?"

Even though she had been anticipating it, Brie felt jittery.

There was something different about this scene. She had not submitted to Marquis Gray's dominance in years. That alone was significant. Additionally, the two-handed flogger he had used for the original scene—and would again use for this one—was a massive and intimidating beast with eighty tails, each leather tail being twenty inches long.

As soon as Sir· pulled the Lotus into the Training Center parking lot, Brie felt her anxiety ramp up.

"How are you doing, babygirl?"

She smiled at him nervously, playing with the white orchid in her hair. "There's so much riding on today's scene, Sir. If I don't get this right, Marquis's flogging scene will be completely cut from the documentary. I'd hate that because it is one of my favorites."

Sir got out of the sports car and walked around to open her door. Taking Brie's hand, he helped her out of the vehicle while telling her, "Don't walk into this scene fearful of the outcome. It is important that you are fully immersed in the experience."

Brie stopped where she stood. "That is very…" She paused, barely stopping herself in time before blurting the forbidden word "wise," and said instead, "…sound advice, Sir."

He looked at her, a smirk playing across his lips.

Once inside the building, they headed to the elevator. Sir nodded to Rachael Dunningham as they walked past.

"Good afternoon, Mr. Davis," she said formally, then called out, "Break a leg, Mrs. Davis!"

Brie waved back at her. "Thank you, Rachael!"

As the elevator headed down, Brie was relieved to find her confidence returning. The Submissive Training Center felt like home to her. Within these very walls, she had discovered who she was. Here, she came to understand that most of the limits she'd had were not based on legitimate fear but simply a fear of the unknown.

This time was no different.

Today's scene was not a chance to fail but a chance to soar. Meeting it with anything less than that understanding would be like clipping her own wings.

As she stepped out of the elevator and started down the hallway with Sir, Brie felt her confidence increasing. Sir escorted her to the room where the scene would take place and opened the door, telling her, "Trust your instincts, babygirl."

Brie smiled. "I will, Sir."

She was excited to see that Marquis Gray was already in the room, setting up his tools for the scene. He stopped what he was doing and held out his hand to Sir. "Good afternoon, Sir Davis. I was pleasantly surprised when Brianna informed me you would be joining us today."

Shaking his hand, Sir replied, "I'm grateful to be here under different circumstances than the first time."

"Ah, yes," Marquis Gray said with a knowing smile. "There was quite a bit of tension between you and me, as I recall."

"Indeed."

Turning his attention to Brie, Marquis Gray said, "Before we begin, I would like to watch the scene again so I can see my skill level at the time. I have improved since, but I wouldn't want that to be too evident."

"Of course," she replied. "Let me set up my camera while you finish setting out your tools. We can go over it together."

Having already taped the floor where the camera needed to be placed, it didn't take Brie long to set up all of her equipment. She hit record, checking to make sure the angle was right.

"Brianna," Marquis called out. "I'm unsure if I have every item we used in the original scene.

"Be right there." Brie grabbed her laptop so they could review the original scene together and verify the tools. Once Marquis felt comfortable to begin filming,

Brie asked to see the eighty-tailed flogger again.

"Do you mean Goliath?" Marquis asked.

Brie giggled. "Is that what you named it?"

Marquis Gray flashed a rare smile. "I thought it was appropriate. Don't you agree?" He walked to the table and picked up the impressive-looking flogger and brought it over to her.

Brie's heart skipped a beat when she saw it again. She had forgotten how truly intimidating it was.

"Touch it," Marquis Gray insisted. "It's important that you re-familiarize yourself with the instrument."

Brie obediently ran her fingers down the length of the long tails. The suede leather was soft to the touch, but she knew it would have a completely different affect when it connected with her skin.

She didn't even realize she'd unconsciously shuddered until Marquis told her, "There is nothing to fear, pearl."

Brie looked up at him, laughing uneasily.

"Do you remember the feel of it on your back?" he asked her.

She nodded. "I remember that I liked it." Then she smiled as she thought back on the scene. "A lot."

He nodded. "I remember."

Brie touched the flogger again, still unable to shake off the uneasiness she felt. "I'm unsure why I feel so nervous."

"From what Sir Davis shared, this would be your first time scening with a flogger since you were rescued from the compound."

Brie shot a glance at Sir. He was watching her intently from the other side of the room. She suddenly realized that he was not here simply for moral support. Sir understood her better than she did herself, and he knew this scene might prove challenging for her.

Snorting, she admitted to Marquis, "I guess I've been so concerned about the documentary that I hadn't even thought about it."

"Your laser focus can sometimes blind you, Brianna," Marquis Gray stated.

Brie looked at him sheepishly and chuckled. "Truer words have never been spoken."

"I have a suggestion for you."

"Please. I'm all ears."

"Hold this," he stated, placing the heavy flogger in her hands. "We both are aware of how important this shoot is to you. However, there is no reason it must happen today."

When she opened her mouth to protest, he held up his hand. "What if we were to play out the scene as we planned—but without the camera rolling? That way, you will not be distracted by the shot and can concentrate on the scene itself."

Brie looked down at Goliath. Although the flogger looked intimidating, she'd experienced its challenging but pleasant thud before. The flogger had never been used as a weapon of punishment—only as a tool of pleasure. There was no reason for her to fear it, except…

Knowing that she needed to trust her instincts, she told Marquis, "If you are willing to schedule another session, I would deeply appreciate having an opportunity to reacquaint myself with Goliath without recording it."

Taking the flogger from her, Marquis Gray replied, "I think you have made an excellent choice."

She instantly felt as if a weight had been lifted from her shoulders and smiled. When she glanced in the direction of the camera, she found Sir standing beside it. He held up his hand to indicate he'd already taken care of it.

She bowed her head to him and then turned back to Marquis. She felt a sense of peace and smiled as she lightly touched the orchid in her hair.

Feeling confident, she formally bowed her head to the trainer and waited for Marquis Gray's first command.

"Undress for me, pearl."

Brie felt pleasant chills knowing the scene had officially begun. Feeling empowered, she slowly removed her clothes. Just as she had the first time, Brie wore a red, two-piece set of activewear that consisted of a halter top and shorts underneath her clothing. It maintained her modesty for the film but allowed for the unhindered sensation of impact play.

Carefully folding her clothes, Brie placed them in a neat pile on the floor.

Standing before Marquis, she felt butterflies when he held out his hand to her. She took it, and the ghostly white Dom drew her close, murmuring, "Do you realize how beautiful you are right now?"

Brie blushed, suddenly seeing herself in a different light. She had walked into this scene today determined to conquer any fears that might be lurking in her subconscious. But that was not how she wanted to approach the rare opportunity she'd been given.

This was a chance for her to reconnect with her past. Brie fondly remembered the young sub who'd stood on stage with Marquis Gray after making the decision *not* to leave the Training Center after being called out for her "encounter" with the Headmaster.

Standing on that stage with Marquis had been the bravest and most difficult thing she had ever done up to that point, and she remembered feeling like the most powerful sub on the planet.

Knowing that's what she wanted out of this scene today, Brie held her head a little higher as she walked to the St. Andrew's cross with Marquis Gray.

He turned her to face it and then ordered, "On your toes."

Brie smiled to herself. She knew Sir was watching her as she stood on tiptoes while Marquis Gray bound her ankles and wrists to the cross. Gently brushing her long hair out of the way, Marquis Gray tied a strip of lace over Brie's eyes.

"Let the pleasure begin..." he whispered huskily to her.

Soon, the sound of Mozart filled the room, stirring her excitement. She'd always enjoyed the care Marquis took with his scenes. He never rushed through them. No, he created a symphony.

Brie licked her lips in anticipation when she heard the sound of a smaller flogger cutting the air behind her. She could imagine Marquis Gray warming his muscles up behind her while Sir watched. The thought of it made her wet.

The moment the tails of the flogger slapped against

her skin, Brie purred in delight.

"Color, pearl?"

"Delightfully green, Marquis."

Continuing with the light stimulation, Marquis used slow, fluid movements as he stroked her with the flogger in time with the music. Once her back was properly warmed up, he set down the instrument.

Moving to her, Marquis caressed her with a strip of lace. Brie smiled when she felt the rough material glide over her skin.

"I see you like the stimulation," Marquis stated, his chuckle low and as enticing as ever.

"I do, Marquis!"

When the song changed to a more spirited melody, Marquis left her to get the next tool. While she waited, Brie remained absolutely still. Her calf muscles began to burn due to the challenging pose she had to maintain, but she knew the position showed off the beauty of her feminine form, which she loved. She especially loved knowing that her Master was watching…

Marquis Gray resumed his position behind her. This time, he used a more thuddy flogger. He timed the strokes to perfectly match the dynamic rhythm of the classical piece. Brie found the combination of the emotional music and the sensation of the flogger transformed the experience into something beautiful and visceral.

"Color, pearl?"

"Emerald green, Marquis."

His warm chuckle filled her ears as he carried her higher. When Marquis put the flogger down at the end of the song, Brie felt an acute sense of loss. But he quickly returned to her, teasing her back with the sensual caress of soft fur. In her heightened state of sensitivity, the simple contact was multiplied many times over, and she moaned in pleasure at the decadent sensation.

"The power of opposing stimuli…" he murmured in her ear.

Brie purred, glorifying in his artful expertise. "Thank you, Marquis."

"I enjoy preparing you to fly."

"I'm so close…" she whispered.

"I know, pearl," he stated confidently as he moved away from her once again.

Brie took in a deep breath, enjoying this extraordinary moment. She was sitting on the precipice, just before she joyfully embraced nirvana.

She shivered when she heard the eighty tails cut through the air as Marquis warmed up his muscles for the bigger flogger. But she felt no fear—only a heady exhilaration.

"Are you ready to fly?" he asked just before the music changed, becoming more intense. It perfectly matched the tone he had set for the final scene.

Although her eyes were covered, Brie could feel the heat of Sir's gaze on her. It turned her on to know he was sharing in this moment.

Channeling the joy of her submission, Brie waited to receive Asher's gift.

She remembered that Sir once described the way Marquis wielded the two-handed flogger was reminiscent of swordplay in both grace and intensity. She imagined his movement now as she heard the tails cutting through the air.

Forcing her body to relax, Brie invited the explosive caress of all eighty tails. When it came, the impact took her breath away and made her whole body tingle, starting at the area of impact and traveling outward.

"Color, pearl?"

It took her a moment to answer. "Greenish-yellow…"

"Good," he murmured. "It's time for you to fly."

Every lash Marquis gave her from that point onward brought Brie closer to the edge as the lashes gradually grew in intensity. It didn't take long before she felt herself flying off the precipice and into subspace.

In that glorious moment, Brie lifted her head and let out a cry of pure joy.

Following her session with Marquis Gray, Brie arrived home only to discover that the entire session had been recorded on her camera. Insatiably curious, she immediately sat down and watched the entire thing from beginning to end two times—once for her own pleasure and then to compare it with the original.

While Brie watched the scene play out, she was struck by the expert way Marquis Gray handled each transition. The trainer's many years of experience were evident as he guided her along, reading her reactions and adjusting accordingly to bring her to the elusive state of subspace through the use of the fearsome-looking flogger.

She was thrilled to see her unfiltered response to each new stimulus as Marquis drew out her pleasure. Thankfully, her reactions and facial expressions naturally mirrored the original without appearing forced. Watching Marquis's powerful movements as he wielded the two-handed flogger was completely mesmerizing and reminded Brie of why she adored the original recording so much.

Brie was luckier than most because she was one of only a few who knew the sensual caress of his flogger. She literally had goosebumps as she watched the eighty tails raining down on her back. When she was finished with the comparisons, she let out an excited squeak and ran downstairs to tell Sir.

She walked up to Sir with a coy smile. "Sir, did you forget to turn off my camera?"

Sir looked up from his work and smiled at her tenderly "No, babygirl. The recording is for you—not the documentary. I understood the reason you didn't want to record it for the film. But knowing the challenge this scene would present for you, I felt you might benefit from watching it for yourself."

Brie broke out in a grin. "Sir, I watched the whole thing and it's amazing!"

Sir nodded in agreement. "You were truly magnificent today."

She blushed as she rushed to him. "It was all Marquis Gray, Sir."

"I know otherwise," he stated, taking her hand and

pulling her to him. "The trust and grace you displayed were inspiring to watch."

Crawling into his lap, she purred, basking in his praise. "I'm so excited because the footage matches the original so well that I won't even need to film a second session."

"Really?" he asked in surprise. "You're using it? That's an unexpected perk."

"It certainly is, Sir." Looking at him flirtatiously, she added, "Would you like to watch it and judge for yourself?"

"I most certainly would, Mrs. Davis…" he replied huskily, grabbing the back of her neck as he claimed her lips.

Nightmares

B rie walked through the field of sunflowers, awash in a sense of wonder. The sky above was a brilliant blue and the warmth of the sun kissed her skin like the gentle caress of a lover.

The hope she felt in her heart seemed boundless and complete. Grazing her fingers over the soft petals of the large blossoms only increased her sense of joy.

She had never felt such a profound feeling of connection with everything around her—the flowers, the trees, and even the large bumble bees flying from flower to flower. Her clarity of mind and spirit left her in a state of awe.

It was so powerful that she began spinning in circles, her arms outstretched as she looked up at the great expanse of sky.

Without warning, she felt herself being dragged down into the earth below by giant hands whose grip was so tight there was no possibility of escape. Brie screamed as she looked up at the blue sky above her, but she was helpless to break free. Before she even knew it, she was being engulfed by the black void underneath.

The darkness enveloped her, squeezing the air from her lungs. The terrifying feeling of being suffocated caused her body to thrash in desperate protest. Thankfully, the violent jerking broke her from the hands of death and she started to claw her way upward.

She headed back to the surface, unwilling to accept defeat. She could see the surface breaking just above her, looking like glittering bits of sunlight hitting the ocean water. Fighting as hard as she could, she came to a point when her body finally stopped struggling. A terrifying calmness took over and she slowly sank back down into the depths—all hope lost.

From above, a hand thrust through the darkness, reaching for her. With superhuman strength, she latched onto it and felt the unseen person pulling her up. But it was too late, and she knew with certainty she would not break the surface in time…

Brie woke up with a start, gasping frantically for air.

"Brie!" Sir called out, his voice riddled with concern.

Struggling to recover from the nightmare, she answered him breathlessly, "Just a dream…"

Pulling her into his embrace, Sir held her tight until she could breathe normally again.

Brie was still plagued by nightmares ever since her rescue. She was uncertain if her experiences as a captive had left this a permanent remnant, like a scar on her soul, that she would have to learn to live with, or if she would outgrow them with time.

Laying there, her body still tingling in fear after the

near death-like experience, Brie decided to take it as a sign that she needed to take action.

There was something she had been battling with. Rather than allowing her inaction to continue to plague her subconscious and steal any more of her energy, Brie decided it was better to face it head-on.

The time had finally come for her to meet with Darius, the boy who had ruthlessly abused her as a child so that she could thank him for his help in saving her life.

"Are you sure you want to do this?" Sir asked when she brought it up to him the following morning.

"As hard as it is for me, I know I need to, Sir. I would not be alive if he hadn't risked defying Holloway by telling Captain what he saw at the compound."

Sir let out an uneasy sigh. "This will not be easy for you, but I stand by your side, babygirl."

Brie hugged him, needing his strength. "I'm going to ask Baron to join us. I found his presence reassuring at our last meeting."

"I will contact him. Do you have any idea when you want to meet?"

She frowned, thinking for a moment. "The sooner the better, I believe. The longer I put it off, the more it's going to weigh on my mind."

Sir made arrangements to meet Darius at a private office Thompson had set aside for them, just as he had before. However, this meeting was going to be different.

Brie wasn't preparing to confront her abuser for all the wrongs that he had perpetrated against her as a child. Instead, she needed to thank him, and that was proving more difficult than she'd anticipated.

Because Brie knew the horrifying abuses that had occurred at the compound, the fact that Darius had been invited to enjoy the "entertainment" made this a hard pill to swallow. Still…Darius had risked everything to save the captives at the compound.

Baron met with them fifteen minutes before Darius was scheduled to arrive. As soon as Baron saw Brie, he gave her an encouraging smile. "How are you holding up?"

"I'm here."

He chuckled in understanding. "That says a lot."

Sir shook Baron's hand. "We certainly appreciate you joining us today."

"I feel very protective of Brianna's well-being," he replied, glancing at her.

Thinking back on their last dinner together, she asked him. "How is Shanice doing?"

"Better. Definitely better."

"I'm happy to hear it." Remembering all of the tragic experiences Shanice shared with her that night, she added, "She is a very strong woman, Baron."

"I agree," he said solemnly. "After her talk with you, I purchased a journal so she could express herself without the need to talk to anyone."

"Has she been using it?" Brie asked hopefully.

"She has. In fact, she's going through the pages so quickly that I'm getting her another one."

"Good," Brie replied, encouraged to hear that.

When Brie heard Darius's voice outside the office, she took a deep breath and sat down, waiting for him to enter the room.

Baron went to the door to greet him while Sir took a seat beside Brie. Grabbing her hand, Sir told her, "Be true to yourself at this meeting."

"I will, Sir," she promised, her heart beating even faster when Darius entered the room.

Baron directed him to sit opposite Brie, then took a seat beside him.

Darius sat back in his chair, staring at her as an uncomfortable silence filled the room.

Sir was the first to speak. "Before we begin, I would like to talk about the altercation between you and I the last time we met."

Darius rubbed his jaw as if he could still feel it. "Yeah, I haven't forgotten."

"Although there is no question that you deserved it for the abuse you inflicted on Brianna as a child, you don't have to worry now. It won't happen again."

Darius snorted. "I suppose I'll consider that an apology of sorts."

"It is a promise," Sir stated.

Turning his gaze on Brie, Darius asked, "So, what exactly is this meeting about?"

Wanting this to be an honest exchange, Brie suddenly noticed that she was crossing her arms in a defensive posture. Before she began, she purposely uncrossed them and leaned forward, looking Darius directly in the eyes. "I was informed that you provided information that helped in the rescue at the compound. I am indebted to you for that."

His gaze was unwavering when he told her, "I had no idea what I was walking into that night."

Brie nodded but told him, "I've struggled to believe that because of the way you acted when you saw me there."

He raised his eyebrows. "I forced myself to act cool despite what was happening around me. I *saw* the way Greg Holloway was eyeing me that night." He rubbed his hands on his pants repeatedly before telling her, "Hell, the minute I arrived, I felt like I was being set up."

"Are you saying you had no idea what was taking place at the compound?" Sir asked him.

"I knew BDSM was involved, but as far as the sex slaves are concerned, I assumed it was just an elaborate game of role-play." Then he looked at Brie. "Until I saw you."

Brie shivered, remembering how betrayed she'd felt when she saw him there.

"I knew you wouldn't be there by choice, and then…" Darius looked away, swallowing hard.

Brie answered for him. "…you saw what happened to Mary."

He nodded slowly. "There was no way that was staged."

Brie closed her eyes, once more seeing the blood and hearing the cruel lashes when Venom delivered Mary's punishment that night.

"Why do you think no one else has reported it?" Baron asked.

Darius sat back in his chair, stating with a dark laugh, "We all knew it was suicide to mess with Greg Holloway."

Brie asked him pointedly, "Then why did you choose to help when nobody else would?"

Darius sat up and crossed his arms, leaning against the table. "You probably don't want to hear this, but I almost didn't."

Brie only nodded, not surprised by his confession. She was well aware of the power Holloway held over everyone in Hollywood at the time.

"What was the deciding factor for you?" Sir pressed.

Looking at Brie, Darius stated bluntly, "I knew the truth would come out eventually." He shrugged. "I didn't want my inaction regarding something so heinous to define me as a man. So, I risked Greg Holloway's fury."

Brie stared at him solemnly. "I'm grateful for your courage, Darius." She added, speaking for all of the other captives, "We all are."

He nodded gravely.

Darius glanced at Sir. "I'm relieved you were able to rescue them all."

Sir answered, his voice gruff with emotion. "Me, too."

Darius stood up and held out his hand to Brie. "So, the two of us live to fight another day."

"Yes, we do," she agreed, shaking his hand. "Without Holloway's shadow hanging over either of us."

After the meeting with Darius, Brie was able to sleep without any nightmares terrorizing her in the middle of the night. As the weeks passed, she believed she'd finally broken the remnants of Holloway's insidious cruelty.

Tono's Secret

Brie was running errands during lunch and happened to pass by Tono's favorite pizza joint. Remembering the tasty pizzas they made, she suddenly had a craving for their sesame chicken with spicy sweet and sour sauce.

While she was waiting in line, Brie's heart skipped a beat when she noticed Tono sitting alone at a table with his back to her. After she paid for her meal, she walked up to see if it was really him.

"Tono?"

When he looked up and smiled at her, she burst out laughing in surprise, "I can't believe you're here!"

"Please, join me at the table," he told her, gesturing for Brie to sit.

Brie immediately sat down, staring at him in stunned silence.

He chuckled, "Would you like a piece of my pizza?"

"No, I ordered a slice. They're warming it up in the fire oven…" She shook her head, unable to believe he was here in the flesh. "When did you get back? I had no idea you were even in town, or I would have made it a point to come see you."

"I have been keeping to myself."

Brie's smile suddenly faltered, and she automatically reached out to him from across the table. Remembering their last conversation, she asked, "Is your mother okay?"

Tono was about to answer when the waitress came up and slid Brie's plate onto the table. "Enjoy!" the girl said pleasantly before leaving.

After seeing Tono's concentrated expression, Brie's heart started to beat faster. "Have things gotten worse with her health?"

His eyes reflected an inner peace when he replied, "Although the situation has become more complex, she is well considering her diagnosis."

"Complex how?"

He looked down at her pizza. "It would be a shame to let that slice of perfection go to waste. Please eat."

"Okay, I will, as long as you tell me what's going on," she agreed, picking up the hot slice even though she no longer felt hungry. Dutifully taking a bite, she smiled as she chewed, waiting for him to speak.

"I made the decision to care for my mother."

Brie immediately stopped chewing, knowing how challenging this was going to be for him, given the woman's difficult disposition. Still, she nodded to show she was listening as she forced herself to swallow the bite.

"Thankfully, I was able to repurchase my home here

in LA. I then brought her here to live with me because the medical staff nearby specializes in her type of brain tumor."

"How did she handle the move?"

He snorted. "Naturally, she needed time to adjust."

Brie chuckled lightly. "I can only imagine. So, how is Autumn handling it?"

She noticed he hesitated before answering, "Autumn was supportive until I explained that I would be acting as her main caregiver."

Brie looked at him sadly. "I'm sorry to hear that, Tono." When he glanced at her plate, she obediently took another bite, chewing slowly so he would continue.

"Autumn hoped we would be able to continue touring once my mother was settled in." He picked up his half-eaten slice and took a bite, closing his eyes to savor the unique flavor of the pizza.

The long, wordless moment of eating together invited a familiar sense of synergy between them.

"I am at peace with my decision to care for my mother," he told her, then smiled. "I have already seen a change in her since coming here, and I remain hopeful that we will both grow through this experience of her death."

Brie wiped her hands, before grasping his hand tightly. "I would like to see her again, Tono."

He seemed pleased by her request. "Okaasan is desperate to see a familiar face."

"Hopefully, she won't mind that it's mine," Brie giggled.

Tono's eyes shone with quiet joy. "We can go right

now—or, rather, after we're finished eating."

"I'd like that," she answered enthusiastically, taking another bite.

Brie texted Sir to let him know about her change of plans. He immediately responded.

Give Nosaka my best, and say hello to his mother for me.

Brie read the text to Tono.

He nodded thoughtfully after hearing it. "My mother will be pleased. In the past, she has mentioned her esteem for Sir Davis for his help with my father before he passed."

As Brie drove up to his house, she felt a sense of déjà vu. She was struck again by how peaceful Tono's house looked with its simple rock garden in front. When she entered the home, she was flooded with memories as she looked at the dark wood floors and the beautiful garden out back.

Tono set his phone and keys on the counter, telling her, "I will start some tea before our visit."

As Brie stood there watching him, she was hit by the ease of their friendship. It felt as if no time had passed between them. Once the tea was brewing, he led her to the master bedroom, which had been filled with all of the necessary equipment needed to care for his ailing mother.

"I have brought a visitor, Okaasan," he stated in a gentle voice.

The nurse attending his mother smiled and bowed to

him before silently leaving the room. Brie noticed the sleeping mat on the floor and realized that Tono must be sleeping there at night.

She looked at him with renewed gratitude, remembering when Tono had slept on a mat beside her own bed while he was caring for her after Sir's plane accident.

While Tono introduced her, Brie approached his mother's bed with trepidation. The petite woman who shared Tono's facial features looked surprisingly healthy to Brie.

"Hello, Mrs. Nosaka."

The old woman squinted for a moment, staring intently at her face.

Brie smiled, wondering if she even remembered who she was.

Mrs. Nosaka snorted and mumbled something to Tono which made him grin. He looked at Brie, telling her, "My mother called you 'the girl who smiles too much'."

Brie laughed, remembering her tense encounters with the woman in Japan. Turning back to his mother, Brie's smile grew even wider. "I am grateful to get to see you again, Mrs. Nosaka."

After Tono translated her words, the woman's expression remained stoic. However, she met Brie's gaze and nodded. Tono's mother had never been an especially warm or emotional person, but Brie was pleasantly surprised to not feel hostility radiating from her.

"I am making tea," he told his mother. "I thought it would be nice to sit out back and drink it together."

"*Hai*," she answered.

130

Brie followed Tono into the kitchen and got out the teacups while he readied the pot. Working together in his kitchen again felt as natural as breathing.

He placed the teapot on a tray and asked Brie to take them out to the garden while he got his mother. Brie watched the nurse follow him back to the room to help.

While she was placing the cups on the tray, Tono received a text. Brie inadvertently read it when it popped up on his screen. What she saw sent shivers down her spine.

The text was from Autumn's mother.

Stay away from my daughter, chink! You are not going to make her a slave to your dragon of a mother. I've never trusted you yellow-skinned, slanty-eyed people.

Brie stood there in shock, sickened by the cruelty of her words.

When she heard the three coming out of the room, Brie quickly picked up the tray and followed them outside, but she couldn't keep her hands from shaking.

After Tono helped his mother settle into a comfortable chair, he joined Brie down on the mat set out there. Tono then poured a cup of tea for each of them, including the nurse, and the four sat in silence while they listened to the peaceful sound of birds.

Brie forced herself to remain calm, but the ugliness of the text continued to swim through her thoughts.

After several minutes, Tono set his cup down and stood up. "Mrs. Davis, would you join me for a moment?"

Brie's heart raced as she stood up to join him.

"We'll be back shortly, Okaasan," he assured his mother.

Mrs. Nosaka nodded in acknowledgment.

Brie followed Tono inside, dreading the conversation they were about to have.

After he closed the door, he turned to face her. She could read the concern on his face when he asked, "What has you so troubled?"

Brie swallowed hard before asking, "Where's Autumn, Tono?"

"She is staying with a friend," he replied evenly. Nodding in the direction of his mother, he said, "All of this has been too much for her."

Brie sighed nervously before apologizing, "I'm sorry, but I accidentally saw a text on your phone. It was on the counter and I glanced at it when it popped up."

Tono frowned. "What did it say?"

Her bottom lip trembled. "It was from Autumn's mother."

He closed his eyes, saying with forbearance, "Ah…"

"Tono, I can't believe the hurtful things in that text!"

Meeting her gaze, Tono told her, "Autumn warned me when we first met that her parents were extremely prejudiced. I dismissed it at the time, certain that once they came to know me, any bigotry they still held would no longer be an issue. I was wrong."

Brie looked at him in disbelief. "How can they misjudge you like that? You're the kindest person I know!"

He looked at her with those chocolate-brown eyes.

"I have come to understand that you cannot convince another person how to feel—no matter how much you might want to."

Brie swallowed hard. "But you deserve their respect, not the horrid ignorance in that text."

He shrugged. "Their opinion of me does not matter."

"Autumn obviously needs to cut those hateful people out of her life! They are clearly too clouded by hatred to have her best interests at heart."

He shook his head. "Family is too important to be brushed aside so casually. I would not want her to disown her parents. Nor would I want her to force me to disown mine."

Tono glanced out a window, gazing at his mother. "This journey with Okaasan is one I am fated to take. Whether it is with Autumn or not must be her choice and hers alone."

Brie understood the truth behind his words, but her heart broke for him just the same. Ever since she had known Tono, he had always been the one to offer help, never asking for it himself. Wanting to help him now, she said gently, "Tono, I support your choice to care for your mother. And I would like to share something that I have learned during my recovery that may benefit you as well."

"What is that?" he asked, taking her hand in concern.

"I understand how easy it is to isolate yourself, not wanting to be a burden to others."

When he shifted uncomfortably, she squeezed his hand.

"But community is everything, Tono! It's wonderful when things are going well and we can all celebrate together, but it's even more important when things get hard. The community support I have received recently has changed how I see things."

Brie smiled at him. "Whenever the community comes together to support someone through difficult times, they each carry a small portion of their suffering for them. But it not only helps the one who is struggling, it also allows everyone to learn and grow from the experience."

She looked at him tenderly. "Please hear me when I say it's important to reach out. So many people in our community would be honored to support and learn from you and your mother."

He nodded solemnly. "I will keep that in mind."

"Good!" she replied, giving him a hug.

Tono nodded toward the backyard. "Would you like to return to my mother and listen to the birds, Mrs. Davis?"

She bowed her head. "It would be my honor, Tono Nosaka."

The Ranch

A s Brie looked out the car window, she could barely contain her excitement now that they were here in Colorado for Master Anderson's wedding! As Sir drove up I-25 on their way to Greeley, Brie stared at the majestic peaks of the Rockies surprised they were still covered in snow despite the fact it was June.

On either side of the freeway were huge grassy fields dotted with cattle.

"Moo moos!" Hope cried out happily, pointing them out to Antony through the car window.

Antony turned his head in the direction she was pointing but looked completely disinterested in the cows.

"I believe Antony takes after his father," Brie teased Sir. "Hope can't get enough of the cows, but her little brother couldn't care less."

Sir smirked at her comment.

Once they finally reached the outskirts of Greeley, they turned off the freeway and headed toward the foothills.

Brie looked around in awe, murmuring, "I can't imagine living with all this space and having nature
surround you like this. From the rugged peaks to the
rolling foothills, it feels like a little slice of heaven."

"Although I agree this area is beautiful, what makes
it 'a slice of heaven' to me is Anderson's family."

The fondness with which Sir said it made Brie turn
to glance at him. She suddenly understood that his
feelings for the Andersons ran deeper than she thought.

Knowing that he had been cheated of having two
parents who loved him and wanted the best for him
made Brie realize that she had a tendency to take her
own parents for granted. They'd always been there for
her. Although her father could be overbearing at times,
she had never once doubted his love for her.

"I can't wait to see them at this ranch I've heard so
much about!"

"You are going to be amazed at his mother's cooking. Mrs. Anderson is a real talent," Sir stated with
admiration.

"The way you say that makes me almost feel jealous," Brie joked.

He winked at her. "No slight intended, babygirl. I've
always admired a cook who can take simple ingredients
and make them taste extraordinary. Mrs. Anderson is
truly gifted in that area."

Sir then muttered to himself, "I heard the same was
true of Durov's mother. It's a shame I never got to meet
her in person…"

Brie sensed a wave of sadness wash over him and
reached out to rub his shoulder. "It must have been hard

on both you and Rytsar that it never happened."

Sir glanced at her, nodding silently.

As they made a turn in the bend, Brie let out a squeal of excitement the moment she spied the large sign carved with a picture of a huge cottonwood tree and the Rocky Mountains in the background. "It's Morning Wood Ranch!"

She quickly turned in her seat and pointed it out to Hope and Antony. "This is where Mr. Anderson grew up!"

Sir slowed down and turned into the long, gravel driveway.

Brie looked up as they passed under the giant sign, grinning. "I guess it makes sense the sign is so huge considering the name of the ranch…and the men involved."

"Indeed," Sir replied, chuckling.

Hope began bouncing up and down in her car seat, crying out, "Horsey, horsey!"

Brie looked in the direction she was pointing and saw a cowboy on a roan horse heading straight toward them at a trot. When he got closer, she realized it was Master Anderson, the groom himself!

Sir slowed to a stop and lowered the window. "Fancy meeting you here."

Master Anderson tipped his hat, then thrust his pelvis forward in the saddle and said, "Welcome to Morning Wood."

Sir shook his head, staring blatantly at Master Anderson's crotch. "I must say, Anderson, I'm not impressed."

Master Anderson threw back his head and laughed.

"Jealousy does not become you, buddy."

Tipping his hat to Brie, Master Anderson grinned. "It's a pleasure to see you, Mrs. Davis."

Leaning down on his horse, he peeked into the backseat of the car and waved at the children. "My mama can't wait to meet the two of you."

Brie stared at him, completely enamored. Master Anderson was in his element and everything she imagined a cowboy to be.

Whipping his horse around in one graceful motion, he tapped his heels into the side of the animal and the horse sprinted off. He turned his head back and called out to Sir, "Follow me!"

"Wow, that horse is fast!" Brie exclaimed.

Sir hit the gas, and the wheels of the car crunched on the gravel. "It's a quarter horse," he informed her. "They're fast sprinters and can outrun other horse breeds in a run of a quarter of a mile or less."

Brie stared at him in amazement. "I can't believe you know that."

"Having a cowboy as a friend will do that to a person."

Her eyes widened as they drove up to the farmhouse. The white two-story home with blue shutters had a large inviting front porch with a swing.

When Master Anderson let out a spirited hoot from his horse, his family spilled out of the house and started waving as the car pulled up.

Brie grinned as she waved back at them enthusiastically. "You can definitely tell they are all related. Except for his mom, of course. She's so tiny compared to the rest of them."

"That's true," Sir agreed. "However, all four children have their mother's green eyes."

Ruth ran up to Sir as he was getting out of the vehicle. "You up for some fishing while you're here, Mr. Davis?"

Sir smiled at her. "You can call me Thane, Ruthie."

Giving him a lopsided grin, she laughed. "Nobody has called me Ruthie in ages!"

"I apologize…Ruth," he said, correcting himself.

Ruth shook her head. "Nah, I kind of like hearing you say it. Brings back good memories."

"Ruthie it is, then," Sir replied, opening the car door to help Antony out of his car seat.

Brie grinned at Sir from the other side of the vehicle as she unbuckled Hope and set her on the ground. Her daughter immediately headed toward Anderson's horse, crying, "Horsey, horsey!"

Master Anderson patted the horse's neck, telling Hope, "This here is Graham Cracker, little darlin'."

Hope looked up at him, repeating the name, "Gam Cacker?"

He nodded, tipping his hat. "You wanna sit on her?"

In answer, Hope held up both hands.

Master Anderson's father walked up and swooped Hope into his arms, helping her onto the horse. Master Anderson then slowly turned the horse around several times to the delightful sound of Hope's laughter.

Master Anderson's mother smiled at Brie as she walked up, while Master Anderson's sisters gathered around, wanting to see the baby. The small woman shook her head in amazement. "It seems like yesterday when Brad told me you had a new baby. I can't believe how time flies…"

Little Antony grinned up at the three sisters as they cooed at him. It was clear to Brie that he was flirting with them.

Staring at her son in amusement, she said, "Children really do make you realize how fast time is flying by." She suddenly caught a whiff of something sweet baking in the house and asked, "Are you already cooking for the wedding, Mrs. Anderson?"

"It's been a weeklong affair for this celebratory feast!" she answered, laughing. She then declared with enormous pride, "I aim to have the tables groaning under the weight of good food. No one is leaving our place hungry after this reception."

"Is there anything I can do to help?" Brie offered.

Nodding enthusiastically, she answered, "After Brad shows you around our place, my girls and I would love to have your company in the kitchen. If you don't mind, that is."

Brie chuckled, glancing at Sir when she said, "I'm not a natural cook like you, Mrs. Anderson. But I take direction very well."

His mom's sweet laughter filled the air. "My son told me about your omelets…but he mentioned you've come a long way since then."

Brie blushed, remembering the disastrous omelet incident at the Submissive Training Center under Marquis Gray's expert guidance.

That poor man…

Shrugging, Brie chuckled. "What can I say? It's extremely easy to improve when you start from zero."

"I'm sure you weren't that bad…" his mother said kindly.

Brie shook her head. "Your son was *not* exaggerating. The man training me has never eaten an egg since."

"Oh, my!" Mrs. Anderson giggled.

Grinning at them from his horse, Master Anderson handed Hope down to Sir. He then swung his leg over, gracefully dismounting the beautiful animal with the adorable name. "Brianna is truly a legend, Ma."

Patting the horse's neck, he pulled the reins over its head to use as a lead. "I wanted to show you the barn where the reception will be taking place tomorrow."

Brie noticed Sir raise an eyebrow, but he said nothing as he set Hope down and grabbed his daughter's hand. Together, they started walking toward the barn.

Making cute faces at the baby, Megan asked Brie, "Can I keep Antony for a bit?"

Her son beamed up at Megan, loving the attention.

"Certainly," Brie answered. "He seems quite infatuated with you."

A pleased blush rose on Megan's cheeks. "He's just so adorable!"

Brie had to run to catch up with Sir. Taking Hope's other hand, the three of them walked together as they followed behind Master Anderson. It was a simple but tender moment between them.

Brie was impressed by the size of the giant red barn. Although it was old, it was obvious that the Andersons were meticulous about the upkeep of their ranch. From the white trim to the vibrant coating of red paint, the structure stood out against the backdrop of the foothills and the bright blue sky.

"This is classic Americana, Master Anderson, if I've ever seen it," Brie told him, impressed by the immensity of the structure. "I've always loved red barns, and this has got to be the prettiest one I've ever seen."

"Pleased to hear that, young Brie," he stated with satisfaction. "This ranch is our family's pride and joy."

"I can tell by the upkeep of this barn alone," she told him.

He gave her a smirk when he slid the large barn door open. "As you can see, the inside needs a tad more work, though."

The interior of the barn was in utter disarray. Old barrels were lying on their sides, with bales of straw strewn everywhere. A mountain of tangled lights lay piled up in the center of the barn. And, to top it off…a flock of chickens was busy pecking at the ground for food.

The moment Hope saw the chickens, she made a beeline for them. The birds scattered in fear at the sound of her excited squeals as she tried to catch one of them.

"This was so not what I was expecting…" Brie murmured to Sir.

Shaking his head, Sir glanced at Master Anderson but said nothing.

It seemed to Brie that Sir seemed as shocked by the state of the barn as she was.

"I know, I know…" Master Anderson chuckled at them both. "We're running a bit behind because of the wedding and all, but that's where you come in," he stated, looking at Brie. "If you're willing, of course."

She crinkled her brow. "What do you need me to do, Master Anderson?"

"My sisters were hoping you'd be willing to get up early and help them tomorrow. While you gals clean out the barn and decorate it for the reception, Ma will finish the cooking. Pa, my buddy Thane, and I will be driving into town to get all the rented chairs and tables so we can set them up. With your help, we will have everything ready before the wedding is set to begin. I guarantee it!"

Brie scanned the messy barn again. "That's an awful lot to do in such a limited amount of time…"

"Trust me, my sisters are hard workers, and the four of you will breeze through this in no time flat. I am fully confident you ladies can knock it out of the park!"

She looked at him dubiously.

"So, is that a yes, young Brie?" he asked with a teasing grin.

Although Brie didn't think the four of them could pull it off, she answered optimistically, "I'm willing to start now, if you'd like."

He swept his hand through the air as if swatting her suggestion away. "There's no need for that. I haven't had the chance to introduce you to my friend yet."

Master Anderson escorted them out of the barn and let out a long whistle. Winking at Brie, he stated, "This is a special friend I want you to meet."

After several minutes, Brie saw a large white dog trotting toward them at a slow pace, its long pink tongue dancing with each step.

"That there is Anya," he stated proudly. Turning to Sir, he added, "She's one of Kiah and Bandit's pups."

"Really?" Sir replied, studying the dog more closely as she approached. "I've never forgotten your two Kuvaszes. I was impressed with how intelligent Kiah and Bandit were and the devotion they showed to your family."

Master Anderson got down on one knee and held out his arms to the huge dog. She immediately ran up to him, wagging her tail. "That's it, old girl. Come get some lovin'."

The dog had the look of a giant golden retriever, but with snowy white fur like a polar bear. Brie had never seen a dog that big in her entire life. She stared at the animal in awe, and then said jokingly, "Hope could almost ride her, she's so huge!"

Chuckling, Master Anderson agreed. "Hope sure could and Anya loves children..." Scratching the dog behind the ears, he explained, "But this old girl isn't as spry as she used to be. Most Kuvaszes only live twelve to fourteen years, but Anya is at the ripe old age of seventeen.

He lifted her muzzle to stare into the dog's big brown eyes. "You've been an important member of this family since the day you were born. Isn't that right, girl?"

Looking up at Brie he added, "Which is why I want her to represent our family at the wedding."

"What do you have planned, Master Anderson?" Brie asked, charmed by the relationship he had with the dog.

Ruffling Anya's thick coat, he told her, "She's going to be part of the wedding party."

Brie put her hand to her mouth. "Oh, my goodness. That's so adorable!"

Master Anderson grinned at Brie, then motioned Hope to step closer to the giant dog. Anya wagged her tail gently as Hope approached her. "Go ahead. You can pet her. She *loves* to be petted."

Brie's heart melted as she watched her daughter reach up to stroke the large dog's white fur with a look of wonder. "Pony!" she cried happily.

"Doggie." Master Anderson chuckled, correcting her. "Her name is Anya."

"An…ya," Hope repeated, petting the dog's fur.

The big dog gave Hope a lick with her long tongue upon hearing her name. The little girl immediately broke out in giggles and looked at Brie.

Staring at the dog with a thoughtful expression, Sir asked, "Why does that name sound so familiar?"

Master Anderson stood up and grinned. "Durov came to visit soon after Kiah had the litter. While he was visiting, the Russian taught my mother all of his *mamul-ya's* favorite recipes." Placing his hand on his chest, he told them, "My mama was both touched by Durov's gesture and heartbroken about the loss of his mother. So, Ma asked if she could honor his *mamulya* by naming the pup after her."

"And Durov agreed?" Sir asked, sounding surprised. "Don't get me wrong, it's a lovely gesture on her part, but I know he was definitely *not* a pet person at the time. I would have expected he'd take that as an insult."

Master Anderson looked at him with a sad smile. "Believe it or not, my mama totally bonded with the guy during his visit. Durov actually cried when she asked him…"

Brie's heart constricted. She could imagine the intense pain Rytsar must have been suffering so soon after his mother's death.

With a twinkle in his eyes, Master Anderson told Brie, "If you can believe it, he's sent Anya a dog toy every month since. That's over two hundred toys!"

Brie shook her head in amazement, remembering the caviar Rytsar sent Shadow as a thank you gift after the black cat saved his life. Glancing down at Anya, Brie felt an even deeper connection with the dog. Petting her on the head, Brie said her name with a tone of reverence, "Anya."

The dog looked up at her with those big, thoughtful eyes and wagged her tail in response. Brie smiled at Master Anderson. "I love that Anya will be part of your wedding ceremony."

Gazing down lovingly at Anya, Anderson stated, "I couldn't imagine having this wedding without my faithful friend in it."

Honorary Anderson

S leeping peacefully, Brie was startled when she heard someone knocking lightly on the door. "Brie, are you up?" Christina whispered. "We're ready to start clearing out the barn."

Gazing at the digital clock on the nightstand, Brie saw it was only four in the morning. She glanced at Sir, who was still sleeping soundly beside her. He hadn't come to bed until two, after treating Master Anderson to a Bachelor Party as his best man.

Brie had no idea what kind of party Sir had arranged, but when he finally staggered to bed and groaned as he lay down, she assumed a lot of alcohol must have been involved.

Not wanting to wake the children, Brie quietly slipped out of bed, put on her robe, and headed toward the door. She was surprised they were starting so early in the morning. But when she thought about the state of the barn, Brie realized it was a necessary evil.

The only way they had *any* chance of getting the

place ready for the wedding reception was to get up before the crack of dawn. Tiptoeing to the door, she whispered back, "Christina, let me get dressed and I'll meet you in a few minutes."

"Okay. We'll be waiting in the kitchen."

Brie fumbled with her clothes as she struggled to dress in the dark. After tying her sneakers, she got up to leave but stopped when she heard Sir turn in the bed.

"Don't work too hard, babygirl," he murmured sleepily.

She turned back to face him even though he was just a shadow in the dark, and whispered, "You saw the condition that barn is in, Sir. I'm just hoping we can have it cleaned and ready before the wedding starts."

"I have no doubt you'll be successful," he stated confidently before turning in the bed and pulling the covers over his shoulder.

Determined to have that barn shipshape for Shey's wedding reception, Brie headed downstairs to the kitchen where she found the three sisters waiting for her.

Ruth held out a cup of hot cocoa to Brie. "Hot cocoa is the best way to start the day!"

She took the warm mug from Anderson's sister and smiled before taking a sip. "I couldn't agree more…"

The moment she finished her cup, Megan handed a flashlight to her. "You'll need this so you don't accidentally step on a rattlesnake."

Brie looked at her in alarm. "Do they hunt at night? I always thought it was too cold for reptiles."

"That's true in the spring, but it's summer now and the nights are warmer."

Shuddering, Brie turned on her flashlight as soon as she walked outside. Megan was right about the temperature. Although the night air was cooler, it was still pleasantly warm. Following the sisters, she was amused by the bouncing lights coming from their flashlights as they walked in single file to the barn.

Megan stopped short before reaching the barn door and set her flashlight at her feet. She whipped off her t-shirt and laid it over a post.

Brie stared in shock when she saw the other two follow suit. "What…what are you girls doing?" she sputtered.

Ruth stopped unzipping her pants and looked up at Brie. "Trust me, Ma won't allow us in the house covered in horse shit. Especially with the wedding taking place today."

Brie didn't move a muscle as she watched all three sisters strip down until they were completely naked.

"Whatcha waiting for?" Christina asked her.

It seemed this was completely normal for these girls. Being an only child, doing such a thing was completely foreign to Brie. She supposed it might be common for sisters to get naked whenever they cleaned the barn. Still…

Brie felt the need to point out, "We're going to be dealing with excrement."

"Far better to get it on your skin where you can easily wash it off with a hose, than to get it on your clothes and throw all of that dung into Ma's washing machine," Megan stated matter-of-factly.

Brie frowned, still not convinced.

Although it sounded somewhat plausible, getting naked to clean out a barn seemed crazy to her.

"Don't feel shy," Ruth said encouragingly. "We're all girls here. You won't be showing us anything we haven't seen before."

When Brie still hesitated, Christine chimed in, "You're an honorary Anderson sister now."

Touched by her innocent enthusiasm, Brie threw caution to the wind and quickly stripped off her clothes and hung them on the post with the others. The morning air was cold enough that her nipples contracted into tight buds as she stood there before them, feeling foolish.

Megan glanced nonchalantly at her chest. "It's much warmer in the barn. The horses and all that dung heat the place up real nice."

Brie gave her a weary smile as she watched Megan pull the barn door open. As the four of them walked into the darkened barn, Brie was surprised at the silence. She didn't hear the welcoming nicker of the horses in their stalls which she had expected would greet them.

"Let me get the lights," Ruth said.

Brie suddenly questioned what the heck she was doing here. Standing naked in the darkness, she thought to herself, *Shey's going to owe me big time for this…*

When Ruth flicked on the power, the barn filled with light, causing Brie to squint. "Wait. What the…?" she murmured as her eyes adjusted to the bright glare of the lights strung along the walls near the ceiling and over the support beams. Goosebumps of excitement rose on her skin when she looked around the barn in blissful shock.

"Who did this?" she asked, turning to Megan.

Grinning, her green eyes sparkled when Megan answered proudly, "Pa, Thane, and Brad spent all night working on it."

Brie scanned the barn again, shaking her head in amazement.

Sheer white fabric hung down from the ceiling on either side of the rafters and was accented by the white fairy lights hung properly everywhere—the same lights that had been lying in a tangled heap the day before. The multitude of soft white lights gave off a warm glow that made the barn look like a rustic fairyland.

The barrels that had been lying on their sides had been fashioned into high-top tables. And all the old straw had been cleared, exposing the wood floors underneath. The bales of fresh straw that had been strewn about were now placed strategically throughout the barn for added seating.

Christina pointed to long strands of garland laid out in neat piles, as well as the buckets of fresh flowers in colors of yellow, white, pink, and blue, and a big box of canning jars. "We get to do the fun part and decorate!"

Looking down at her naked body and then at the three sisters, Brie asked, "So, why did we have to get naked again?"

The three immediately broke out in uproarious laughter.

Brie shook her head in confusion. "What am I missing here?"

"Christina and I will get our clothes while Megan explains," Ruth informed her as the two younger sisters burst out in fresh giggles as they walked outside.

Turning back to Megan, Brie demanded, "Girl, spill the beans!"

"Okay, okay…" Megan said, holding her palms up toward Brie, as she tried to stop herself from laughing. "Just give me a second." It took Megan several tries to stop laughing long enough to tell her.

As Brie waited, a smile played on her lips at the sheer absurdity of this moment.

"My brother thought you would enjoy getting a taste of what Thane went through on his first visit to the ranch."

Brie stared at her with her mouth wide open. "Are you saying what I think you're saying?"

Megan nodded. "Yep! Brad and my father convinced Thane that they always clean out the stalls naked. And, just like you, Thane didn't believe it at first. But when he saw Brad and Pa strip down to their birthday suits, he did exactly what you just did. However, they never let on that it was a joke."

Brie covered her mouth as she imagined Sir buck naked in this very barn. "So, they all just cleaned out the stalls until they were done?"

Megan grinned and nodded her head.

"I can't believe it," Brie exclaimed, shaking her head in amusement. "But I bet my man looked awesome doing it!"

The two sisters returned with everyone's clothes. While Brie was slipping on hers, she asked, "When did he finally find out that it was just a prank?"

"Not for a long, long time, from what my brother said," Ruth replied, her face flushed from having laughed so hard.

Brie looked at the three girls and started laughing again. "So, that's what the two meant whenever they mentioned 'mucking out the stalls'!" When she envisioned it playing out in her mind, it made her laugh so hard that she found it difficult to breathe. "Oh, my…oh, my…"

Brie's infectious laughter made the other three start up again. It took several minutes before the four of them were able to calm down long enough to work on the task at hand.

But Brie couldn't stop grinning as she helped Megan with the garland. "That has to be the funniest prank I've ever heard of!"

Megan's eyes flashed with amusement. "And now you are part of that memory."

She snorted in disbelief. "How was your brother able to convince you to do this?"

Christina piped up. "It didn't take any convincing."

Brie looked at the child's impish grin and teased, "You are a naughty little thing, aren't you?"

Christina framed her face with her hands and blinked demurely, the picture of pure innocence.

Ruth laughed. "Don't be fooled by that innocent face, Brie. She's the best prankster in our entire family."

Looking at Christina with new admiration, Brie muttered, "I better keep that in mind in the future…"

Giving Brie a friendly slap on the back, Megan stated warmly, "This little prank was the perfect way to initiate you into the Anderson Family."

Brie stared at all three of the girls, saying with a full

heart, "I'm tickled to be part of your crazy family."

The girls embraced her in a long, three-way hug before Ruth announced, "Now, we'd better hurry and get started decorating the place. Ma said she's making cinnamon rolls for breakfast, and they are perfection when they are hot out of the oven!"

Brie and the girls spent the next few hours joking with each other as they decorated the barn. After they hung the last strand of garland made from dried flowers and artful vegetation found in the area, the four of them finished by creating pretty floral arrangements for each table using the canning jars as vases.

Brie felt a deep sense of pride when she stood back and saw how beautiful the barn looked. "I don't think I've ever seen a prettier venue for a reception."

Ruth wrapped her arm around Brie and nodded in agreement.

Looking at her watch, Megan said, "Well, would you look at that? We're going to just make it in time to watch Ma take those cinnamon rolls out of the oven."

Christina bolted to the barn door, calling back, "Last one to the house is a rotten egg!"

Brie chased after the three sisters, laughing as she gazed at the sun rising over the plains, marking this special day. Master Anderson was claiming Shey as his wife this afternoon. Little did his soon-to-be bride know that on this very night, she would find out that the man she just married was a millionaire. Brie couldn't stop smiling to herself just thinking about it.

When she entered the warm kitchen, Brie was shocked to see Ghost Pepper sitting beside Master Anderson. The cat was staring intensely at Anderson's mom while she worked in the kitchen.

Master Anderson and the black feline turned to look at Brie in unison. It was uncanny and gave Brie a shiver. It was as if the two were one.

"What the heck is Ghost Pepper doing here?" she asked Master Anderson. "Did you really fly him all the way from LA?"

Looking down at the black cat, Master Anderson grinned. "He refuses to leave my side these days. I can't say I mind."

He then looked over at his mother scurrying around in the kitchen. "It seems that I might have some competition, however. Ghost seems right smitten with my mama."

Brie giggled as she watched the cat follow Mrs. Anderson's every move, his tail twitching in excitement.

The moment Sir walked into the room, he glanced at Brie with an amused expression on his face.

Master Anderson nodded to him before asking Brie, "So, how did you enjoy mucking out the barn this morning?"

She frowned when she answered. "It was…" Pausing for a moment, Brie glanced from him to Sir, then to Master Anderson's mother and father, before her lingering gaze landed on his three sisters who had perpetrated the prank, "Hilarious!"

Master Anderson slapped her on the back as his family joined in his laughter. "Welcome to the family, young Brie."

Brie didn't miss the mischievous glint in Sir's eyes when he walked up to her and pulled her into his warm embrace.

Grinning up at him, she said, "I can't believe you let me walk into that, Sir…"

He raised an eyebrow. "I've been acutely aware of how much you've wanted to know what happened between Anderson and I on my first visit to this ranch. However, I also knew the only way for you to truly understand was to experience it yourself."

She giggled. "I agree, although I'm very grateful I didn't have to muck out those stalls in the buff."

He leaned in close, kissing her lightly on the lips. "I insisted they spare you that part of the experience."

Brie stood on tiptoes and kissed him, confessing quietly, "Oh Sir, how I wish I'd been there when Anderson and his dad pranked you. I bet you looked magnificent cleaning those horse stalls…"

He chuckled. "It was certainly a day that will live in infamy."

She smiled up at him. "I can't believe how much work you did last night."

Turning to address the other two men in the room, Brie said, "All three of you worked so hard! Here I thought you were whooping it up last night, but the entire time you three were breaking your backs instead."

"They did work hard, didn't they?" Mrs. Anderson said proudly, wiping her floured hands on a towel before grabbing her oven mitts to get the cinnamon rolls out of the oven.

"And we just finished making it look even better!" Christina declared.

"I'm sure you did, little lady," Anderson's dad stated with obvious pride. "You take after your mother in that way."

Turning to his wife, he said with a pleased smile, "You've always had a special touch for making everything beautiful."

Brie thought it was particularly endearing when he leaned down to kiss his wife, especially considering how tiny she was compared to her tall hunk of a husband.

The three girls groaned in unison while Master Anderson ribbed them, "Not in front of the children, Pop!"

His father winked at his four kids. "You *do* realize that it was the immense love I have for your mother that brought all of you into the world."

"Eww…" Christina cried, sticking her fingers in her ears.

"Way to make our minds go there, Pa," Megan teased.

Mr. Anderson wrapped his arms around his wife and lifted her up. "I love this gorgeous woman, and I don't give a damn who knows it!"

The kitchen timer suddenly went off, filling the room with a high-pitched ring.

Placing her back down, Mr. Anderson watched his wife become a whirlwind of energy. Putting on the oven mitts, she ran to the oven to get the cinnamon rolls out while simultaneously ordering her kids to set the table.

Brie stood back, amazed to see how Master Anderson, Megan, Ruth, and Christina moved in synchrony, each sibling doing their task with no questions asked as they set the table in no time flat.

Although it might have seemed strange for people who knew Master Anderson as the Headmaster at the Training Center to take on such a role, Brie found it exceedingly heartwarming.

The Anderson Family was truly a unit, and the love and respect the children had for their parents, as well as for each other, was inspiring.

Love in Many Forms

It seemed like the entire city of Greeley had come out to celebrate Master Anderson's wedding. A passel of neighbors were busy setting up the numerous tables for the reception dinner. The wedding ceremony itself was slated to take place under the shade of a large cottonwood tree near the house where another group were lining chairs up in straight lines for the ceremony.

Brie was standing on the porch steps with Master Anderson when a big truck caked in mud and dust pulled up, and Master Anderson's mom came running out of the house.

"Joe!" she cried excitedly, "I can't wait to finally see it!"

The man got out of the truck and grinned at her as he slowly pulled back the tarp. "I think you're going to like it, sis!"

"This is truly a masterpiece!" Master Anderson exclaimed as he walked up to the truck to look. Staring at the wooden arch his uncle had carved by hand, Master

Anderson shook his head and paused for a moment before clearing his throat, "I'm more touched than I can say, Uncle Joe."

Joe smiled warmly at his nephew. Running his fingers over the intricately etched wood, he said, "I spent many a late night on this baby because nothing less than perfection would be good enough for my favorite nephew on his wedding day."

As the men set about getting the heavy arch out of the truck, Master Anderson's mother glanced at her watch and cried, "Oh, my goodness! The bride-to-be should be arriving any minute. I'd better get back to the kitchen!"

Master Anderson looked at Brie and grinned. "I'd better skedaddle, then. I see a truck heading our way, and it looks like Willis' ol' Chevy."

Brie looked down the long drive and saw a green truck bumping its way down the dirt road. When the old truck pulled up, she spotted Shey and her mother sitting in the front.

An older gentleman with white hair and a battered old cowboy hat got out of the vehicle and walked around, insisting that Shey and her mom stay put so he could open the door for them.

Brie ran down the porch steps to greet them. "Happy wedding day!"

Carefully handing Brie the garment bag containing her wedding dress, Shey confessed to Brie, "I'm so excited, I'm shaking all over."

Shey's mother laughed as Mr. Willis helped her out of the truck next. "My poor daughter has been too excited to eat anything this morning."

Grinning at Brie, Shey said, "My stomach is too full of butterflies."

Master Anderson's mom opened the screen door and gestured to Shey to follow her inside. "Hurry, honey! We don't want my son seeing his beautiful bride-to-be before the ceremony."

While they headed upstairs with Anderson's sisters following behind, his mother called up, "I'll bring up a plate of goodies to you girls."

Somewhere in the farmhouse, a grandfather clock chimed the hour, and Brie suddenly realized how soon the ceremony would be taking place. Heading to the guestroom, she quickly changed clothes, putting on the simple, sleeveless dress with an asymmetrical skirt that flowed whenever Brie walked. The cornflower blue color of the material reminded Brie of the sky on a bright summer's day, and she liked that it complemented her honey-colored eyes.

Heading back to assist the bride, Brie found the large bedroom buzzing with excitement as Master Anderson's three sisters, who had already changed into their dresses, were now busy styling Shey's hair and helping with her makeup.

Since Brie had yet to see the wedding gown, she asked if she could take a peek inside the garment bag hanging from the closet door.

"Of course!" Shey answered, then gently warned, "Be careful when you take it out, though. It was my grandmother's dress, and the fabric is really delicate."

Slowly unzipping the garment bag, Brie was mindful

as she eased the ivory gown out and held it up so everyone could see. All the women in the room murmured in approval when they saw her wedding dress. It was a vintage A-line gown, with delicate sheer sleeves that matched the strip of chiffon decorating the waist of the dress.

"Shey...it's stunning!" Brie told her.

Shey smiled as she reached out and lightly traced her fingertips over the fabric, saying wistfully, "My grandmother passed away two years ago, but I still think about her every day..."

Gazing at the beautiful dress, Brie completely understood why Shey cherished it so much. "What a lovely way to honor your grandmother."

Shey asked her, "Do you mind helping me into it?"

"I would love to," Brie answered. Following Shey behind the curtain the girls had set up, Brie slipped the dress over her head and buttoned up the back of the dress. Although the dress was simple, the fitted bodice complemented the full skirt, and the chiffon accents gave it an elegant touch.

"It looks amazing," Brie gushed.

"I think so, too," Shey murmured happily, running her hands down the skirt with a look of joy on her face.

When Shey stepped from behind the curtain, her mother smiled, nodding as she gently touched the chiffon. "I really thought you should have had a new dress, modern and white—not ivory. But..." She gazed into her daughter's eyes. "I was wrong, Shey, it looks perfect."

Shey had tears in her eyes as she gave her mother a

hug.

Mrs. Anderson walked into the room carrying a tray of miniature sandwiches, plus a number of sweets. The moment she saw Shey in her wedding dress, Mrs. Anderson stopped in her tracks. "I can't tell you how lucky I feel that you chose my son!"

Shey laughed lightly. "I'm the lucky one. You raised an exceptional son, Mrs. Anderson. Brad is as good as they come—incredibly smart, funny, kind…" She then blushed when she added, "…and exceedingly romantic."

"Are you sure you're talking about my brother?" Megan joked.

Mrs. Anderson gave her daughter an amused look, then told Shey, "Brad is a stubborn soul, and he insisted he wasn't willing to settle down until he found his soul mate." Walking up, she cupped Shey's cheek lightly. "I will be forever grateful he did just that."

Brie was moved by the obvious love that Mrs. Anderson had for Shey. Even though it was something she had never experienced from her own mother-in-law, she could imagine the powerful advantage of having two mothers, one from birth and the other through marriage, loving and supporting you through life. It was a priceless gift.

Brie heard a familiar voice call out from downstairs, "*Moye solntse*, give your *dyadya* a hug!"

Brie glanced at Shey. "Do you mind if I say hi to Rytsar?"

"Not at all!"

"I'll go with you," Mrs. Anderson said excitedly. "I haven't seen Anton in ages!"

They hurried downstairs to find Rytsar in the hallway, lifting Hope in the air and smiling at her. The moment he set the little girl down, he noticed the two women standing there. Knowing it had been a long time since Mrs. Anderson had seen him, Brie hung back.

"I've been looking forward to this moment for so long, Anton!" Anderson's mother laughed, rushing to him.

Rytsar bent down to give the tiny woman a heartfelt hug. "I agree, Mrs. Anderson. It has been much too long. I'm grateful this wedding gave me the opportunity to see you again."

"You should know I plan to make blini tomorrow for breakfast in honor of your visit."

Rytsar looked over at Brie and winked before telling Mrs. Anderson, "You should not go to any trouble for me."

"Nonsense! I want to spoil you just like your dear mother would."

His smile suddenly disappeared, and he looked at her thoughtfully. "I had forgotten how much I miss the selfless kindness of a mother. Thank you."

Mrs. Anderson reached up and patted his strong jaw. "She is always with you in spirit, Anton. I will just be her hands tomorrow when I make you breakfast."

"You are a priceless gem, Mrs. Anderson," he stated in a solemn voice.

She smiled at Rytsar proudly. "I feel the same about you. You are the Russian son I never had."

He burst out laughing. "*Da*. I am your stronger and far more handsome son."

She slapped his arm, giggling as she held out her arms to Hope. "Did you know I saved you a special treat to eat?"

Hope eagerly climbed into her arms and pointed toward the kitchen.

Rytsar turned to Brie and spread his arms wide. *"Radost moya."*

She rushed to them, smiling as he enfolded her in his powerful embrace. Even though it had only been a couple of days since seeing him last, she felt the familiar butterflies that being so close to Rytsar always caused.

"I'm so glad you made it safely," she murmured.

Her head bounced lightly against his chest when he chuckled. "It was an uneventful flight, but I'm looking forward to the four of you joining me on my jet after the wedding."

She looked up at him and confessed, "You know, I still haven't gotten used to the idea of flying on a jet. I realize it doesn't faze you, but this girl grew up in a small town in Nebraska where going to McDonald's was a rare and special treat."

He stroked her hair, refusing to let her go just yet. "A special treat, was it?"

She nodded enthusiastically. "It really was! As a kid, whenever my parents bought me a hamburger and small fries, it was pure heaven."

He let out a low chuckle. "My poor *radost moya*. Your idea of heaven was a simple fast-food hamburger while mine was blini, piroshki, and medovik cake made from scratch."

Brie giggled. "If you put it that way, it does sound a

little pathetic."

Squeezing her tight before letting go, he told her, "Head back upstairs and take care of the bride. I do not wish to deprive her of your attention."

Brie squeezed his hand before heading up, but she stopped on the stairs and glanced back. Rytsar was still watching her, a pleased look on his face.

"*Dyadya!*" Hope called to him. "Antony wants you."

Rytsar chuckled and turned, walking toward the kitchen. "What? Is that *moy gordost* I see?"

Brie smiled to herself as she continued up the stairs. She was glad that her children were lucky enough to have such a devoted *dyadya*. Because of the past trouble with Sir's half-sister, and the fact that Brie was an only child, her two children would never have known the selfless love and devotion of an uncle without Rytsar in their lives.

Brie watched as Shey stared out the window at all the people, growing more anxious for the ceremony to begin.

"I haven't seen Brad *all* day!"

Her mother laughed. "That's tradition, sweetheart."

Letting out an exasperated sigh, Shey told her, "I know, Mum. But I've been cooped up in this room for hours when all I really want is to be in Brad's arms."

Her mother patted her on the hand. "There'll be time enough for *that*…young lady."

Shey shot a look at little Christina and then sputtered, "Jeez, Mum…I didn't mean it like that! I just meant that it's hard being separated when I can hear his voice downstairs."

"I totally get it," Brie assured her with a laugh. "I feel that way about my husband even though we've been married for years now and have popped out two kids together."

Megan spoke up. "I have to admit, even though my brother can be a real pain in the…" She glanced at Shey's mother and said politely, "…bum. He really is a nice guy."

Despite all the happiness in the room, Brie noticed that Christina looked sad. "What's wrong, Christina?"

The little girl's bottom lip trembled when she said, "Once Brad gets married, he won't have any reason to come back home."

Mrs. Anderson looked at her daughter with sympathy. "It's the way of life, sweetie. A man leaves his mother and the woman leaves her home. They are meant to become one so they can start their own family together."

Brie crouched down so she was on the same level as Christina. "I'll tell you a secret."

Christina looked at her sorrowfully. "What?"

"Your brother will always come back because he loves you too dang much. Plus, there's no better prankster in the world than you."

Christina nodded, a smile peeking out behind her frown.

Mrs. Anderson grinned at them both and asked

Christina, "Do you want to get our special surprise for Shey?"

"Yes!" Running to the closet, Christina pulled out a large square box and handed it to her mother.

"Shey, I know you didn't want to waste money on flowers for your wedding, so Christina helped me grow these in our garden." Opening the box, she lifted a wreath made of tiny white flowers called Baby's Breath, with strips of ivory satin hanging down artfully in the back.

"You made this?" Shey asked, tearfully.

Mrs. Anderson wrapped her arm around Christina when she answered, "Yes. We knew it would look perfect with your grandmother's wedding dress."

Shey's mother handed her daughter a tissue. "Now, now…you don't want to go spoiling your makeup, sweetheart."

Dabbing her eyes, Shey asked, "Would you put it on for me, Mum?"

When Mrs. Allen took the wreath and placed the flowers on Shey's head, Brie gasped in delight. The floral wreath matched the simplicity of the dress but added an elegant touch.

"You look like a princess!" Christina exclaimed.

Brie nodded. "You certainly do."

Shey smiled, telling Mrs. Anderson and Christina. "Thank you both."

"It has been our joy to watch these flowers grow, knowing they would crown your head on this day," Mrs. Anderson replied, looking at Shey lovingly.

Shey's mother grabbed her purse and pulled out a

small jewelry box, offering it to the bride. "Nana's dress is something old, Mrs. Anderson made you something new, so I have something borrowed for you to wear."

When Shey opened the box, her eyes lit up. "I know these earrings! Da gave them to you as an anniversary present."

Mrs. Allen took the blue topaz earrings from the box and smiled. As she put them on for Shey, she explained, "You were our miracle baby, sweetheart. We'd given up on ever having kids. The day he gave me these earrings for our anniversary was the same day I found out I was pregnant with you."

After Shey and her mother exchanged a heartfelt hug, Ruth cleared her throat. "Naturally, Megan and I wanted to give you something special that is blue. Any guesses as to what it is?" she asked, handing Shey a large gift bag.

Shey shook her head, laughing. "I have no clue what is in this bag. In fact, I'm almost afraid to look after hearing what happened to Brie."

Riffling through the tissue paper, Shey pulled out a baby blue garter belt. "Well, isn't that perfect!"

Megan held up a blindfold in the same color. "We got this for our brother so he would match you when he takes the garter off."

Shey blushed. "I'm nervous about that part. I really don't know how my father is going to react."

"Don't be concerned about that," Mrs. Allen assured her. "Your father had the whole reception hall in stitches when he went for my garter." Mrs. Allen's smile was wistful when she added, "He's always known how to make me laugh…"

Shey grinned. "I guess you and I have the same taste in men, Mum."

There was a knock at the door and Brie heard Shey's father ask nervously, "Can I come in?"

"Of course, Da!" Shey cried, hurrying toward the door.

Brie pulled out her phone and hit record, wanting to catch his reaction. The moment Shey's father entered the room and saw his daughter in her wedding gown, his whole face lit up.

He stood there in silence, his eyes filling up with tears. Shaking his head in disbelief, he told Shey in a hoarse voice, "My sweet little girl…you're all grown up."

Shey smiled shyly at him.

"A true vision of light…" His voice faltered, and he quickly wiped his eyes. "I can't get over how lovely you are."

Shey took his hands and squeezed them tightly, whispering, "Thank you, Da."

He glanced down at his watch and said solemnly. "It's time."

Shey immediately cried out, "Finally!"

Brie laughed as she and the rest of Shey's bridal party headed downstairs to get in line while Shey remained behind with her father.

Glancing back at the two of them, Brie was reminded of her own wedding day and the feeling of anticipation she'd experienced as she waited with her father. There was something sacred about the moment just before two souls commit to loving and supporting each other for a lifetime. Whether it was a wedding or a collaring, there was reason to celebrate the beauty of such a union.

Brie smiled when she went downstairs and spotted Rytsar with Hope. He was standing in the foyer, dressed in a dark blue tux and a black tie. Hope's brown hair was done up in cute little pigtails with blue ribbons. She looked adorable in her blue and white gingham dress and blue cowgirl boots to match.

"Mama!" her daughter cried as soon as she saw Brie.

Brie rushed to her, rubbing noses with Hope. "Aren't you the prettiest darn flower girl the world has ever seen?"

"*Da*, she is," Rytsar agreed proudly.

Hope pointed excitedly behind Brie and cried, "Anya!"

Brie turned to see the huge Kuvasz trotting up to them from the direction of the kitchen. Surprised to find the dog in the house, Brie broke out in giggles when she spied the blue velvet pillow strapped to her torso, with the wedding bands tied onto it with satin ribbon. "Oh, my goodness! Is Anya the ring bearer?"

"Anderson insisted," Sir chuckled as he walked up carrying Antony. He leaned in for a quick kiss, then reached down to pet the large dog.

Anya looked up at Sir with trusting eyes, wagging her tail slowly.

The interaction between them moved and surprised Brie. Although Sir had come to respect Shadow, she had never seen him connect so naturally with an animal as he was right now with Anya. It was touching to see.

Mrs. Willis walked up to Sir and held out her hands. "I'll take that cute little boy from you now."

Brie smiled at the woman. Sir had once shared that the Willis's were parents of Master Anderson's childhood friend, Paige. Tragically, the young girl had died in an accident when she was only ten.

Brie was extremely grateful that Mrs. Willis had offered to hold Antony during the ceremony since Brie, Sir, and Rytsar were all part of the wedding party. The fact that Mrs. Willis and her husband were actively involved in Master Anderson's wedding was a testimony to the strong bonds they still had with him even after all these years. Thanking her for the help, Brie waved goodbye to Antony as she walked away, telling him, "Be good for Mrs. Willis."

Turning to face Sir, Brie looked him up and down in appreciation. "I must say, you look devastatingly handsome as best man, Mr. Davis."

He inclined his head toward her and smiled. "Thank you, Mrs. Davis, and you look stunning in that bridesmaid dress." Leaning closer, he whispered, "Although I look forward to tearing it off of you later…"

Brie giggled, feeling the heat rise to her cheeks as she looked at the other people in the room, secretly thinking, *I can't wait!*

"Until then," Sir murmured, kissing her on the lips.

"Get a room, you two!" Master Anderson teased when he entered the kitchen with Ghost Pepper walking beside him.

Brie's heart skipped a beat when she turned and saw him. Master Anderson was completely swoon-worthy in his stylish black tux. The suit jacket had a distinctive western flair and with it, he wore a bolo tie, black jeans, and fancy leather cowboy boots. However, it was his familiar black Stetson that completed the look.

Mrs. Anderson ran up to her son with a radiant smile. "You look as handsome as your father did the day we were married!"

He tipped his hat to her. "That's quite the compliment, Ma. I know how head over heels you are with the man."

Her green eyes twinkled when she told him, "I've dreamed of this day ever since I held you in my arms."

Taking off his hat, Master Anderson leaned down to give her a peck on the cheek before placing it back on his head and holding an arm out to his mother. "Shall we? I'm hankering to see my beautiful bride."

Exchange of Vows

Everyone in the wedding party quickly lined up as Master Anderson made his way to the front door and waited for the music to begin.

Brie handed Hope the flower basket and knelt down beside her. "Remember, you follow Anya and spread the petals on the ground just like we practiced for our friend, Mr. Anderson."

Hope looked up at the handsome cowboy, and her eyes grew big. When he tipped his hat at her, Hope giggled and held up the basket to him.

"You got this, little lady," he grinned.

A lone guitarist started playing outside, marking the beginning of the ceremony. Master Anderson glanced down briefly at Ghost Pepper, and the two locked eyes. The cat stood up and rubbed his head against Master Anderson's pant leg before turning his gaze toward the door.

Master Anderson then turned to his mother and said with a playful smirk, "Let's do this thing."

As Brie watched him leave, her heart started to race. She understood the significance of this moment in Master Anderson's life. She clearly remembered when he had shared with her about the pain he'd suffered after losing his first love, Amy. He had been certain she was the one, and his heart was completely shattered when she chose someone else.

Years later, when Amy asked Master Anderson to meet her husband, Troy, he'd asked Brie to join him at the restaurant, unable to face them alone. Although the meal was an uncomfortable affair, the couple seemed truly happy, which only broke Master Anderson's heart more when he found out Amy was pregnant with Troy's child.

At the time, Master Anderson couldn't envision his life without her and mourned the loss of that relationship. Of course, he couldn't know that Shey would enter his life years later while he was on his way to LA to take on the role of Headmaster of the Submissive Training Center.

Brie had always had a good feeling about Shey. Not only was she obviously in love with Master Anderson, but she enjoyed exploring BDSM with him as well. Having watched Brie's first documentary before they even met, Shey already knew who he was and his unique talent with the bullwhip. She appreciated every aspect of the man—from his clever pranks to his intense love of animals. And Shey certainly shared in his love for animals, based on the fact that both Ghost Pepper and Anya were part of their wedding party.

Brie moved to stand beside Rytsar, who wrapped his

arm around her possessively. When she met his gaze, he said in a soft, intimate tone, "You look quite fetching today, *radost moya*."

She smiled, laying her head on his shoulder. Brie felt extremely grateful that he was the one walking with her down the aisle today.

As best man, Sir was the first to follow behind Master Anderson. Before leaving, he glanced back at Brie and winked before joining the groom, and she immediately threw him a kiss.

Brie eagerly watched as the youngest sister, Christina, was escorted out by one of Master Anderson's old high school friends.

Ruth went next, escorted by Sebo Vari. Master Anderson had explained when he introduced Sebo to Brie earlier that the two had become friends through Dominus Toth, the man who had mentored Master Anderson as a Dominant when he was in college. Brie knew that Master Anderson held the late Dominus Toth in the highest regard and found it touching that he was being honored in this way on Master Anderson's wedding day.

Hearing murmurs behind her, Brie turned around to see Shey coming down the stairs, holding a colorful bouquet made from the same flowers they'd used to decorate the barn for the reception.

The bride truly looked like a radiant dream come true.

Rytsar squeezed Brie's arm, letting her know their time had come. She turned, facing forward as Rytsar escorted her out the door to the sound of the lone guitarist strumming the simple but exquisite melody as he sang "There is Love" by Peter, Paul, and Mary.

It wasn't until that moment that Brie realized Mrs. Anderson had referenced the lyrics earlier when the women were gathered upstairs. The powerful meaning behind the words in the beautifully haunting song caused Brie to tear up as she looked at Master Anderson standing under the wooden arch, confidently waiting for his bride. She smiled when she saw Ghost Pepper sitting at his feet while Sir stood beside him—his eyes locked on her.

Brie glanced at Rytsar beside her, who kept his gaze forward as he walked in slow, measured steps to the tempo of the music. It suddenly struck her that he'd been robbed of this moment with Tatianna and would never know this joy. It pricked her heart.

When the two of them reached the end of the aisle, Rytsar released her arm and turned to face her, giving Brie a slight smile and nod.

Brie joined the line of bridesmaids and waited in anticipation for Hope's entrance. Everyone began laughing good-naturedly when Anya appeared. She walked toward Master Anderson, her tail wagging slowly and her head held high, while the pillow secured to her back swayed with every step.

There was a unified "Aww…" when Hope appeared next with her flower basket. The little girl immediately froze, looking bewildered when she saw the huge number of people staring at her.

Brie motioned Hope to continue, but she remained rooted to the spot, looking as if she were about to bolt back into the house. Wagging her tail, Anya turned around and walked back to Hope, licking her on the cheek.

Giggling, Hope gleefully followed behind the dog as she started back toward Master Anderson. Midway down the aisle, however, Hope remembered she was supposed to be scattering the petals. She beamed a smile at Brie as she spread the rose petals on the ground just like they'd practiced.

Brie couldn't have been prouder!

When Hope reached the end of the aisle, she dropped her basket and ran to Brie while Anya approached Master Anderson and stood still as he untied the rings from the satin pillow on her back.

Brie swept Hope into her arms and gave her a kiss, while Rytsar quickly snatched the basket off the ground and held it behind him just as the official bridal song began.

Turning toward the house, Brie watched as Shey and her father slowly walked down the aisle toward Master Anderson.

When Brie looked to Master Anderson, her heart completely melted catching the expression on his face. He was staring at Shey with a look of wonder, and the devotion in his eyes stole her breath away.

Brie heard him murmur, "Breathtaking…"

The smile on Shey's face was equally as radiant when she returned his gaze.

Pastor Paul held a Bible in his hands and smiled at the crowd, stating formally, "You may be seated." He then looked at Shey's father and asked, "Who gives this bride to this groom in marriage?"

Mr. Allen stated proudly for all to hear, "I do."

Master Anderson gently took Shey's hands in his, looking at her tenderly. "Hello, darlin'."

Shey's smile grew. "I've missed you!"

People in the audience chuckled hearing Shey's cute confession.

"Feeling's mutual," Master Anderson replied with a wink.

Pastor Paul then addressed the gathering. "Friends, we have come here today to share in the joy of Brad Anderson and Shey Allen's wedding. You hold a place in their hearts reserved for those that they have chosen to call 'family' and they are deeply grateful to every one of you here. Your love has helped to shape our bride and groom into the people they are today."

Master Anderson and Shey stared at each other intently, seemingly oblivious to everyone in attendance.

Pastor Paul turned to face Master Anderson and had to clear his throat to get the groom's attention. Smirking at the crowd, Master Anderson confessed, "I can't help it. My bride is too dang beautiful!"

Someone in the back let out a long whistle of appreciation and the crowd chuckled in response.

Then a wave of seriousness washed over the gathering, and everyone fell silent.

Smiling at Master Anderson, Pastor Paul asked, "Do you, Brad Anderson, take this woman to be your true and wedded wife? Do you solemnly promise before God and these witnesses to love, cherish, honor, and protect her, in sickness and in health, in poverty as in wealth, and to forsake all others and be faithful to her so long as you both shall live?"

Master Anderson looked deeply into Shey's eyes, stating confidently, "I do."

The pastor then turned to the bride.

"Do you, Shey Allen, take this man to be your true and wedded husband? Do you solemnly promise before God and these witnesses to love, cherish, honor, and protect him, in sickness and in health, in poverty as in wealth, and to forsake all others and be faithful to him so long as you both shall live?"

The moment the pastor mentioned the part about "in poverty as in wealth," Brie smiled to herself, knowing that later tonight Shey would become privy to the immense wealth she had just married into. What Brie wouldn't give to see the look on Shey's face when he told her!

Brie knew Master Anderson's mentor Dominus Toth had instructed him to keep the inheritance a secret in a letter after his death. He wanted there to be no doubt in Master Anderson's mind that Shey was marrying him purely out of love and not for his money. The fact that Shey wanted the wedding to be held at the ranch to keep costs down attested not only to her love for Master Anderson but her wish for a bright future as a couple.

Shey let out a shy giggle before answering, "I definitely do."

Smiling warmly at her, Pastor Paul told those in attendance, "The bride and groom have chosen to recite their own vows."

He then nodded to Shey. "You may begin."

Her hands were trembling slightly when she took the

ring that Master Anderson held in the palm of his hand. Smiling up at him bashfully, she said, "I don't want to get this wrong."

He winked at her. "No chance of that, darlin'."

Slipping the ring partially onto his finger, she looked up and said in a tender voice, "The day we met in person, I knew you were the one. I think it was the kindness in your eyes." She then laughed. "Or maybe it was because you snuck your cat into the hotel."

Several women giggled in the crowd.

"I was smitten and had to hide how completely head over heels I was with you when we played our first game of poker together."

Master Anderson tilted his head, a smile playing across his lips when she mentioned their poker game.

"And here we are, Brad, about to be married and, somehow, I'm even more in love with you now. How is that even possible?" she asked, her voice full of wonder. "I am honored that I get to be your wife and can't wait for the wild adventures ahead. Because if there's one thing I know…being with you means my life will never be dull."

He chuckled.

Glancing down at the ring, she vowed, "I promise to love you well and never leave your side." She finished sliding the wedding band onto his finger and looked up at him with a huge smile. "With this ring, I thee wed."

Master Anderson stared at her intently for a moment before he began. "Shey Allen, I will never forget the day I met you." He turned her hands palm-side up. "I was introduced to the magic of these hands first, but then came to know the beautiful soul behind them. I love your gorgeous red hair and the twinkle in your eyes, but it's your love of life and your kindness that have stolen my heart."

He placed the ring partially on her finger, stating, "This ring is my sacred gift to you. It is a symbol of my love and a sign that from this day forward, my love will always surround and protect you." Slipping the ring fully onto her finger, he added in a solemn tone, "With this ring, I thee wed."

Master Anderson then broke out in a grin, stating, "You'll never be able to get rid of me now!"

The entire assembly erupted in applause and joyous laughter.

Brie's glance darted to Mr. and Mrs. Willis standing in the back. Mrs. Willis was bouncing Antony in her arms, her face glowing as she stared at Master Anderson and Shey. Despite the tragic loss of their daughter Paige as a child, the couple was fully invested in Master Anderson's happiness. Brie believed Paige was with them in this moment, certain the young girl must be rejoicing with her best friend on his wedding day.

Pastor Paul stated in a formal voice, "By the authority vested in me by the state of Colorado, I now pronounce you husband and wife." He then broke out in a warm grin when he told Master Anderson, "You may kiss the bride!"

Sweeping Shey up into his arms, he gave her a long and passionate kiss to the sound of celebratory whistles as all of the people wearing cowboy hats threw them into the air.

Brie looked at Sir standing across from her, remembering the joy of their own wedding day. She then glanced at Rytsar and smiled, deeply grateful that the three of them could share in this moment with Master Anderson.

After being single for such a long time, the sexy Dom had finally found a woman who was not only in love with him, but who also celebrated his kinky ways. Shey was the perfect "shoe" for Master Anderson in every way.

When the couple finally broke their embrace, Shey was left breathless and trembling. The two then turned to face their friends with radiant smiles.

Pastor Paul announced with pride in his voice, "May I present to you, Mr. and Mrs. Anderson!"

Difference

B rie was busy getting the children ready for the trip back to California when she found herself staring out the window of the ranch house, watching the prairie grass swaying in the breeze. She was struck by how peaceful it was and smiled to herself, thinking of Master Anderson as a little boy here.

It thrilled her heart to know he and his new bride were currently on a long flight headed to a luxurious honeymoon where they could explore the many different animals of Africa. Brie couldn't wait to hear about all of their adventures on their return, as well as Shey's reaction to her new financial status, and she smiled to herself.

"What are you thinking about, *radost moya*?" Rytsar asked, popping his head into the bedroom.

She grinned. "Just thinking about Master Anderson and Shey."

"It was a fine wedding."

Her grin grew wider. "Yes, I thought it was absolutely perfect."

Rytsar gave her a private wink, saying, "The barn wasn't too bad, either."

She stopped packing and felt the heat rise to her cheeks when she recalled the sexy romp she'd enjoyed in the hayloft the night before with both men. "Yes, I think the barn may have been the best part of the whole weekend."

"I quite agree," Sir stated, stepping into the bedroom. "By the way, the vehicle just arrived."

Rytsar immediately grabbed two of the suitcases and told Brie with a mischievous glint in his eye, "I have another surprise for you."

Before she could question him on it, Rytsar headed out of the room.

Her mind latched onto the obvious and her jaw dropped. Turning to Sir, she asked, "Are we headed to the Isle?"

He chuckled, zipping up the suitcase she'd just finished packing. "Not that I'm aware of."

Brie was still pondering what Rytsar was up to while they were boarding his private jet a short time later. After buckling the kids in their car seats, Brie sat down and dug out her tablet, looking for an animated movie for Hope to watch during the flight.

She heard a commotion at the door hatch and was surprised to see Maxim hurriedly enter the plane just seconds before it was scheduled to take off.

"For you, Mrs. Davis," he said, breathing hard as he thrust a brown paper bag at her.

Brie opened it up and glanced at Rytsar, laughing in

delight when she took out a single hamburger and small fries. "My little piece of heaven…"

Rytsar nodded, an amused look on his face.

She was touched that he'd remembered. Picking up a crunchy fry, she broke it in half and handed a piece to both children. "Have a taste of Mommy's childhood."

She looked back at Rytsar, who was smiling to himself.

The captain came out to inform them the jet had been cleared for take-off.

Sir immediately checked the children's seatbelts before sitting down next to Rytsar. Occupying the chair opposite her, Sir buckled up. Brie noticed the tight grip he had on the armrest. When he caught her staring at his hand, he loosened his grip and gave her a tight smile.

Rytsar noticed the exchange and elbowed Sir. "You will never guess where we are headed."

Sir turned to him. "Los Angeles, I assume."

"*Nyet*. I have a little detour planned. Any guesses, *moy droog*?"

"It can't be Fiji," he stated.

"Correct."

Rytsar glanced at Brie and caught her disappointed expression. Chuckling, he said, "Keep guessing, comrade."

Sir indulged him and rattled off a litany of destinations that all sounded wonderful to Brie, but Rytsar just shook his head.

"Fine. I give up." Sir huffed, tired of guessing.

Just then, the captain announced over the intercom that the plane had reached altitude and they were free to unbuckle their seatbelts.

Sir turned to Rytsar with a smirk. "I see what you did there, Durov."

Brie suddenly realized that the guessing game had simply been a ploy to take Sir's mind off of the takeoff. It was subtle but strategic. Brilliant!

She smiled at Rytsar, appreciating his kindness. "So, I guess that means there's no detour after all," she joked.

The mischievous look in his eyes returned when he said, "*Nyet.*"

The jet landed in Moscow eleven and a half hours later.

During the flight, Rytsar explained he had been re-quested to speak at a symposium on the topic of human trafficking. "They asked me to talk about the Tatianna Legacy Center and the success rate of the survivors who go through our program."

"What an honor! You must be so proud," Brie told him.

"*Nyet,*" he replied. "I only feel pain knowing that I haven't been able to do more."

Sir frowned. "You can't look at it that way, old friend. Every person you help gives back the future that was ripped from them."

"But they shouldn't have lost it in the first place!" Rytsar declared angrily, pounding his fist on the armrest.

Hope whimpered, responding to Rytsar's open dis-tress.

"Do not fret, *moye solntse*," he said soothingly, smiling at her.

Keeping his calm, he told Sir in a lower voice, "If I could, I would rid the world of every slaver in existence, *moy droog*—whatever the personal cost. Instead, I am left trying to stop the tide of casualties they create. It's like desperately trying to hold onto water while you watch it drain from your hands."

"But you are making a difference, Rytsar," Brie insisted. "And when this documentary is finally released, I hope to add a million more dollars to your efforts."

He nodded to her. "It is appreciated, *radost moya*."

But Brie could see by the forlorn look in his eyes that he would always be haunted by the ones he couldn't save.

Picking Hope up, Brie whispered in her ear to give her *dyadya* a hug. She nodded eagerly and ran to him as soon as Brie set her down.

Rytsar's ready laughter filled the cabin as he lifted Hope high and then hugged her tight. But Brie knew that sound belied the heavy burden of guilt he carried with him constantly.

When they arrived in Russia in the late afternoon, Brie saw that Rytsar's driver was waiting for them, along with the nanny who had watched their children during their last visit to Russia when they'd visited the salt mines of Yekaterinburg.

Brie held out her hand to the young woman. "It's lovely to see you again, Innessa."

Making a quick curtsy before she took Brie's hand, Innessa stated in disbelief, "I can't believe how much the children have grown, Mrs. Davis."

Brie smiled at her kids. "I feel exactly the same way!"

Once they were on the road, Rytsar hit a button that raised the partition so the driver and nanny would not be able to hear them. He said in a low voice, "I am taking you to a place that means the world to me."

Brie's eyes lit up. "Oh, I can't wait to see it!"

She immediately turned to Sir and asked, "Do you know where we're headed?"

He shook his head, chuckling. "No clue, babygirl."

Rytsar gazed at Sir intently. "Nobody knows, *moy droog*. This is a secret I've kept since I was twenty-one."

Sir tilted his head. "I thought there were no secrets between us, brother."

Rytsar snorted in amusement. "There may be one or two. How about you? Any secrets I should know about?"

Sir smirked when he answered, "I plead the Fifth."

Brie looked at them both, wondering what other secrets the two still kept from her and from each other.

Looking at his watch, Rytsar told them, "We'll have just enough time to visit before we head into Moscow for the symposium. I don't expect the event tonight will take more than a couple of hours." He straightened the cuffs of his suit and cleared his throat before looking out the window.

Rytsar looked extremely uncomfortable, and Brie

wondered if he might be nervous about speaking at the event.

"You're going to do a great job," she assured him.

He turned his head and reached out to stroke her cheek but said nothing. Briefly glancing at the two children, he again stared out the car window.

When the vehicle rolled to a stop at the crest of a tall hill, Rytsar lowered the partition. "Stay here with the children, Innessa. We will be back shortly."

"Yes, *Gospodin*."

Rytsar exited the vehicle with Brie and Sir following close behind him. Brie looked around at all the tall trees covering the top of the hill overlooking Moscow. "This is beautiful."

"*Da*, it is," he agreed with satisfaction, then commanded, "Come. Follow me."

The three walked down a narrow path between the trees that eventually opened up to a valley below. Rytsar stared at a modern building with large windowpanes nestled between the hills surrounding it. There was an impressive garden on the west side of the building with wandering paths through manicured flower beds, and strategically placed stone benches throughout to sit and enjoy the scenery.

"What is this place?" Sir asked him.

Instead of answering, Rytsar stared at it long and hard before reaching into his pocket and pulling out his wallet. He momentarily looked down and took out a photo, holding it out to them. "I had this picture taken the day I had to leave them behind." His voice caught and he shook his head before taking a moment to regain his composure.

Brie took the picture from him and held it up so she and Sir could see it. In the old photo, Rytsar was down on one knee, surrounded by four teenage girls. Brie was shocked by how young he looked in the picture, but what struck her more was the expression on Rytsar's face.

It was so full of love and hope that it gave her goosebumps looking at it. "Who are they?" she asked, unable to take her eyes off the photo.

"They were the first," he answered.

She had no idea what he meant.

Sir took the photo from her to study it more closely. Then he asked in disbelief, "Did you have a shelter for survivors before the Tatianna Legacy Center?"

Rytsar nodded, letting out a tortured sigh.

"Why did you keep it a secret from me?"

Turning to face Sir, he said, "I had to. My brother Andrev sabotaged the project. In one fell swoop, he destroyed Dr. Volkov's impeccable career and forced me to abandon the girls in this picture."

Brie studied the young women's faces more closely and noticed that one wore a strained smile and had tears in her eyes.

Rytsar noticed who she was looking at and told Brie in a tender voice, "That was Lada. She was the first to come to me."

Brie looked up and noticed a tear running down his cheek. "What happened to her, Rytsar?"

He frowned, looking back at the large building. "Through a third party, I was able to secure this building for the girls, so the program could continue and grow. But the only way to truly keep all of them safe was to disappear from their lives completely."

Rytsar glanced back at the photo she held in her hand. "That was the last time I saw any of them, *radost moya.*"

Sir put his hand on Rytsar's shoulder. "I knew your brother was a worthless piece of shit, but I had no idea he betrayed you like this."

Rytsar's voice was strained when he shared, "That bastard not only betrayed me but Dr. Volkov and the innocent girls in this picture."

Looking back at the building, he confessed, "I come once a year to visit this place, hoping against hope that those four girls survived."

Brie walked up to Rytsar and wrapped her arms around him in support. "I'm sure they did."

Rytsar swallowed hard, then nodded to her as he took the photo and carefully placed it back in his wallet.

A heaviness settled over them as the three walked back down the path to the vehicle.

As they rode into Moscow, Brie had time to reflect. She couldn't believe that the Tatianna Legacy Center was actually the second facility Rytsar started.

Even at a young age, he had been on a path to making a positive difference in the world. It was a shame it had come at such a deep, personal cost to him—one that still haunted him today.

When they pulled up to the convention center where Rytsar was slated to deliver his presentation, Innessa joined them, and they followed Rytsar into the building as a group.

A professional-looking woman met them at the entrance. "Thank you for coming, Mr. Durov," she said in Russian.

Brie noticed Hope instantly perk up and realized that her little girl might be mastering Russian at a faster rate than she was under Rytsar's tutorage.

"If you'll follow me, I'll escort you and your guests to your table," the woman told him pleasantly.

"Thank you," Rytsar replied in a formal tone. Brie noticed him staring at the woman for several tense seconds before shaking his head and reaching out to take Hope from Brie. Rytsar insisted on carrying the little girl as they followed the woman down the hallway.

Sir glanced at Brie and gave her an encouraging smile as they entered a large convention room filled with elaborately set tables. Brie had naturally assumed the symposium would be held in an auditorium with rows of theater seats, not this fancy affair.

They were led to a table near the front. Brie sat down beside Rytsar and offered to take Hope from him, but he assured her that he didn't mind. He then smiled at Hope as he bounced her on his knee. Brie suspected that her daughter was providing Rytsar with a sense of calm.

Before the event officially began, they were treated to a traditional Russian meal that included some of Brie's favorite dishes, including caviar with blini, piroshki, and beef stroganoff.

Once the plates had been cleared, all eyes turned to the stage. Brie noticed Rytsar suddenly straighten up in his chair when a distinguished-looking gentleman walked onto the stage and the people around them started clapping, including Rytsar.

After seeing Rytsar's reaction, Brie openly stared at the man, wondering who he was.

Holding up his hands to the audience, the gentleman quickly quieted the room. "Please, I'm only here to introduce the first speaker for this evening. A man who has made it his life's work to provide quality care to the survivors of human trafficking. It is my pleasure and honor to introduce to you Anton Durov."

Rytsar gave Hope a kiss on the forehead before handing her to Brie. She noted his huge smile as he approached the stage. Holding out his hand to the master of ceremonies, Rytsar gave the man a vigorous handshake before turning to the audience.

"Please, give Dr. Volkov the reception he deserves."

Brie stood up with Sir, joining in the applause. She felt honored to be meeting the esteemed doctor in person. Not only was he a good friend of Rytsar's, but he was also the same physician who was personally committed to overseeing Lilly's mental care.

After the applause eventually quieted, Dr. Volkov left the stage so Rytsar could speak. Brie sat transfixed as she listened to Rytsar share the story of Stephanie, the young woman he saved years ago and who now ran the Tatianna Legacy Center.

In Rytsar's speech, he disclosed the number of survi-

ok*Craving His Touch*

vors who had attended the Center up to that point and the percentage who had completed the program. He then shared the names of those who had not survived despite the professional care they'd received.

"We must never forget those who lost their lives," he stated somberly. "Every one of them had a future that was stolen from them…and those they loved."

After ending on that somber note, the room remained silent as Dr. Volkov returned to the stage.

"Anton Durov, your passion and commitment to the survivors has not gone unnoticed."

Rytsar looked at him strangely but then glanced around as the large room was suddenly illuminated with bright light.

"Everyone here tonight has come to thank you. They are the product of your ongoing commitment to the mission you began over fifteen years ago, and they want you to know they not only survived but continue to flourish."

As Dr. Volkov read off the names, each person in the room stood up. Rytsar looked over the crowd, shaking his head in disbelief with a look of amazement on his face. When the name Lada Belova was called, Brie noticed the woman who had greeted them at the entrance stand up.

Rytsar immediately jumped off the stage and walked to her, his arms outstretched. Brie had to wipe away her tears as she watched their emotional embrace.

As Brie scanned the crowded room, her eyes blurry with tears, she looked at everyone in the audience with a sense of awe. So many people—so many lives—were represented here tonight. They were all connected because of Rytsar's singular passion to save the broken.

He was proof that one person could truly make a meaningful difference in the world.

The Cabin

The symposium lasted until the wee hours of the morning. Every person in attendance wanted to personally thank Rytsar and share their story, as well as introduce him to their spouses and children. It was wonderfully inspiring for Brie, and she could not even imagine how much it must mean to Rytsar—though she saw it on his face.

When they finally left the convention center, her children had already fallen asleep under Innessa's care and didn't stir even when they were buckled into their car seats. Brie was completely exhausted as well and ready to follow them into dreamland. Laying her head against Sir's shoulder, she sighed in contentment as her eyes fluttered closed.

"Durov, where are we headed?" she heard Sir ask as she was drifting off to sleep.

Curious to hear the answer, she lifted her head and heard Rytsar say, "Feel free to go to sleep, brother. I hadn't planned on the engagement taking more than a few hours." He snorted. "As poignant as this night has been, we are leaving tomorrow night, and I am not a man to be denied."

"What are you talking about?" Brie asked him groggily.

Rytsar turned and flashed her a grin. "Go to sleep, *radost moya*. I want you well rested."

Sir laid her head back on his shoulder and kissed her forehead. Too tired to protest, Brie fell back to sleep and didn't stir until she felt Sir lay her down on a soft bed and cover her with a warm blanket.

Sometime later in the night, she woke up again and instinctively reached out for Sir. Surprised to find he wasn't there, she opened her eyes and was momentarily disoriented. Looking around the room as the moonlight shone through the window, she suddenly recognized exactly where she was.

The cabin!

Brie squeaked and threw back the covers. Tiptoeing out of the bedroom, she headed toward a flickering light down the hallway. There she found both men silently playing a game of chess by candlelight. Brie found it exceedingly charming.

Rather than disturb them, she quietly headed back to bed, smiling as she fell back to sleep.

"Rise and shine, *radost moya*!" Rytsar commanded, his booming voice filling the bedroom.

Brie wiped the sleep from her eyes and sat up, grinning at him when she saw he was holding both children in his arms.

"Did you even get any sleep?" she asked, then turned to look at Sir, who was sitting up in bed beside her. "Either of you?"

Sir only smiled in answer.

"Out of bed, sleepyheads!" Rytsar commanded with a smirk.

Looking at Antony, he said, "I think it's time your *dyadya* teaches you and your sister to make some of my *mamulya's* dishes, starting with my favorite one for breakfast."

Brie loved the idea.

Once Rytsar left with the kids, she quickly got out of bed to dress. As she was slipping on her socks, she told Sir, "I can't believe he brought us to the cabin during the night. This is an unexpected treat!"

"I agree," Sir stated, pulling a sweater down over his head. "Well worth the drive, although we only have today to enjoy it."

Brie bit her lip as she put her hands on his toned chest. "This is the place where we had our first three-some…"

"Yes, it is," he murmured, swooping in to give her a kiss. "I have fond memories of that encounter, and we plan to add a new memory today."

Brie shivered when she felt the electricity of his touch as he placed his hand on her back and led her out of the bedroom.

Walking to the kitchen, Brie saw her children sitting

on the counter. Rytsar set a large bowl in between the two, telling them, "This first dish is called syrniki. It's similar to your mama's pancakes, but mine are much better."

Rytsar looked up at Brie and winked.

"Before a good chef begins, they always wash their hands," he told them solemnly. One at a time, he helped both kids soap up their hands, rinse, and then dry them.

After he had washed his own, he clapped his hands together and smiled at them. "Now, it's time to cook!"

Hope and Antony clapped their hands, responding to his enthusiasm.

Rytsar pulled out a white brick from a package on the counter and showed it to the children. "You start with farmer's cheese. You need to crumble it into little pieces." He handed them each a small piece and then showed them how to break it up into the bowl.

Hope snuck a bite when she thought Rytsar wasn't looking.

"I saw that, *moye solntse*," he chuckled, ripping a bite-sized chunk off the brick, and popping it into his mouth.

Rytsar then produced two eggs. Holding one in each hand, he tapped them on the counter and cracked them two-fistedly into the bowl in one fluid motion like a magician.

Hope clapped her hands wildly. "Again, again!"

He chuckled. "We only need two eggs."

Brie looked at Rytsar in admiration. "I've never seen eggs cracked like that before. I'm impressed!"

He nodded to her with an air of sexy arrogance.

Taking out a measuring cup and a spoon, Rytsar instructed Hope to fill it halfway with flour. Hope took the task seriously, sticking out her tongue as she filled up the cup. Rytsar praised her for a job well done, then held the cup for Antony so he could pour it into the bowl.

Rytsar added some sugar next, which he let the kids taste, and then dramatically sprinkled a generous pinch of salt.

Sticking his bare hands into the mix, he started massaging the ingredients, encouraging the kids to help him. Once he was satisfied with the consistency, he took a handful out and formed it into a ball before patting it into a thick little pancake. "You must pat it for me for good luck," he told the children, holding it out to them.

Hope smacked it hard and he shook his head. "*Nyet, nyet…*" he instructed. "Gently. Like patting Little Sparrow on the head."

Antony gave it a little pat and looked up at Rytsar expectantly.

"That's right, *moy gordost.*"

Hope tried again, lightly patting it this time.

When Rytsar nodded approvingly, she smiled.

After making five of the little pancakes, he helped the kids dredge them in flour.

"Now for the magic!" he announced, pouring some oil into a warm pan. "You want to cook it on medium-low."

Turning to Hope, he asked, "What do you want to cook it at?"

"Medum low."

"Very good, *moye solntse!*"

Rytsar then placed the five doughy pancakes in the

pan. Holding up his fingers, he said, "We cook them for five minutes on each side until golden brown."

He turned to address Brie. "How long, *radost moya?*"

Brie giggled when she answered, "Five minutes."

"Vewy good, Mommy!" Hope cried.

Brie grinned at her.

When the syrniki were done, Rytsar put one on each plate. Grabbing the two children, he carried them to the table amid peals of their laughter. Brie and Sir then set each plate on the table.

Rytsar headed back to the kitchen, returning with a bowl of powdered sugar. "The final touch," he stated dramatically. Sprinkling each syrniki with a dusting of powdered sugar, he told the children, "Look how I make it snow."

Standing back, he spread his arms wide and smiled at Hope and Antony. "Enjoy the pillowy pancakes that you have made!"

Brie looked down at her plate. "It looks delicious."

Sir lifted his syrniki with his fork and examined the other side. "Durov, it looks a little charred to me."

"Never mind your papa. He knows nothing," Rytsar assured the children. "A little black around the edges makes them tastier."

Looking at Antony's dark syrniki, he grabbed the powdered sugar again. "You need more snow on that, *moy gordost.*"

Rytsar then leaned over to Brie and whispered, "In truth, I never could pan-fry them correctly—not even under my *mamulya's* watchful eye."

Brie giggled, thrilled to discover this part of his past.

Pointing to the bowls of sour cream and several different jams on the table, Rytsar told the children, "It's not complete without a dollop on top. Which one would you like?"

Brie was charmed by his entire cooking lesson. Grinning down at the charred syrniki sitting on her plate covered in powered "snow," she felt nothing but love in that moment.

"What would you like?" Rytsar asked her, interrupting her thoughts.

"Sour cream, please."

"Excellent choice, *radost moya*. Inside your chest beats the heart of a true Russian."

While they were eating the first batch, Maxim finished cooking the remaining syrniki and then placed the plate on the table. Brie noticed how perfectly browned each one was and secretly smiled to herself.

"I must say, old friend, the symposium last night was truly inspiring," Sir told Rytsar as he took a bite of his burnt syrniki and smiled at Hope, who had been staring at him intently, anxious for his reaction to the breakfast she helped make.

"I agree, brother. Seeing Lana and her little brood of babes…" He sat back, patting his chest with an open hand. "My heart has never been so full!"

"Someone needs to write down all of their stories," Brie told him. "It would be an inspiration to new survivors to read them and know what's possible in their future."

"Agreed," Rytsar stated. Snapping his fingers, he told Maxim. "Call Titov and see if he can help make that happen."

"Yes, G*ospodin*."

As Rytsar took the last bite of his syrniki, he chewed slowly, gazing at Brie with a smoldering look in his eyes.

Rytsar joined Brie outside while she was pushing both kids on the new swing set he'd had installed.

She glanced at him, shaking her head, as he walked up. "A castle spire for a slide? Don't you think that's a bit much—even for you?"

Rytsar looked at the elaborate wooden structure and shook his head. "N*yet*. And I will tell you why."

He took over swinging Antony so she could concentrate on Hope. As they swung the children in tandem, he admitted, "When I purchased this land, I brought Anderson out here to this very clearing."

"I didn't know that."

He nodded. "I asked him what I should do with the eight-hundred acres, and he suggested I build a rustic cabin rather than the deluxe vacation home I was planning. I visited this same clearing a year later."

Rytsar paused, looking at the cabin he had given her as a birthday gift. "I envisioned it just like this."

Turning back to her, he added, "The vision I had was so strong—so real—that I felt if I just reached out, I could literally touch it."

"Wow," she murmured, feeling a quickening in her spirit.

"But that's not all…" Rytsar glanced at the large play structure again. "I saw this, too. All of it."

Glancing at Hope for a moment, Rytsar confessed, "When I built the original swing set for a baby I hoped you would have someday, I had yet to truly believe…"

"Believe what, Rytsar?"

He snorted, his blue eyes meeting hers. "What you see now?" He glanced at the new swing set with the castle spire. "*This* is what I envisioned all those years ago, *radost moya*—and that vision included your children."

Brie's jaw dropped. Staring at him in shock, she was suddenly struck with a realization. "Is that why you were so sure Hope would be a girl?"

He nodded.

Maxim, along with several of Rytsar's men, came out to join them.

"Keep the children entertained for me," Rytsar ordered, smacking Maxim on the chest good-naturedly.

"Come, *radost moya*," he ordered in a sultry voice as he headed to the cabin.

Defying Gravity

"*Moy droog,*" Rytsar called out when he entered the cabin with Brie.

Sir walked out of their bedroom dressed for a trek in the woods. When he produced a set of furry boots from behind his back, Brie broke out in a grin.

"Take everything off, téa. These are the only things I want you to wear."

Her heart raced, remembering when she wore furry boots outside in the snow while tied to a tree. This would be a whole new experience since it was a lovely summer day.

Brie immediately disrobed, quickly following Sir's command. As she undressed, she thought about her favorite dubstep song. Gyrating her hips to the beat of the song in her head, she took off each piece of clothing, giving each motion a seductive flair. She made sure to caress her breasts and ass as she bared herself to both men, imagining it was their hands against her skin.

Once she was completely naked, Brie lowered her

head and waited in anticipation.

Sir approached her, commanding in a low, sensual voice, "Lean against him."

Rytsar wrapped an arm around her, and she obediently leaned against his muscular chest for support as Sir lifted one leg and slipped the first boot on. Zipping it up, he did the same for the other.

Standing again, he held out his hand to her. She took it and he twirled her around once, stating. "Damn fine, wouldn't you agree?"

"*Da…*" Rytsar answered huskily, leaning into her throat to give her a love bite.

Weak in the knees and covered in goosebumps, Brie squeaked when the Russian picked her up and slung her over his shoulder.

Sir grabbed a tool bag off the floor and gave her ass a playful slap, telling Rytsar, "Lead on, old friend."

The Russian headed to the door opposite the one he and Brie used to take the children out to the play area. Brie felt the thrill of vulnerability when he carried her out into the wide-open.

Brie smiled to herself, enjoying the erotic feel of the breeze caressing her naked butt, as she bounced with every step Rytsar took while he walked down a dirt path leading into the woods.

Sir followed behind them, staring at her in a lustful way that let her know he was already contemplating the erotic things he planned to do to her.

"I know every trail, river, and lake on this property," Rytsar stated. "Where do you think I am going to take you?"

Feeling flirty, Brie answered, "Wherever, whenever, and as many times as you want."

His warm chuckle filled the mountain air. "You certainly have a cheeky sub, *moy droog*," he said, giving her a stinging slap on the ass.

"The cheekiest," Sir replied, winking at Brie.

As the forest grew dense and the air cooled around them, it caused her nipples to harden. Being carried out into the forest by two handsome men was an exhilarating thrill, especially knowing they were about to have their way with her.

Rytsar's progress slowed as he worked his way up a steep hill. When they neared the top, the trail suddenly opened up into a clearing surrounded by a thick grove of trees. Bright sunlight shone down from above, warming Brie's cool skin.

He set her down on her feet, wiping the sweat from his brow before physically turning Brie around so she could see why he had brought her up here.

There, in the center of the clearing, were four tall trees. A large, wood-framed bed had been suspended with chains attached to the tree's limbs high above.

Rytsar walked up to the bed and smiled at Brie as he pushed on it. She squeaked when she saw it swing freely. "Oh...that bed looks like fun."

"It should prove entertaining, eh, comrade?" Rytsar asked, raising an eyebrow at Sir.

Sir stared at the suspended bed with interest. "Defying gravity will make for a stimulating challenge."

Addressing Brie, Sir asked, "Are you prepared to fly in a completely new way, téa?"

She felt shivers of desire as she looked at the bed hanging on its chains from the tree limbs. "Yes, Master! Shall I take off my boots?"

"Oh, no…I plan to fuck you hard in those boots."

Brie squeaked when Sir picked her up and carried her to the suspended bed. Laying her down on it, Brie felt it sway gently underneath her. The feeling reminded her of a boat being lightly rocked on the ocean.

Rytsar grasped one of the thick chains supporting the bed and shook it, stating with a wicked grin, "It is sturdy enough to hold a bull, *radost moya*."

The bed rocked more powerfully, causing Brie to giggle as she instinctually spread her arms out to brace herself.

Rytsar glanced at Sir. "This will be entertaining."

"As long as one of us doesn't get seasick," Sir chuckled.

Both men quickly undressed, tossing their clothes into the tool bag while Brie watched. Sitting up, she bowed her head as they approached her.

With her heart racing, she asked Sir, "How may I serve you, Master?"

"We will begin with something simple," Sir stated.

Turning to Rytsar, he said, "You deep-throat her while I eat her pussy."

Brie shivered in excitement as Rytsar moved to the edge of the bed and grasped a chain in each hand.

"Present your lips to me, *radost moya*."

Brie slowly crawled to him while he kept the bed steady. She carefully lay on her back while he let go of the chains to pull her body closer to him, positioning her head so it hung just a little off the edge of the bed.

Brie looked up at him expectantly and opened her lips, sticking out her tongue invitingly to him.

Once she was in position, Sir climbed onto the bed. Brie immediately felt it swing in response to his motion, making her stomach flutter. After spreading her legs wide, Sir settled between them and began teasing her clit, first with his fingers and then with his tongue.

Rytsar looked down at Brie hungrily as he guided his cock into her mouth. Quickly grabbing the chains again, he controlled the motion of the bed. Brie grasped his shaft with her hand to help control the depth as she relaxed her throat to take him more deeply. He then eased his cock farther down her throat, groaning as he watched her lips encase him.

Rytsar began swinging the bed in a slow but steady motion. The overall movement reminded her of a sex swing, but instead of her body being cradled in the mesh of a swing, the bed felt much more open and free.

Sir groaned, responding to the increased movement as he licked and teased her clit. Because the swinging bed felt so different, Brie found the experience incredibly erotic and was seriously turned on sharing this new experience with them.

Rytsar ramped up the length of each stroke but kept the motion slow as she deepthroated him. Sir responded by intensifying his attention on her clit.

The rocking motion added to the dual stimulation, and she soon found herself highly aroused.

"She's so wet," Sir murmured between her legs. "We should take advantage of it and change positions."

Rytsar pulled out and leaned down, kissing her passionately on the lips before commanding, "Present that fine cunt."

Brie remained on her back while he helped turn her, repositioning her body so her pussy was now on the edge of the bed where her head had been.

Sir lay down beside Brie, his cock inches from her face. She grasped his shaft eagerly, wanting to please him. Purring with desire, she licked the head of his cock before taking him into her mouth.

Rytsar grabbed her legs and lifted them straight up, crossing them at the knees and resting her ankles against his chest. He grasped them tightly with one hand while he guided his shaft into her wet pussy. Brie let out a gasp as she took his full length in that challenging position.

"*Blyad!*" he exclaimed huskily, growling in satisfaction.

In response to his vocal pleasure, Brie moaned around Sir's shaft. It took several moments for her body to adjust to the depth of his cock as the bed swung back and forth.

Concentrating her attention on Sir's cock, Brie sought to create the same intensity for him that she was feeling.

Rytsar started swinging the bed at a faster tempo, pumping his cock deeper into her pussy. It drove Brie wild, and she began sucking Sir's cock with more vigor. She lost herself for a moment, reveling in the erotic taste of his precome.

"Slower," Sir ordered through clenched teeth.

Brie immediately released his cock and pulled back

for a moment, allowing his libido to ebb before she opened her mouth to take him again.

The feeling of Rytsar's spirited fucking, along with the motion of the bed as she and Sir swung in tandem, had her body buzzing at a dangerously high level.

When she took Sir's cock into her mouth again...that feeling of the ridge of his cock moving in and out of her mouth while she was being fucked by Rytsar turned her on so fiercely that her eyelids fluttered.

Brie completely bypassed teetering on the edge of a climax and jumped straight into a powerful orgasm. Her whole body stiffened, then trembled uncontrollably as her orgasm rocketed through her, covering Rytsar's shaft with her watery excitement.

Sir pulled out immediately, almost joining her against his will. Rytsar had to do the same, and the Russian slapped her hard on the ass for it.

"Naughty, *radost moya*," he teased.

Brie mewed softly, still captive to the intensity of the climax as her entire body shuddered in ecstasy for several more seconds.

Once it passed, Sir gave her an amused look and tsked. "Coming without permission, téa?"

Still flying high from the orgasm, she responded to him with a smile. "I'm completely at your mercy, Master."

"Yes, you are..."

Sir glanced at Rytsar. "If we don't want this to be a five-minute session, we will have to try something different."

Staring at Brie, Rytsar said lustfully, "I suggest we

both give it to her."

Brie whimpered, too turned on to have any self-control. If they needed to punish her, she would accept it with a repentant heart. But she suspected she might come even harder in the process.

Rytsar turned and rummaged through the tool bag for a moment. When he returned, he tossed a tube of lubricant and a hand towel to Sir, then handed him two strips of cloth.

"Secure her to the chains after I sheathe my cock in that disobedient pussy."

Brie hid her smile as Rytsar joined the two of them on the bed, making it swing wildly with his rough movements.

"Maneuver slowly," Sir cautioned him. "Finesse is needed to navigate this bed or you'll send one of us tumbling off it."

Rytsar didn't seem to care. With his eyes trained on Brie, he flopped down on the swaying bed, ordering, "Mount your Russian."

Turned on by his sexy demand, Brie moved with the grace of a feline as she slowly made her way to him. With strong arms, Rytsar grabbed her by the waist and lifted her pussy just inches above his hard cock. Using his muscular body to balance herself while the bed still swayed beneath them, Brie slowly lowered herself, letting his rigid shaft fully penetrate her.

Rytsar closed his eyes and sucked in a deep breath, obviously enjoying the wet constriction of her freshly come pussy.

Using slow movements, Sir attached one of the ties

to a suspension chain and then tightly secured Brie's wrist to it. With a seductive grin, he then did the same with the other, leaving her helpless to both their sensual desires.

Sir had to steady himself as he coated his cock liberally with lubricant and then wiped his hands with the towel. Tossing both off the bed, he told Brie with a wicked glint in his eyes, "You have made your Master nearly come twice against his will. Not only that, you have come without my express permission. Prepare for your punishment, téa."

Brie said in a properly repentant tone, "I willingly accept my punishment, Master. I deserve to be punished as *hard* as you like."

"That is a given," Rytsar assured her, tightening his grip on her waist as he thrust his cock deeper.

Sir smacked her ass, warming her skin with his hand. The delightful sound of her spanking echoed throughout the forest. He then positioned himself behind her, making the bed sway again with his movements.

Brie stared deep into Rytsar's eyes as Sir pressed the head of his cock against her ass. She opened her mouth, moaning softly when he breached her opening.

"That's it, *radost moya*...let your Master claim you."

Brie loved the feeling of her body being challenged in this way, and she forced herself to relax even more so she could fully take both men.

Sir's claiming of her was slow as he allowed her body to adjust to their double penetration. Then the two men began thrusting, but their rhythm was completely off, which was a new experience and they immediately stopped.

"Let's try that again, *moy droog*," Rytsar stated, unconcerned.

Repositioning himself, Sir grasped Brie's waist as he slowly began thrusting again. But as soon as Rytsar joined in with his thrusts, their rhythm was interrupted once more.

Brie was confused. The two were normally so in sync that it was never a problem.

Reasoning it out, Sir told Rytsar, "Instead of alternating our thrusts, we must synchronize them with the swinging of the bed."

Giving Brie a playful slap on the buttocks, Sir teased her ass with the head of his cock before easing it back into her. Throwing her head back, Brie purred, her body primed and ready for their pleasure.

Sir did not hold back this time, fucking Brie deeply with each stroke as he slowly built the tempo, causing the bed to move with him. Rytsar lifted his head to suck on her nipples and play with her breasts, sending electrical currents of pleasure straight to her pussy.

Brie's heart started to race when the bed began swaying faster, causing that fluttering in her stomach to return.

The moment Rytsar wrapped his arms around her and began thrusting in tandem with Sir, Brie cried out in pleasurable surprise. The swinging action increased the sensation of their movements, making them stronger and more intense.

The experience of combining the thrill of flying in rope with the decadence of being taken by both men was incredible. Brie soon felt herself losing touch with her surroundings as she gave in to the multiple sensations they were creating.

It seemed the three of them were being carried away on the same wave of pleasure. The moment she felt her clit begin to pulsate of its own accord, the two men groaned in unison.

Unable to stop her climax, Brie fully embraced it— and she was grateful she did when she felt both men pumping her in tandem as they filled her with their essence. The high of subspace made their dual thrusts pure ecstasy but it was gloriously frightening in its intensity.

When the familiar tingling grew even stronger, Brie gratefully accepted her fate as she flew to even greater heights, blissfully defying gravity.

Act of Love

Brie came back from their trip to Russia feeling incredibly refreshed and ready to tackle the next round of edits for her documentary. She felt great about the changes they'd made to the documentary so far, but it still needed more tweaking. Although it caused her a lot of stress and sleepless nights, it was worth it to make this film as perfect as possible.

Sir had already left earlier that morning to meet a client in Long Beach, so Brie was in charge of the children for the day. She had already set up her office with plenty of toys so Hope and Antony could entertain themselves while she worked.

Sitting down at her computer, Brie put on her headphones ready to view the newest edits waiting for her approval. But not more than five minutes into it, she heard the faint sound of a doorbell. Stopping the video, Brie took off her headphones and heard the doorbell ring downstairs.

Glancing at the time, she saw it was only nine. Since

she wasn't expecting any visitors or packages, Brie put her headphones back on and hit play. Unfortunately, whoever was at the door wouldn't let up!

Brie threw off her headphones in frustration, ready to let loose on whoever was disturbing her morning…until she got a text from Mary.

Hey, you there? I'm at the door.

Brie immediately headed downstairs and opened the door for her. "What are you doing here?"

Mary brushed past her. "I refused to mess with your trip, so I waited until you were back from Russia."

Brie could tell Mary was distressed and asked, "Are you okay?"

"I'm fine." Her voice was grave when she turned to face her. "This isn't about me, Stinks."

A feeling of dread swelled up inside Brie. "What happened, Mary?"

"You need to promise me you'll stay calm."

"Okay…" Brie muttered, fear prickling her skin.

Mary took her by the shoulders. "While you were gone, Todd was rushed to the hospital in critical condition."

"What?"

Mary tightened her grip on Brie. "Don't start freaking out on me, Stinks. Just listen. He's now out of ICU and recovering."

"What happened to him?" Brie cried, her stomach twisting into knots.

"Todd got gored by a bull."

"What?" Brie frowned and shook her head. "That doesn't make any sense!"

"I know, I know…" Mary agreed. "It was a freak accident."

"Freak accident!"

Hope started crying upstairs, obviously reacting to Brie's emotional outburst.

Brie stopped and took a deep breath. "It's okay, honey!" she called up to Hope. "Mommy was just surprised by something Aunt Mary said. Everything is okay…"

It felt as if this was all a bad dream. Brie stared numbly at Mary, tears filling her eyes.

Mary squeezed her shoulders harder and explained, "Todd was taking Kaylee on a hike in the foothills when they crossed paths with a rogue bull that had broken through a fence."

Chills coursed down Brie's spine when she asked, "What happened to Kaylee, Mary?"

"Don't worry, she's okay. The kid only suffered minor scratches and bruises."

Mary put her arms down and took a step back. "Todd protected her with his body, which saved her life."

Brie stared at her mutely, unable to speak.

"The crazy part is the whole thing was caught on a nature livestream in the park."

Brie brought her hand up to her mouth. "Oh, my God…"

"Yeah," Mary said in an uneasy voice. "The attack was brutal. It's a miracle either of them survived."

Brie remembered Master Anderson telling her once how dangerous bulls were. He warned her never to turn her back on a bull, no matter how docile they seemed, stating firmly, "They're killers."

"Please tell me he's going to be okay, Mary!"

She nodded. "It was dodgy there for a bit with his one kidney and all…but the doctors feel confident he's out of the woods now."

Brie shook her head, heartsick knowing everything Faelan had already suffered. "How is he do-ing…mentally?"

Mary sighed. "Better than I would be." She met Brie's gaze, adding, "But I think he could use another friendly face at that hospital."

Brie stared at her numbly, still in shock from the news. She grabbed her phone and called Sir first. After explaining what happened, Sir encouraged her to go with Mary. She then texted Rytsar and was grateful he was able to watch the children without any advance notice.

On the drive, Mary warned her, "He looks pretty bad. Todd not only suffered multiple broken bones, but he was in the operating room for hours while they repaired the gaping hole in his side where the bull gored him."

Brie shuddered.

Brie felt her nerves kick in when she entered the hospi-tal. She had a severe aversion to them after spending months taking care of Sir, following his plane accident.

Keeping her head down, she blindly followed Mary into the hospital room wearing a pasted smile on her face. Brie immediately felt a wave of relief when she saw Marquis Gray in the room, standing beside Faelan's bed talking to him.

Marquis Gray looked up when the two entered the room and smiled when he saw Brie. "It's good you came."

She nodded and then bravely turned to face Faelan. The poor man's right leg was suspended in traction, while his left arm was completely covered from shoulder to wrist in a white cast. Brie let out a small gasp when she met his gaze. Not only was Faelan's forehead bandaged, and he had two black eyes, as well as a badly bisected lip held together with sutures.

She looked at him, overflowing with sympathy. "Oh, Faelan…"

He stared back at her through his swollen eye and said in a hoarse whisper, "You should see the other guy."

She burst out in nervous laughter, then caught herself and frowned, thinking it was inappropriate to laugh when Faelan was in so much pain. "I'm sorry this happened to you."

"Me, too," he answered.

"Thank God you were able to save Kaylee."

He wore a haunted expression on his face and simply nodded.

Marquis Gray spoke up. "She's doing well, Todd."

Brie smiled at Marquis Gray, grateful to know Kaylee was with them. The little girl would naturally feel safe with the couple since they had cared for her when she was still an infant.

Looking around the hospital room uncomfortably, Brie asked Faelan, "Did they say how long you'll be here?"

He only growled and looked away.

Marquis Gray answered for him. "The physician said six to eight weeks, but she is leaning toward eight because his single kidney is under duress and it's slowing the healing process."

"You can't catch a break," Brie told Faelan sadly.

He snorted. "It's fucking hard not to lose hope."

Marquis Gray looked at Faelan thoughtfully for several minutes and then said, "You are a man of great courage, Todd. It's not something you manufacture—is it in your DNA. I realize how bleak things look for you right now. However, I encourage you to think of your life as a tapestry made of moments so intense, they leave an indelible mark. Moments of love, heartache, triumph, and loss. You can't see it now, but the tapestry you are creating is so much bigger and far grander than you can imagine."

Faelan groaned. "I'd take a simple life any day, Asher."

Marquis Gray clasped his right hand, wrapping it with his other, stating with conviction, "It is my honor and privilege to know you." He then nodded solemnly before letting Faelan's hand go.

Brie was deeply moved by Marquis Grays's statement, because she felt the same way about Faelan.

Addressing Mary and Brie, Marquis Gray said, "I will

leave so you can visit."

After he'd gone, Mary joked, "Well, I don't know if you're all *that* and a bag of chips, Todd. But at least you're famous."

Faelan looked at her oddly. "What?"

"One of the media outlets shared that livestream recording of the bull attack last night."

Faelan frowned. "Did you see?"

"Yeah." She shrugged. "It was impossible to turn away once it started playing on my phone."

Faelan glanced at Brie. "Have you?"

She shook her head.

Faelan pointed to his iPad.

Mary picked it up and raised an eyebrow. "You really want to watch it?"

He nodded.

"If you say so…" Mary started searching YouTube. She suddenly stopped, staring at the screen with a shocked look on her face. "Oh, wow…"

"What?" Brie asked anxiously.

"The video already has over six hundred thousand views."

Faelan waved Mary to him and then nodded at Brie to join him.

Too curious not to watch, Brie leaned in with trepidation when Mary pressed play.

The video began by showing Faelan walking behind Kaylee on a dirt trail…

Kaylee is taking slow but enthusiastic toddler steps down the trail. She keeps looking back to make sure her daddy is watching her, and each time she does, she almost loses her balance.

Faelan claps in encouragement and gestures for Kaylee to keep going.

Kaylee suddenly stops and starts pointing at something out of the range of the camera. She jumps up and down as if she's excited to see it.

Faelan runs full speed toward her and falls on top of Kaylee just as the rogue bull charges into the scene with its head lowered.

Its head and horns hit Faelan full force and he is knocked away from Kaylee.

The bull sees the child and rushes at her, its vicious horns lowered again. Faelan crawls back on top of Kaylee, taking the impact as the bull thrashes its head, trying to rip Faelan apart.

When the bull steps back for a moment, Faelan repositions himself to cover Kaylee completely. Then the bull goes at him again and tosses him around violently as it continues to thrash its head.

Suddenly, the bull hooks one horn under Faelan, and the force of its head shake sends him flying in the air.

The bull turns to face Kaylee again. The little girl's mouth is open and she's crying hysterically.

Lowering its head, the bull starts pawing the ground...

Faelan throws his bloody body in front of Kaylee to shield her from the attack.

Out of nowhere, a four-wheeler appears and shoots

across the screen, momentarily distracting the bull. Faelan takes the opportunity to grab Kaylee with one hand, stumbling badly as he drags her out of the view of the camera.

The bull turns in Faelan's direction and lowers its head again, but before it can charge, the four-wheeler returns and the driver waves his cap wildly at it, driving right past the bull. With its sights now focused on the vehicle, the bull runs out of the camera's range in hot pursuit, heading in the opposite direction of Faelan and his daughter.

Brie could barely breathe after the terrifying video ended.

"Strange. It looks like it happened so fast." Faelan paused for a moment. "But it felt like an eternity to me."

Brie looked over his body again, noting all of his injuries, fully appreciating how lucky he was to be alive.

"You really are a hero, you know," Mary told him.

"No," he stated emphatically. "Just a parent."

Tears pricked Brie's eyes when she told him, "That was the most extreme act of love I have ever seen."

Faelan looked at her and said in a choked voice, "I couldn't let her die, blossom."

A knock on the door caused the three of them to turn in unison. A nurse walked in holding a bouquet of flowers. "Pardon me, Mr. Wallace. Would you like the flowers in your room?"

Faelan looked at them with disinterest. "Sure."

The nurse walked to the back of the room and placed the flowers on the counter. She was followed by a string of other nurses, each carrying a bouquet.

Faelan stared at them, speechless, while they watched the long line of nurses fill the room with flowers.

He looked confused and asked Mary, "What's going on?"

She snorted. "Better get used to it, Todd. You're famous on social media now."

"Good grief…" he muttered.

Brie was silent on the drive back to the house. She could not get that video out of her mind. It was as horrifying as it was inspiring.

Later that night, when she was getting her children ready for bed, Brie stopped for a moment, taking in the simple joy of her bedtime routine as a parent.

Looking tenderly at Hope and Antony, she told them, "If I had to choose between your life or mine, I would always choose yours. You *are* my life."

Part of Mine

It touched Brie how quickly the community rallied around Faelan after the accident. Moved by the heroic and selfless display of protecting his daughter, people all over the world reached out with cards and donations to support in his healing.

Those that knew him well made a personal commitment to visit him at the hospital as moral support, including Sir.

"I understand what he is going through better than anyone," Sir explained to Brie as he got ready for one of his weekly visits. "The man almost died in that freak accident and now faces months of recovery from numerous injuries that will remain with him for years—both physically and mentally."

Understanding that, Sir had committed to visiting Faelan three times a week to help him through the depression and to encourage him with his physical rehabilitation. His renewed connection with Faelan seemed to rekindle the relationship they once had in the beginning, when Sir mentored him during Faelan's training at the Dominant Training Center.

Sir had the advantage of knowing Faelan when he was just starting out on his path as a Dominant. He understood the man behind the heroic act—both his strengths and his weaknesses. That history between them allowed Sir to encourage and challenge Faelan in ways that others could not.

However, Sir wasn't the only one. He mentioned that he would often see Marquis Gray, Tono, or Mary at the hospital supporting Faelan as well. It made sense to Brie since each one of them had developed a deep connection to Faelan over the years.

Because Brie knew that Mary was not only busy with work but was also helping to care for Caden *and* regularly checking in on Faelan, it came as a welcomed surprise when Mary asked Brie to meet her at the cafe like they used to…before the kidnapping.

Despite their near-fatal encounter with Holloway, it seemed their lives were beginning to fall back into their normal routines. It felt good on a soul level.

Thankfully for both of them, interest in Holloway's victims had quickly died down after the announcement that a popular movie couple was divorcing amid wild accusations of infidelity and mudslinging. The two were embroiled in a public battle of he said/she said, drawing America's eye away from what she and Mary endured at the compound.

Although it had taken a couple of news cycles, it seemed the public had finally satiated their perverse hunger to know the gory details of the torture suffered by the kidnap victims and, for that, Brie was grateful. It gave her and Mary the freedom to finally move about without the press constantly hounding them.

However, it did not prevent perfect strangers from coming up and asking inappropriate questions about their experience at the compound—or even requesting a selfie!

While Sir had done an excellent job of shielding Brie from the fallout whenever he was by her side, he couldn't be with her twenty-four/seven. For times such as this, when she was navigating public spaces, Brie resorted to dark sunglasses, oversized t-shirts, and baseball caps to make herself less recognizable.

Today, she'd been successful in walking into the cafe without incident. The moment she spotted Mary at a table, she lowered her head and walked up to her quickly. Settling in the chair opposite her, she murmured, "Wow… It's been a while, hasn't it?"

Mary set down her phone and glanced at Brie with disinterest. "Took you long enough, Stinks. I've been here for over fifteen minutes already.

Brie looked at her watch and frowned. "You said you wanted to meet at two, and it's three minutes before that."

She huffed. "I see you've forgotten your training. Funny…when you were the top graduate of our class."

Brie chuckled in response to Mary's surliness and picked up the menu to see what new specialty drink they had for the week. "For your information, Mary, the rest of the world doesn't hold to the idea that unless you are fifteen minutes early, you are actually late."

Mary lowered her sunglasses momentarily, giving Brie a condescending look. "We are not part of the common world, subbie. I should report you to Marquis Gray and let him dole out an appropriate punishment."

Brie smirked. The idea of another flogging session with the trainer sounded just lovely. "Please do."

Sliding her sunglasses back up, Mary snorted. "Sorry, Stinks. I'm not that nice."

"True…" Brie agreed, deciding to try the café's Caramel Dream. "You want me to order for you?"

"Don't bother. I already placed my order."

As if on cue, one of the servers walked up holding a large cup and saucer and set it on the table next to Mary. "I hope you like it!"

Mary gave her a curt smile before looking at Brie and then nodding to the counter. "Better hurry before my latte gets cold."

Although Mary was acting as abrasive as ever, Brie still felt an underlying affection for her friend. They had weathered so many storms together, and she seriously couldn't imagine her life without Mary Quite Contrary in it.

Once her own latte was delivered to the table, Brie picked up the large cup and blew on it, appreciating the generous drizzle of caramel they'd put on top. "So, what did you want to talk about?" she asked before taking a sip.

Mary's expression turned grim. "After what happened to Todd, I've been thinking about what you said."

Brie tilted her head. "I have no idea what I said. You're going to have to give me a little more than that."

Sighing heavily, Mary stated, "About my sperm donor."

Brie set her cup down, surprised Mary was bringing up her biological father. "What are you thinking?"

Mary didn't answer right away, taking several leisurely sips of her latte first. "I realize everything I believed growing up was manipulated by Greg Holloway. That fucker shaped my life the day I was born and made it into a living hell."

Brie nodded but said nothing. She knew Mary wasn't the kind of person to appreciate a gush of sympathy and kept it to herself, although her heart secretly broke for her friend.

"I've got nothing to hold onto. No basis for my existence."

Brie looked at her sadly. "I can't imagine how that feels."

"No, you can't," Mary snapped. "You may have gone through a couple of rough patches as a kid, but you had a stable childhood and two parents who actually loved you."

"I did."

Mary looked down at her cup and said in a fragile voice, "I've felt adrift without an anchor for such a fucking long time…"

Brie instinctually reached out to touch Mary's hand and was surprised when she didn't pull away.

She confessed to Brie, her voice full of pain, "Every time Marquis Gray and Celestia ask me to look after the baby, I'm reminded of how similar his background is to mine. His mother left him, but not by choice—not like mine did. The kid has no idea who his father is, and maybe he never will."

Mary took off her sunglasses to wipe her eyes. "You can't know how alone that makes a person feel. I have no roots, Brie. No family to come home to for the holidays, nothing…"

Holding up her hand when Brie opened her mouth to speak, Mary said, "I know, I know, I have you and big boobs, but it's not the same."

"No, it's not," Brie quietly agreed.

"The kid is going to be all right. He's got Marquis and Celestia now."

"And you," Brie added.

"True. I'm never going to abandon that kid like my mother abandoned me." Mary picked up her coffee cup and took another sip. The cup made a gentle clinking sound when she set it back down on the saucer.

Mary stared at her for a long moment. Brie noticed she swallowed hard before saying, "I feel a strong need for connection beyond friendship or sex. I want…" She swallowed hard again, forcing back her emotions. "I want to feel a connection with my past that doesn't include pain or betrayal."

"You deserve that, Mary."

"So, I was thinking…" She paused again, taking a deep breath. "I want you and big boobs to come with me."

"Where?"

"To meet the man in New York."

Brie's heart started to race. She was hardly able to believe what she was hearing. After the horrific way

Holloway had manipulated Mary's first meeting with her biological father, Brie was surprised but extremely proud that she still wanted to make contact.

"I'm honored that you want me to go, but I'm under such a killer deadline right now with the release of the film coming, I don't have a minute to call my own these days except on the weekends. But I'm sure Lea can go."

Mary didn't even hesitate. "Then I'll book a flight there, we'll stay a couple of hours, and then we can fly back. Just a quick in and out—like he did to my mother."

Brie shook her head at Mary's self-deprecating joke. "Look, I wouldn't want you to do that on my account."

"I wasn't planning a family reunion, Stinks. This gives me the perfect excuse to keep it brief." Mary leaned forward. "I can't face him alone. Not after what happened…."

Brie looked at her sadly and nodded.

Sitting back in her chair, Mary stated, "Having both of you with me would make it less uncomfortable. And if he turns out to be a total asshole, the three of us could easily take him down."

"Yes, we could."

Letting out an uneasy sigh, Mary told her, "I don't know what I am more scared of. Him being the total dick I think he is or…finding out he's not."

"Unfortunately, that's not something you can know until you come face to face."

Mary frowned as she finished off the last of her cup. "That's why you have to be there for me. I need you to talk me down off the ledge if things go south. I can't handle any more shit. I'm done."

"I can understand that. But are you sure it's not too soon after everything that's happened?"

Her eyes darkened. "I feel like I am falling down a black hole." She then shook her head, adding, "I can't stop thinking about him. But I'm unsure if my need to see him is my sick need to sabotage myself or my chance to take back something that Holloway stole from me."

Grabbing her purse, Mary suddenly stood up. "Either way, if I don't do something drastic, it may be too late." Brie watched with concern as Mary held out her hand to her, palm down. It was shaking uncontrollably.

"I feel like a ticking time bomb, Stinks. Something is about to give…"

After the long flight, Brie was feeling tired and achy as she piled into the cab with Mary and Lea. Mary explained that Jason, her biological father, moved to New York the moment he learned Greg Holloway was dead.

"Does he have family here?" Brie asked, shouting over the harsh blare of the cabbie's horn.

Mary sneered, "No, the idiot still has aspirations of making it 'big' now that Greg kicked the bucket."

Lea frowned, looking confused. "Why didn't he return to Hollywood then? At the very least, it would have saved you this long trip and travel expenses."

"I'm grateful he moved to the other side of the country! There's no possible chance of accidentally meeting that fucker on the street." Mary visibly shuddered. "God, I can't think of anything worse."

Glancing out the window, Mary abruptly ended the conversation.

Although she would never admit it, it was obvious to Brie that Mary was feeling nervous. Who could blame her? Mary knew next to nothing about the man. Growing up, she'd had no idea he even existed.

When the cab pulled up to a row of upscale townhouses, Brie exclaimed, "I didn't know he had the kind of money to afford a place like this…"

Mary stared up at the unusual white brick townhouse. Each window had black ironwork and was accented with red terracotta tiles. Shaking her head in disbelief, Mary turned to the cab driver. "Are you sure this is the right place?"

"Yes, lady," the cabbie answered irritably.

"Maybe he's secretly rich!" Lea squealed excitedly as she opened the cab door and got out.

After tipping the cabbie extra to stay until she'd confirmed that her father lived there, Mary got out of the cab to join them.

"What are you thinking?" Brie asked her as they stared at the black steps that led up to the door.

"I honestly don't know what to think…" Mary glanced at her watch anxiously and hesitated for a moment.

"You don't have to go through with this," Brie told her.

"What the fuck am I even doing here then?" Mary growled. After a moment, she turned on Brie accusingly. "This is your fault!"

Lea reached out to pat Mary on the head. "Now, now…we all know that nobody, and I mean *nobody*, can make Mary Wilson do anything she damn well doesn't want to."

Mary snorted. "Well, that's true." She stared hard at the door and grumbled, "Might as well get this over with…like pulling off a fucking Band-Aid."

Starting up the steps, Mary suddenly stopped halfway and turned around to yell at the cabby. "Don't you go anywhere until I give you the word!"

He flipped her the bird but remained where he was.

Satisfied, Mary continued up the stairs with Brie and Lea following after her and rang the doorbell. The three of them huddled together, Mary in the middle, as they waited for the door to open. When it finally did, Mary stared at the man, her mouth agape.

Her father was taller than Brie expected, and he had a classically handsome face. But the thing that struck her was how much his daughter looked like him. They both shared the same hair color, and his face looked like a masculine version of Mary—though both of them had refined features.

Brie knew that Jason had been a famous actor in Hollywood when he was young, but she hadn't expected him to be even more attractive now that he was middle-aged.

Mary continued to stand there gaping at him, un-characteristically mute.

The cab driver blared his horn, startling Mary out of her stupor. Turning her head, she screeched, "Get the fuck out of here, asshole!"

"Bitch!" the cabbie yelled as he hit the gas and disappeared down the street.

Mary turned to face Jason again.

"I'm glad you were able to come, Mary," he said, looking happy to see her.

She just snarled. "Let's get this over with…"

Jason stepped aside, motioning the three of them to enter his home. Mary brushed past him without a word. Brie simply nodded, but Lea held out her hand to him and giggled. "Knock, knock."

He cleared his throat as he shook her hand, asking in a confused voice, "Who's there?"

"Adam."

He looked over at Mary questioningly but dutifully answered. "Adam who?"

"Adam my way, I'm coming in!"

He gave her a bemused smile, then shut the door behind her. "Please head upstairs and make yourselves comfortable."

Brie followed Mary up the colorful tiled staircase, marveling at the white walls, dark wood rafters, and decorative items of blue that gave the interior a Mediterranean feel.

Once upstairs, Mary crossed her arms and turned to face him. "There's no way you own this place, Jason."

He chuckled. "No. It's owned by a friend of mine who is allowing me to stay here while I reestablish my acting career."

Mary snorted sarcastically. "You *do* realize you're no different than every other poor sap trying to make it on Broadway, right? Only difference is, you're a washed-up

Hollywood actor who is a hell of a lot older than everyone else."

He smirked at her but chose not to reply. Heading to the bar area, he asked, "Rum and coke, right?"

Mary frowned. "How could you possibly know that?"

His tone was somber when he told her, "That's what you had that night."

Mary's face suddenly drained of color. "Oh…"

Brie could only imagine how uncomfortable it must be for the two of them. Lea, on the other hand, was blissfully ignorant.

Mary had never told another soul, other than Brie, about the night Holloway had tricked the two into engaging in a scene of fellatio. Wanting to be grossly entertained, Holloway had commanded Mary do it, knowing that neither had any reason to believe they were related.

Jason nodded curtly to Mary, acknowledging the unwanted memory they shared. After several moments of uncomfortable silence, he asked Brie and Lea what they wanted to drink.

After making a round of drinks, Jason returned and gave Brie and Lea theirs, before handing Mary her drink. "What happened that night has no power over us. We were not in control. Best to purge all thoughts of it."

Mary held up her drink, "I'm fucking all for that!"

He smiled stiffly before taking a sip of his drink.

Lea looked at both of them, clearly wondering what they were talking about. Rather than pry, she asked, "Would you like to hear another joke?"

The two turned in unison and stated emphatically, "No!"

Lea glanced at Brie and giggled. "Well, at least they agree on something."

And just like that, the awkward tension in the room was broken, and it was all thanks to Lea.

Jason smiled at his daughter as he took a seat. "Thanks for coming, Mary."

She stared at him for a moment before saying guardedly, "I'm still uncertain if this was a good idea."

He chuckled good-naturedly. "I've actually wanted to see you for quite some time. However, I wasn't sure how you would react."

She raised her eyebrows. "I can guarantee you that if you had tried, I would have kicked you in the balls and run in the opposite direction."

Jason nodded, and that cynical smirk that reminded her of Mary suddenly appeared on his lips. "Hence the reason I've chosen to remain here. I would *never* force you to do anything, Mary. Not after everything you've been through." Brie saw tears form in his eyes. "I'm sorry for what that bastard did to you…"

Mary frowned and snarled back, "I'm not here to talk about that."

He set his drink down and sat back in his chair. "Fine. Take the lead, Mary. I'll answer any questions you have for me."

For the next two hours, Mary grilled him relentlessly, never giving him a moment's break. In the course of those two hours, they learned he had traveled to Morocco to escape Holloway. Unlike Mary, he knew what the man was capable of and understood that his life was forfeit if Holloway ever discovered where he was.

Brie felt sad when Jason informed Mary that he suspected her mother was dead. Jason then shared that he'd kept tabs on Mary and her mother through private investigators over the years. One of the investigators confirmed through photos that her mother had been spotted getting into a vehicle with Holloway, but she hadn't been seen since.

Although Mary responded by saying, "Good riddance!" Brie worried that the news hurt Mary more than she was letting on.

At one point in the conversation, Lea picked up a newspaper lying on the coffee table and pointed to a picture of Jason on the front page. "Are you really starring in the Broadway show *Moulin Rouge*?"

His smirk returned when he glanced at Mary. "Seems I still have what it takes, even though I'm 'all washed-up'."

Mary rolled her eyes, looking decidedly disinterested. But Brie knew Mary well enough to tell that she was impressed.

"I hear you take after your old man," Jason stated, his smirk suddenly transforming into a genuine smile. "I was impressed by the versatility you showcased in your films. Few actors I know can fully commit to the wide range of roles you were given. Truly a rare talent."

Mary looked at him incredulously and snapped back, "Don't try to patronize me with false accolades."

He leaned forward, his expression open and earnest. "Even if there was no connection between us, I would feel the same watching you act."

Mary waved her hand dismissively. "Whatever…"

"Would you like to come to my performance to-night…?" He looked at Brie and Lea, adding, "All three of you?"

Lea immediately perked up. "Oh, my goodness, that would be incredible! I've always wanted to see a show on Broadway!"

Mary gave her a sideways glance. "We'll pass."

Slumping in her chair, Lea looked at Brie and pouted her bottom lip.

"My friend Brianna," Mary stated, gesturing to her, "is currently under an extreme deadline with her second film. She only came at my insistence, and we have to fly back to California immediately."

Jason glanced at Brie. "I enjoyed the insight you brought to your first documentary and I'm looking forward to the next one. It's coming out this summer, correct?"

Brie was surprised and humbled that he knew about her films and was about to respond when Mary suddenly jumped to her feet. "We have to go now."

Standing up in solidarity, Brie and Lea prepared to leave. Jason quickly shook both their hands and then turned to face Mary. Grasping her hand firmly, he told her, "I hope we can see each other again, without any time constraints."

Mary eyed him distrustfully. "Don't hold your breath."

"You'd fit in just fine here, you know," he said chuckling lightly. "You have the New Yorker attitude down pat."

"She does, doesn't she?" Lea blurted, turning to Mary. "Your surliness would be considered completely normal here."

Mary rolled her eyes at Lea.

"Would you like me to drive you to the airport?" Jason offered.

"No!" Mary replied a little too quickly. Trying to make light of her blatant brush-off, she said jokingly, "I prefer to soak in the New York experience in the backseat of a cab."

Brie was impressed that Jason took Mary's brusque response in stride. "Then let me escort you out." After opening the door, he told them, "Safe travels back to Los Angeles."

"Thanks, Jason," Lea replied enthusiastically. "And I'll take you up on that offer next time I come."

He chuckled. "Good."

Looking at Mary, he stated in a serious tone, "If this is the last time I see you, I need you to know that although I haven't been a part of your life, you have always been a part of mine."

On the plane ride home, Brie could tell Mary was growing more and more agitated. She understood that her friend suffered from serious trust issues due to everything she'd experienced in her life, so it didn't surprise Brie that Mary had chosen to treat Jason the same way she once treated Brie.

But something deeper was going on. Brie could feel it in her bones.

"What are you thinking, Mary?"

Mary had a haunted look in her eyes. "I have a really bad feeling..." she murmured ominously, then looked out the airplane window.

"About Jason?"

"No."

Brie glanced at Lea questioningly.

"Don't leave us hanging like that, girl," Lea teased.

Mary turned to look at them both, her gaze growing darker. "I have a sinking feeling that my mother was one of Greg's earliest victims. And I bet my life that her body is hidden somewhere at that fucking compound."

Brie gasped in horror, sickened by the thought...

The Premiere

Several weeks before the release, Mr. Cummings called to inform Brie that she needed to choose a gown for the upcoming premiere.

"I'm sorry, Mr. Cummings, I simply don't have the time to go shopping for one," she informed him as she sat at her desk, going over the final edits that Michael Schmidt had sent her. "If you could pick one like you did before, I'm certain it will be perfect."

He chuckled. "That evening was nothing compared to this event. You must look the part," he insisted. Brie was about to protest until he said, "...which is why I have arranged for a private showing so all the designer dresses will be in one place for you to try on."

She let out a sigh of relief. "Okay, that I can do. Thank you!"

"I'm here to serve," he replied cordially.

"When is the showing?"

"Anytime you like."

"Would this Wednesday night work? It's the only

time I have free this week."

"Wednesday it is, Mrs. Davis. I'll have a driver come pick you and Mr. Davis up."

Brie smiled to herself. The idea of spending a night trying on beautiful gowns sounded like a fun escape. "Thanks again, Mr. Cummings. That sounds lovely."

"My pleasure, Mrs. Davis."

After Brie got off the phone, she took a moment to appreciate just how crazy her life had become. That little girl from Nebraska, eating her McDonald's hamburger and small fries, was about to go to a private showing so she could pick out a designer gown for the grand premier of her second feature film.

Who would have thought?

Brie felt as if she was dreaming when Mr. Cummings greeted her at the door of an upscale boutique on Rodeo Drive that had closed early for this private showing. He nodded to Sir before ushering the two of them inside and introducing them to several attendants who eagerly walked them to the back of the store.

One of the attendants handed them champagne while each dress was brought out and the shop assistant shared interesting facts about each designer and explained the special details of the dress. Brie was familiar with the designers' names but knew little about them, so she found it fascinating.

It came as a complete shock to Brie when the shop

assistant then informed her that the gowns displayed had been specifically created by the designers for her premiere.

Brie immediately turned to Sir, completely speechless.

"Accept it in the spirit it was given," he advised her. Looking at the six dresses hanging on display, he said, "These were created with you in mind. I suggest you put aside who designed them and simply choose the one that resonates with you."

Brie appreciated his suggestion. This night wasn't about the designers who'd created these dresses; this was the premiere of a film she had fought for and almost died for. Everything surrounding the premiere needed to be authentic and represent not only her but the documentary itself. Once she realized that, it made the dress selection an enjoyable experience.

Fully indulging her girly side, Brie tried on each gown and turned in the three-way mirror to admire it. One of them was more of a fashion statement than a dress. The bold color choice of orange and dark blue, along with the unusual lines of the gown, made it interesting, but it didn't speak to her as a woman. Several were classy and more traditional in shades of either white or black, but they didn't wow her.

The one she gravitated to the most was the one she saved to try on last. The rich purple dress was striking even on the hanger. However, the moment she put it on, and the assistant zipped up the dress, Brie felt a surge of energy course through her.

When she turned to face Sir, she heard his audible

gasp and knew he felt it too.

Looking in the mirror, Brie was mesmerized by the way the sequined gown was contoured to her body. The full-length dress had long sleeves and a high neckline in the front. But what made it so unique was the multiple gold art-deco sunbursts that accented the dress. The design was reminiscent of the Golden Era of Hollywood, but the color of the dress was unusual and bold. For Brie, the pièce de résistance was the plunging back of the gown that exposed her small brand—something both she and Sir appreciated.

As Brie turned slowly in front of the mirror, she found herself admiring the dress from every angle—and falling in love with it. The gown both infused her with a sense of power and radiated classic elegance. That was exactly how she wanted to step out on the red carpet.

She smiled at Sir and announced, "This is the one."

"I agree, babygirl."

Brie turned to Mr. Cummings. "Please thank all the designers and let them know how deeply appreciative I am. But this is the one I want to wear for the premiere."

"It is an excellent choice, Mrs. Davis."

Turning to Sir, Mr. Cummings added, "A matching tux will be provided."

Sir raised an eyebrow. "Not a purple one, I hope."

The man chuckled. "No, Mr. Davis. I assure you it will be black and quite tasteful."

Sir nodded, then turned to Brie with a smirk. "As much as I love you, babygirl, I do have my limits."

She giggled before throwing herself into his arms.

The marketing for the film leading up to its release was unlike anything Brie had ever seen. Mr. Cummings informed her that the advertising agency was given a generous budget and instructed to relentlessly promote the film in a variety of different news mediums to hit every demographic.

The hype for the release was off the charts, and it wasn't confined to just America. People around the world were reaching out to her on social media to let Brie know how excited they were about seeing the film.

Michael Schmidt, and the entire team who had worked with her on the film, were enthusiastic about the documentary's release, and that created a tremendous energy in advance of the premiere.

Because of the buzz surrounding the film, the elites of Hollywood had begun courting Brie, many asking her to attend their private parties. In response, she had to ask Mr. Cummings to come to the house so she could discuss the situation.

"How would you like me to respond to them, Mrs. Davis?" he inquired, taking out a pen and notebook.

Brie smiled wistfully when she told him, "You know, ever since I was a kid, I have dreamed of making it big in Hollywood and becoming part of the 'in crowd'." She smiled as she thought back on it. "I imagined what it would be like to be friends with famous directors and the hottest stars, getting invited to the best parties and having a stack of awards on my mantel…"

She laughed at herself. "While I was slaving over my homemade movies on the weekends, I would tell myself that someday I would become part of the inner circles of Hollywood."

"An admirable goal," he stated.

Brie shook her head. "Mr. Cummings, I've seen the best and the worst that Hollywood has to offer. I realize now that I am, and will always be, only an observer to it all."

"There's no reason to think that," he protested.

"While I might be able to achieve all those things that I dreamed of…" She smiled at him warmly. "…I find I have no desire to reach that particular status anymore. I know it would require all my focus and energy, and I have better things to do with my life."

Brie glanced out the back window at her children playing on the beach with Sir.

Turning back to Mr. Cummings, she explained, "I prefer to observe those glamorous parties and the stars in the limelight from afar. I understand that people in Hollywood want to attach themselves to me right now. It's not that they care about my work or the message of the documentary; they just want to be part of the buzz."

He nodded his agreement.

"So, I would appreciate it if you would turn down every invitation I receive." She chuckled, adding, "Even if it would flatter my ego to attend."

He looked at her in concern. "Are you certain that is what you want, Mrs. Davis?"

"Absolutely," she responded with confidence. "I want the premiere to be focused on the message of the documentary and the many people who have poured their energy into making this film a reality...including you."

He nodded, a look of admiration in his eyes. "I will send them your regrets, Mrs. Davis."

"Thank you."

As he turned to leave, she suddenly felt the urge to ask him point blank, "Mr. Cummings, who is my bene-factor?"

He sighed heavily as he turned around to face her. "I have asked myself that question every day since I was given this assignment." He looked at her with regret. "I am sorry to report that I still cannot answer that question for either of us. Should I ever find out, you will be the first to know."

She nodded, unable to hide her disappointment.

After he left, Brie headed out back to join her family. As she watched Hope and Antony laughing as they played in the water, she was struck by a sense of profound gratitude.

Brie sincerely hoped that someday she would find out her benefactor's identity so she could thank whoever it was personally.

The night of the big event, Sir's aunt and uncle insisted on watching the children for them. When they arrived, Judy immediately set their son Jonathan down so he could join their kids. When she saw Brie, she gushed, "I can't tell you how proud we are. This is such an incredible day for you!"

"It really is," Brie agreed, hardly able to contain the excitement she felt about the premiere.

"It has been years in the making," Sir stated as he walked up to greet his aunt.

"Just look at you two…" Judy shook her head in amazement. "You look like professional models!"

Brie glanced at Sir, quite taken by the suit Mr. Cummings had sent him for the event. The tailoring of the black tux was exceptional, but Brie deeply appreciated the single vent cut into the back of his jacket because it accentuated Sir's firm ass. The purple tie and cufflinks sent with the tux matched the hue of her dress, and both bore the same art-deco sunbursts.

"Turn so I can see the dress," Judy begged her.

Brie happily obliged, smiling when his aunt complimented her on the long strand of black pearls that were draped down her bare back. "Sir got them for me years ago for Christmas," she stated, "and I thought they'd look perfect with this dress tonight."

"You look absolutely elegant," Jack told her, his eyes twinkling with pride.

She grinned at him. "Not too shabby for a little tobacco shop clerk, huh?"

"Not shabby at all, I'd say," he replied with a wink.

When the doorbell rang again, Sir went to answer it.

Brie was relieved to see it was her parents. "I was starting to get worried that you wouldn't make it in time."

Her father shook his head as he walked into the

house. "Traffic was a bear!"

Brie noticed her mother looking as pale as a ghost and asked, "Dad's driving?"

Her mother simply nodded.

"I wasn't about to have your mother miss this big event, little girl. Not on my watch!"

Brie giggled as she gave her father a hug. "Well, I'm grateful you both made it safely and in one piece."

When she went to hug her mother, Brie noticed tears in her eyes. "No need to cry, Mom. This is a happy occasion."

"I'm just…" She pulled a tissue from her purse and dabbed at her eyes. "You are the most amazing person I know, sweetheart. From that shy little girl who hid behind the camera as a child, to our college graduate working in a tobacco shop to make ends meet…even after the terrible things that happened to you recently, you've *never* given up on your dreams."

Her dad nodded in agreement. "God broke the mold when He made you, little girl."

Brie smiled at them both, then glanced at Sir. "I wouldn't be here today if it weren't for all of you."

Sir winked at her, then glanced at his phone when it buzzed. "Looks like the limousine should be pulling up any second."

After giving a quick round of hugs to the adults and planting a quick kiss on each of her kids' heads in an attempt not to get lipstick on them, Brie followed Sir and her parents outside to meet the limousine.

While the vehicle was pulling into the driveway, Brie noticed Rytsar walking up the road from his beach house. He looked incredibly attractive in his four-piece suit and dark red tie. Holding out his arms to Brie, he stated in admiration, "With you around, *radost moya*, no light is needed."

Brie blushed, remembering the power of that poetry line in the letter he had written to her in Mexico. "I'm so grateful that you can join us tonight!"

He hugged her tightly. "It is an honor to be asked."

Rytsar then greeted her parents, before slapping Sir on the back. "What does it feel like to be married to a famous director?"

Sir grinned, looking at Brie with pride in his eyes. "Surprisingly, it feels the same as being married to my wife."

Brie's heart melted when she heard his reply.

Rytsar chuckled, "True enough, *moy droog*."

Thankfully, the limo ride was not tense like it had been for her first premiere. In fact, the drive there was full of lively conversation between her parents and Rytsar as they made their way downtown.

"Brie," Sir said, taking her hand to get her attention. "I have a surprise for you."

Turning to him, her eyes widened when he pulled a thin satin box from his jacket.

She lifted the lid and was touched to see a gold bracelet. She held it up, smiling when she saw the two condors in flight with their wings outstretched. It matched the necklace he had commissioned for her to commemorate her first documentary.

Brie looked at him with tears in her eyes. "I love it, Sir."

He smiled as he put the bracelet on her wrist before kissing the back of her hand.

As they drew up to the theater, Brie felt a thrill of excitement…at least, until she saw the shocking number of reporters crowding the entrance. Even with the hype surrounding the film, the sheer number of reporters far exceeded anything she'd expected.

As the limousine was forced to slowly pull to the curb due to the crowd, Brie suddenly realized that most of the reporters gathered outside the theater were not entertainment journalists. She immediately shot Sir a worried glance.

Sir gazed deep into her eyes, the picture of calm.

Brie gently rubbed the condors on her bracelet and then smiled at him, clearly hearing his command that night she was collared: *Exude elegance and poise, confident in the knowledge you are mine.*

Looking to her parents, Brie instructed, "We are going to ignore any reporter who is not here to talk about the film."

They both nodded but her mother looked nervous.

"I'm here for you," her father stated firmly. "No one is throwing eggs at my little girl tonight."

She giggled. "Thanks, Daddy."

When she glanced at Rytsar, he winked as he discreetly punched his fist into his palm. She grinned at him, appreciating his silent support.

Brie took a deep breath as she watched the driver walk around the vehicle to open the limo door. Sir exited first and then held his hand out to her.

Feeling confident with her entourage, Brie took his

hand and gracefully exited the vehicle with Rytsar directly behind, her parents following.

"Mrs. Davis, look over here!" one of the reporters shouted.

Brie looked up at Sir instead and smiled. This was the moment she had fought for, and she felt an overwhelming sense of power and calmness. Smiling back at Rytsar, Brie scanned the multitudes clamoring to get a photo of her.

She was touched to see Captain, Master Nosh, Mistress Luo, and Mr. Gallant had come to stand guard on both sides of the red carpet.

Brie held her head a little higher, walking the red carpet as if she owned it—fully taking in this moment of triumph. Despite Holloway's attempts to destroy her, the man no longer existed. She had survived, and she was here now, premiering the film he'd sought to obliterate.

It took them considerable time to make it down the red carpet, but Brie enjoyed every moment as she shared her enthusiasm for the film, as well as her admiration for the people who were represented in it. She made it a point to pass by any journalist asking questions about Holloway or her captivity.

Just as they were about to enter the theater, Brie heard a loud commotion behind her. She turned and was shocked to see the throngs of reporters clamoring around Faelan, who was making his way down the red carpet alone on crutches.

"I can't believe he came!" Brie told Sir, touched to see him.

Rytsar nodded to her before walking back to join

Faelan, but Brie remained where she was. She wanted Faelan to fully experience the outpouring of love that both the press and the public had for the young father and hero.

When he finally joined her, Mr. Cummings had the attendants open the doors so she and Faelan could enter together.

"I can't believe you came with your broken leg," she cried over the din of shouting reporters behind them.

Faelan laughed. "Nothing could keep me away, blossom."

Brie stopped for a moment and looked back, astonished by the sheer number of people gathered outside. This premiere went far beyond anything she could have ever imagined.

So many factors had played into this night—from surviving the horrors of the compound and Holloway's subsequent death, to Faelan cheating death at the horns of a bull and the concentrated efforts of her mystery benefactor.

This premiere was truly a dream come true…and the film hadn't even started rolling yet!

Sharing Their Voices

Gratefully taking the arm that Sir offered her, Brie followed Mr. Cummings as he led them into the packed theater and escorted them to their reserved seating. There she saw that all of her friends who were involved in the film were already seated. Brie made it a point to shake their hands before she sat down.

Coming upon Master Coen first, she held out her hand. "I appreciate you and raven traveling all the way from Australia to be here tonight," Brie gushed, shaking the trainer's hand enthusiastically.

She turned to his submissive raven, who looked as cute as ever wearing her pigtails and a schoolgirl outfit similar to the one she wore for the spanking scene they were in. "I'm so glad you could make it."

She moved on to formally shake Marquis's hand. "I can't tell you how excited I am to see how the audience reacts to our scene together."

He squeezed her hand tightly and smiled. "I am too, Mrs. Davis. You never compromised your vision and I commend you for that."

She nodded to him, touched by the compliment.

Brie's eyes lit up the moment she saw Autumn had come in support of Tono's scene. "It's wonderful to see you, Autumn."

Autumn grinned. "I'm so happy for you, Brie. I can't wait to watch this film and see all the changes!"

Tono smiled as he glanced at the white orchid in Brie's hair. Taking her hand, he said, "I'm grateful I get to continue this journey with you, Mrs. Davis."

She leaned in, telling him, "Your support of my films has always meant the world to me, Tono." Before she pulled away, she whispered, "I wouldn't be here without you."

Brie shook Baron's hand next. "Baron, I will never be able to thank you for all you've done for me, starting with our first scene together."

"It's been my pleasure, kitten," he told her with pride in his eyes.

Boa was sitting beside him and stood up. Clasping hands with him, she said, "I know the audience is going to go wild when they see your scene tonight. I still get goosebumps watching it."

His eyes sparkled. "My Mistress is looking forward to seeing it on the big screen."

"Yes, I saw Mistress Luo outside," Brie commented. Looking up, she spotted his Mistress entering the theater. "And there she is now…"

Looking in her direction, he told Brie, "She insisted on keeping guard over you."

"Please thank her for me."

Brie moved on to Master Anderson and Shey. "I don't need to ask how the honeymoon went because I can see it in your faces."

Master Anderson shook Brie's hand, grinning. "I'm right proud of you, young Brie. I recall how I found you in that hospital room, watching over Thane. Two children and two premieres later? You're unstoppable, darlin'."

Tears brimmed in her eyes. "Thank you, Master Anderson."

Next, Brie went in for a handshake with Ms. Clark but suddenly felt the urge to hug the woman.

"Oh!" Ms. Clark cried out in surprise and immediately stiffened, but then returned the hug. When she pulled away, she told Brie, "I know you never felt I gave you enough credit. But it wasn't that, Mrs. Davis…"

She paused for a moment, opening her mouth as if she was about to say something more. Suddenly having a change of heart, she stated abruptly, "Congratulations are in order." Then she sat down.

Brie nodded, but was left wondering what Ms. Clark was afraid to say.

"Stinky Cheese!" Lea called out. Brie turned to see she and Mary were sitting together.

Before she could even reach them, Lea ran up, grabbed her, and started jumping up and down excitedly. "It's happening…it's finally happening!"

"I know," Brie giggled. "It's taken long enough, but we're finally here."

"I'm so freakin' proud of you, girlfriend! So, in honor of this night, I have a special joke—"

"Step aside, Lame-o," Mary interrupted. "It's my turn to hug the cheese."

Brie laughed as Mary gave her a long and heartfelt hug. "I'm really proud of you, Stinks."

When the two pulled away, they both had tears in their eyes.

"We made it," Brie whispered, her bottom lip trembling.

"Fucking yeah, we did," Mary declared, hitting her on the arm.

Mr. Cummings walked up to Brie and smiled warmly. "It's time to head up to the stage, Mrs. Davis."

She nodded to him and then turned to Sir.

He stood up, wrapping his arms around her. "Your time has come, babygirl."

She looked up at him and smiled. "*Our* time, Sir."

Giving her a tender kiss, Sir let her go.

As she walked up to the stage, Brie heard the theater quiet. After she reached the podium, she looked at the packed theater in amazement and took time to soak in the moment before she began.

"Hello. I'm Brianna Davis, director of the documentary you are about to see."

Cheers rang through the theater, most emanating from the reserved section.

She smiled as she explained, "My intention when I created this second documentary was to showcase the wide variety of experiences one can explore under the BDSM umbrella. With so many misconceptions out there, I wanted to present BDSM in a way that would not only entertain you but also expose you to the beauty that can be found in the lifestyle."

She looked around the room, her smile growing when she said, "I hope, as you watch the various scenes played out by people trained and experienced in BDSM, you will not only identify with the sensual aspect of the scene but discern the connection and trust that it builds between the partners who engage in it."

Glancing at different individuals in the audience, Brie continued, "I filmed a variety of scenes and dynamics to engage and challenge any preconceived ideas you might have. I trust the quality of each scene will speak for itself."

Brie gestured to her friends sitting in the audience. "It took a community of dedicated people to make this documentary."

She added with humor, "I would not have been able to make it without them…literally."

The audience responded with laughter.

"In all seriousness, I hope this documentary gives voice to every person out there who wants to be accepted and loved in whatever manner they choose to express that love. Your love is beautiful and powerful."

Taking a deep breath, she announced with great pride, "And now, I give you our film…" Brie bowed her head as the titles came up on the screen behind her.

She looked up to meet Sir's gaze, smiling as she walked off the stage. Returning to the group, she sat down between Sir and Rytsar and grabbed both of their hands as the lights went down.

The film began with the scene both Brie and Michael Schmidt agreed was the most profound and visually stunning: Marquis's skill and grace with the eighty-tailed flogger. The dual perspective of Marquis's and Brie's voiceovers as they shared their own unique viewpoints on the connection they experienced during the session and the importance of trust as Dominant and submissive as their scene played out set the tone for the rest of the film.

Tono's scene with Lea followed. Brie was swept away as she listened to the haunting flute music fill the theater. She could feel the rope on her skin as she watched the performance unfold. The connection he established with Lea at the beginning played out throughout the scene as he slowly and sensually bound her in the rope, ending with her flying in Tono's jute.

Brie heard murmurs of appreciation in the crowd.

Then came Rytsar's scene, which was starkly different. He explained the dynamics of his sadistic dominance and how it influenced the scene when he introduced his sub to a new tool. Brie could feel the girl's genuine alarm as she stared at the electric instrument Rytsar held in his hand. However, it was clear by the lust in her eyes, that her desire outweighed her fear. The audience watched in collective anticipation as she bravely pressed her nipple against the instrument and cried out in painful pleasure. The erotic dynamic between the two was unique and thoroughly fascinating to watch.

Baron's sensual reenactment of Brie's first sex-swing lesson moved the audience, while his sultry voice rang out in voiceover as he explained the purpose of punishment in the D/s dynamic. Brie enjoyed watching their scene, as well as Baron's explanation of the ways punishment can build a deeper level of trust between a Dominant and submissive.

Ms. Clark's session with her male and female submissives showcased a completely different but equally compelling dynamic. Watching the seductive way the Domme designed the scene between her two subs, teasing and challenging them in equal measure, was extremely arousing. It reminded Brie why Ms. Clark had earned the devotion of so many submissives throughout her years as a Domme.

The film continued moving from scene to scene, building in intensity. The audience watched Master Coen's titillating spanking session with raven, then the more intimate and sensual oral scene between Faelan and Mary.

Master Anderson's bullwhip scene with Boa had been unanimously chosen by the team as the climax for the film. The intense power play between the skilled Dominant and the male sub was so provocative that it still had the power to make Brie wet. She found herself squirming in her seat beside Sir and heard the soft gasps of people around her, letting Brie know they found it equally stimulating.

To end the documentary, Michael Schmidt filmed the mountainous landscape surrounding The Sanctuary. The beautiful scenery was the perfect backdrop for Gannon's impassioned speech about his mission for the commune he'd created, while still keeping its actual location private.

Gannon's commanding voice filled the theater. "We share everything at the Sanctuary, including our kinks.

You would be surprised by how satisfying sex can be when societal limitations are stripped away. We are not just a bunch of kinksters but a true community in every sense of the word."

The documentary ended with Gannon's wish for the future. "I hope my vision for The Sanctuary will inspire other communes like it. America has been bound by laws and prudish traditions for too long. It is time to open our minds and embrace something far greater…"

The credits ended with an "in memoriam" for Gannon and a short camera recording that Lea took of Shadow watching the TV screen intently, slowly wagging his tail back and forth as he watched his late owner share his mission statement for the Sanctuary. Brie heard sniffling in the audience.

When the lights finally came up, the entire theater broke out in applause.

Brie motioned to everyone involved in the film to stand up with her and the audience gave them a thunderous standing ovation.

Afterparty!

B rie had planned a huge party for all her friends the weekend after the film was officially released in theaters. Mr. Cummings encouraged her to invite everyone she knew, informing her that her benefactor was covering the bill.

He suggested she approach the event without a budget in mind. "Extravagant gala" was the term used in the instructions he had been given.

An extravagant gala sounded very formal to Brie, and she was tired of going to events that didn't include children when hers were such an important part of her life. So, rather than go with that theme, Brie decided to hold the party on the beach.

However, she did hire the event planner Mr. Cummings recommended and embraced his suggestion not to spare any expense.

Brie planned to invite every person she knew and make this a gathering no one would forget!

The morning of the big party, Brie was startled awake by a stray sunbeam hitting her face from the window. When she glanced at the bedside clock, she was shocked by how late it was.

Confused by the silence in the house, she quickly slipped on her robe and rushed out of the bedroom to find out what was wrong.

"There you are, sleepyhead," Sir said, sitting on the couch as he casually flipped through a newspaper.

"Why didn't you wake me, Sir?" When she didn't see Hope and Antony, she immediately followed up by asking, "Where are the children?"

"In answer to your first question, I thought you deserved some extra sleep after your tremendous accomplishment. As far as the children, our resident *dyadya* is taking them to get donuts and won't be back for a few more hours."

Brie smiled, remembering those decadent donuts Rytsar loved. "Can you tell him to pick us up a box?"

"He already promised to bring back several boxes to celebrate. He mentioned something about you being a donut hog…"

Brie burst out laughing but protested in her defense, "I couldn't help it, Sir. Those donuts were really that good!"

Sir chuckled as he continued to read the newspaper. It struck her as odd because they never had the newspaper delivered anymore. Thinking back on what he said about "her tremendous accomplishment" and Rytsar wanting to "celebrate," Brie asked, "Did something happen, Sir?"

He smiled as he slowly folded the newspaper and patted the area next to him on the couch. Brie hurried to sit down. "What's this all about?"

Sir pointed to the newspaper. As Brie scanned the headline, her jaw dropped.

Provocative Documentary Setting Records!

Brie gasped as she quickly scanned the article and murmured, "One million in profits worldwide in the first three days, and set to break over two million the first week…" She looked up at Sir in disbelief.

He nodded. "You did it, babygirl. You said you were going to make a million with this film and donate it to the Tatianna Legacy Center, but you've far exceeded that goal."

Tears rolled down her face as chills of providence washed over her. "I never thought that was even a possibility, Sir…"

He reached out to caress her cheek, smiling when he told her, "It seems when you dream, you dream *big*, babygirl."

She just nodded in shock, then looked back at the newspaper, unable to believe it.

Standing up, Sir held out his hand to her. "To celebrate this momentous accomplishment, I have planned a celebratory scene for you this morning."

Already on an emotional high from the remarkable

news, Brie took his hand and followed him into the bedroom caught up in a wonderful daze.

Sir instructed her to take a quick shower while he set up his scene. When she was done toweling off in the bathroom, Brie headed out to the bedroom to find the door of their secret room open and Sir standing at the entrance, dressed only in black sweatpants.

"Come to your Master," he ordered in a low, silky voice.

She walked to him, barely feeling her feet touch the ground. With deep joy, she knelt in front of him and bowed her head.

When she felt his hand touch her head, the electricity of the connection they shared flowed through her entire body. "Stand and serve your Master, téa."

Brie rose to her feet and looked at Sir, her love for him so intense she found it difficult to breathe.

Leading her into the room, Sir commanded, "Lay face down on the table."

Her heart beating like hummingbird wings, Brie climbed onto the table and lay down on the leather, her head turned so she could watch Sir as he approached.

"First, I bind my goddess to the table..." He took her left wrist and buckled the cuff. Brie felt her pussy growing wetter as he moved around the table to bind her other wrist and then her ankles.

He leaned down and whispered in her ear, "My helpless beauty."

Brie moaned softly, having already fallen under his sensual spell.

"Now, your Master is going to warm up that lovely

back of yours." Sir moved to a table with the candles he had set out. Lighting them one by one, he allowed them to burn for several minutes.

"Which color would you like first?"

"Purple," she purred, already anticipating the warmth of the wax on her skin.

Sir picked up the pillar candle and slowly poured the hot wax on her back. Goosebumps rose on her skin as the warm wax rolled down the sides of her back, leaving ticklish trails until they cooled.

Sir took his time covering her in various colors, including her ass and thighs, as he turned her into a piece of art for his own enjoyment—and hers.

Once he was satisfied, Sir blew out the candles and picked up his phone, taking several pictures before setting it back down.

Brie watched as he covered the floor around the table with plastic before selecting a dual set of floggers from the wall. Smiling at her, he said, "Instead of a knife, I am going to use these to remove your wax, téa."

She gasped in delighted surprise. "That sounds dreamy, Master."

Sir then gently turned her head to face forward, explaining that he wanted to protect her from any flying wax.

Taking a stance beside her, Sir started out slowly, lightly striking her skin with the two floggers. He then gradually increased the strength and speed of the lashes until the tails began to dislodge the cooled wax.

With skill and precision, Sir twirled the tails round and round, causing the wax to fly off in pieces. Soon,

Brie was treated to a kaleidoscope of colors as the wax flew all around her.

After finishing with her back, he moved to her ass, taking his time there. Brie loved his focused attention and moaned in pleasure as he covered her body with the thuddy caress of his dual floggers.

By the time he was done, she was flying on the beautiful sub-high he had created.

Unbinding her ankles, Sir ordered her to tuck in her knees as he joined her on the table. Grabbing her waist, Sir rubbed his rigid shaft between her ass cheeks, teasing her with the hardness of it.

"What do you want, téa?"

"My body wants to be fucked deep and hard, Master."

"Then deep and hard you shall have." Tightening his grip, Sir plowed his cock into her. Taking the fullness of him stole her breath away. Brie's eyes fluttered closed as Sir stroked her with his shaft. He reminded her of how well he knew her body by bringing her to the edge again and again, only to stop and start up again a few seconds later, slowly building her up toward the mind-blowing release that was coming.

When he deemed she was ready, he commanded, "You will count us down."

Brie's heart skipped a beat. "Yes, Master."

Wanting to fully take in all the sensations of this moment, Brie closed her eyes before she started counting.

"Five...four...three...two...one..." She gasped as he thrust even deeper and she felt her pussy begin to pulse.

Brie screamed in primal ecstasy as he wrapped his arms around her, squeezing her tightly as they came together in perfect and breathtaking unity.

After the news of the documentary's success and Sir's incredible scene, Brie had been flying on an emotional high all morning. That joyful peace remained even as she watched the event planner and their staff running around to make sure the caterers and entertainment were ready for the day's event.

This party was going to have it all!

From two separate catering companies for culinary variety to professional entertainment for both the children and the adults—including pony rides, live music, and top-shelf liquor served by renowned mixologists—no expense had been spared.

Rather than dressing in formal wear for this party, Brie had requested that her guests come in beach clothes so they could enjoy the sand and the ocean.

Dressed in a cute one-piece bathing suit and a stylish cover up, Brie happily padded barefoot to the door when she heard the doorbell ring. She couldn't wait to greet their very first guests!

She was thrilled to see it was Tono at the door. He was dressed in swim trunks and looking as handsome as ever. His mother was sitting in a wheelchair with wide wheels designed specifically for the beach. Brie had purchased it for her with the unlimited party budget and insisted Tono keep it so his mother could enjoy as many sunsets on the beach as she wanted during her final days.

It was impossible for Brie not to notice that Autumn wasn't there with him. Inviting them both inside, Brie gave Tono a quick hug and then told his mother, "Mrs. Nosaka, we've set up a tent out back to provide you with an abundance of shade."

The old woman nodded to Brie, the slightest of smiles on her lips.

Mrs. Nosaka smiled at me!

What might have seemed like a tiny gesture to some was a huge victory in Brie's book.

She grinned as Tono pushed the wheelchair inside and headed toward the French doors that led out to the beach. Before Brie even asked, he told her, "Autumn had to fly out yesterday. She had the rare opportunity to perform in Dubai at a private Kinbaku Exhibition with a colleague of mine, but she asked me to extend her sincerest apologies to you."

Brie shrugged. "There's certainly no need for apologies, but I'm glad I had the opportunity to see Autumn at the premiere."

"She was grateful to see you, as well," he told her, smiling.

Tono then stopped for a moment and turned to face her. "I must congratulate you, Mrs. Davis. It appears your documentary is garnering considerable attention since its release and only continues to gather steam."

Brie squeaked happily. "Can you believe it, Tono? We've already made a million dollars for the Tatianna

Legacy Center!"

"Truly inspiring," he agreed, his eyes reflecting the same overflowing joy she felt.

She looked at him tenderly, full of love for him. "It wouldn't have been possible without you."

Mrs. Nosaka pointed toward the French doors, making a clicking sound with her tongue to get Tono's attention, breaking their heartfelt moment.

"*Hai, Okaasan*," he said, winking at Brie as he started pushing his mother toward the door.

The doorbell rang again.

"I'll meet you out there, Tono…" Brie called back as she ran to answer the door. Many doorbell rings later, their house and the surrounding beach out back were overflowing with guests in swim trunks and bikinis. Even her parents had dressed in the spirit of the party, wearing bathing suits that looked like they were made in the 1980s.

Brie sat in a lounger on the beach with Lea and Mary on either side of her. "Who would have guessed that on our first day at the Submission Training Center the three of us would be chilling here at the beach, celebrating our second feature film together?"

"Not me," Lea sighed happily, sipping on her fruity drink as she stared at Hunter playing volleyball with some of the other Dominants. "Just look at him…" she said dreamily, "…there he is looking so fine with all of those muscles rippling every time he jumps up to spike the ball."

"If you'd like, I could go de-pants the guy so you can ogle even more of his 'fine' body," Mary offered.

Lea reached across Brie to slap Mary on the arm. "Don't you dare!"

"So, Stinks," Mary said in a casual tone, turning to Brie. "What are you planning to do with all that moolah coming in?"

Brie smiled when she thought about it. "My deepest desire is to donate everything the film makes for the first month straight to the Tatianna Legacy Center and other centers around the world like it."

She then looked at Mary with a serious expression. "But the truth is, you fought hard for this film, too. I think you should get paid extra for the sacrifices you made."

"Don't need it. Don't want it," Mary answered. Snarling in irritation, she reminded Brie, "I already have enough on my fucking plate dealing with Holloway's damn fortune."

Mary frowned slightly as she scanned the crowd. It appeared she was looking for someone.

Lea immediately noticed and asked, "What's up, Mary? Got a hot date meeting you here?"

She slumped back in the lounger. "No. I…" Her voice trailed off and she suddenly looked uncomfortable.

Brie nudged her. "Who did you invite, Mary? It's okay. I don't care if you invited the entire Rams football team. Trust me, we've got enough food and liquor for everyone!"

Mary sighed, admitting to them both, "I invited Jason."

Brie and Lea sat up in their chairs at the same time, staring at her.

"You invited your dad to come?" Lea asked in hopeful disbelief.

Mary scoffed. "He's not my *dad*."

Brie was excited to hear it but kept her response appropriately chill. "How did that come about?"

Mary shrugged nonchalantly. "He called the day the documentary released, and we've been talking since. I told him if he wanted to fly out, he could meet me here…"

Brie took that as a good omen for Mary. She had genuinely liked Jason after meeting him in person. So, if Mary was talking to him, that must mean she liked the man, too.

Watching all the young children making sandcastles on the beach tickled Brie's heart. With so many of them around the same age, she could imagine them growing up together and forging friendships that would last a lifetime—not unlike what she had.

Jonathan suddenly grabbed Hope's hat off her head and laughed when Hope got up and started chasing him. She loved seeing them play together. "Those two sure are becoming inseparable."

"I gotta admit, he's a damn cute kid," Lea remarked.

"He sure is," Brie agreed.

Brie turned to Mary. "I can't wait to see if Caden and Antony become good friends."

"Yeah," Mary said, glancing at the group of children playing. "I'm glad the kid won't be growing up alone like I did."

"With all the 'baby talk' lately, I've been looking up new jokes," Lea announced excitedly. "I've got one your kiddos will love, Stinky Cheese."

Brie laughed. "I'm already worried now…"

Lea elbowed her. "Don't be! It's really cute."

Grinning, Brie braced herself for it. "Give it to me."

"How do we know that the ocean is friendly?"

Mary shook her head, warning Brie not to answer, but she did anyway. "I don't know Lea. How do we know the ocean is friendly?"

"It waves!" Lea answered, giggling hysterically.

"Oh, hell…" Mary groaned. "I'm not mentally equipped to handle ten years of kid jokes. Just shoot me now."

Lea reached across Brie to slap Mary again. "It's funny, admit it."

"Never."

Brie looked at Mary and shrugged. "I actually thought it was adorable. Thank you, Lea."

Lea sat back in her lounger, looking pleased as punch while Mary let out a tortured sigh.

When Brie caught sight of Baron strolling down the beach with Shanice, she quickly excused herself from the girls and ran to catch up with them.

"I'm thrilled to see you both here!"

Shanice stood extra close to Baron, and Brie couldn't help noticing that Baron had one arm wrapped around her waist protectively—it was truly a swoon-worthy moment.

"We can't stay long," Baron explained, "but we wanted to share in congratulating you on the success of the film."

Brie laughed. "I keep telling people it was a group

effort."

"That may be true, but you were the one who spear-headed it. Without your vision…" He glanced around at all of the people gathered. "…none of this would have happened."

When Brie looked at Baron, she felt deep gratitude for the difference he'd made in her life. Smiling at the two of them, she said, "We have all kinds of food and drink, so *please* don't hold back. Also, just in case I don't see you before you leave, please grab your gift bags on your way out. Lea and I had a ton of fun picking out every single item in those bags."

Baron chuckled and glanced at Shanice. "We look forward to checking them out later."

"Brie!"

She turned to see Faelan motioning to her from a chair at the kid's craft area.

"Go, go…!" Baron insisted.

Nodding to him, Brie turned to Shanice. Realizing how difficult this party must be for her social anxiety, Brie told her, "Thanks for coming today, Shanice. It means more to me than you know."

Brie then ran to talk to Faelan, anxious to share her exciting news with him. She found him helping his daughter Kaylee glue shells on a picture frame.

"I'm glad you called me over, Faelan. There was something I wanted to talk to you about."

Faelan looked up at her from the chair. She noticed he was wearing his eye-patch again and looked extremely tired. "I'd stand to shake your hand properly, but my bum leg is still healing." Holding up his hand instead, he gave her a high-five. "I always knew you were special, blossom. I just didn't realize you were millions of dollars special…"

She laughed. "You know that old saying. A person is known by the company they keep…"

"Hey, if that's true, do you mind rubbing a little of that million-dollar magic on me?"

"Funny you should mention that…" Brie said excitedly as Sir came walking up beside her. "Ever since the premiere, I've been getting tons of requests for speaking engagements. They want me to share details about the different scenes and talk about the ins and outs of BDSM. But the fact is, I'm not interested in traveling."

Faelan frowned, agreeing with her as he glanced at Kaylee. "I would never leave my little girl to go traipsing around the country on speaking engagements."

Sir spoke up. "But have you ever considered doing a podcast, Wallace? Considering your extensive knowledge as an experienced Dominant and your popularity with the media right now, this would be the perfect time to jump in."

"Yes!" Brie cried. "Instead of you needing to travel, special guests could come to a home studio at your house. You could even video the podcasts and put them on different media outlets without ever having to leave your home. It would give you the opportunity to heal and be a stay-at-home dad at the same time."

Faelan nodded slowly, a half-grin playing on his lips. But then he shook his head. "But why me when you could easily make more bank doing that yourself?"

Brie snorted. "I don't have time. I plan to start working on Alonzo's documentary as soon as possible."

"Huh…a podcast could be quite an opportunity," Faelan said, sounding as if he was intrigued.

Seeing that he was truly interested, Brie couldn't hold back any longer. She felt like she was going to burst because she'd been thinking about it for days. "Faelan!"

He looked up at her questioningly. "Yeah?"

"Do you remember that time when I told you about the vision I had all those years ago…" She pointed at Sir, herself and Faelan. "…when the three of us were talking in Sir's hospital room? That vision about you hosting a show called 'The Voice of Reason?'"

"Sure…" he replied with a smirk.

"I still remember it as vividly as the day I had it!" she gushed. "You were in charge of a show that debunked the myths around BDSM, and you would bring experts in to teach your audience how to practice it safely and effectively. I still get goosebumps when I think about it because it's happening…now!"

His smile suddenly froze. "Oh, hell…" Faelan rubbed his jaw. "Although I legitimately thought you were hallucinating that day when you told me, I've never forgotten it." Brie then saw Faelan physically shudder when he told her, "That's freaky, Brie. Like *seriously* freaky."

"I *know!*" she agreed, laughing wildly.

Sir nodded listening to Brie, then told Faelan, "I'd be happy to help should you need anything, or if there's a topic you are unsure about. If I can't answer it for you, I'll find someone who can." He took out his wallet from the pocket of his swim trunks. "I happened to meet a very capable woman who is a publicist specializing in the podcast industry. She has connections that may prove helpful for you."

Sir handed him a business card. "Her name is Semper Brooks."

Faelan took the card and stared at it, looking thunderstruck as he rubbed the top of his daughter's head absently.

"Hey, Davises!"

Brie turned to see Master Coen walking up to them, the trainer's big muscles as impressive as ever. "Appreciate you two having this little shindig before raven and I fly back to Australia tomorrow."

"Of course!" Brie told him. "I actually scheduled the party with you two in mind because I didn't want you to miss it!"

Master Coen looked around at all of the people gathered and shook his head in disbelief. "Amazing to see so many familiar faces here."

"Your name still comes up in social circles," Brie assured him. "Do you think you'll ever come back to the States?"

"Not on your life," Master Coen answered, motioning raven to him. "We love it down under. In fact…"

Raven pulled an envelope out of her beach bag and handed it to Master Coen. She then grinned at Brie.

"We are no longer accepting any excuses from you two." He gave the envelope to Sir, who immediately opened it and chuckled, showing the tickets to Brie. "Four airplane tickets with no expiration date. Bring your kids and stay a while," he commanded.

Brie grinned at the two of them, hugging the tickets to her chest. "I've always wanted to visit Australia."

Ms. Clark joined them. "I see you gave them the tickets."

"I certainly did," Master Coen answered.

Ms. Clark smiled at Brie and Sir. "Then I suppose I'll see you there, too."

Brie chuckled. "What do you mean?"

Master Coen answered for her, "I've invited Samantha to join my team of instructors."

Sir stared at Ms. Clark. "Really? That's unexpected news, Samantha."

She wore a thoughtful expression when she explained to him, "I've come to a stage in my life where I need a drastic change." She glanced at Master Coen. "When the two of us started talking, he made a pretty convincing case of why I should consider his offer."

Brie was surprised by the news. "Do you know anyone in Australia?"

"Other than Coen and raven? No. And the idea of that is what attracts me the most."

Brie noticed Ms. Clark glanced briefly at Lea. The look in the Domme's eyes made Brie wonder if Ms. Clark still had lingering feelings for her friend, and that made her sad.

Turning her attention on Sir, Ms. Clark said, "You must be proud of Brianna's work, Thane."

Sir smiled at Brie. "I am."

Ms. Clark nodded, staring at him with a wistful expression. "Strange...you used to remind me so much of my brother Joseph that it hurt me just to look at you. But that's not the case anymore. You've changed, Thane."

She then glanced at Brie briefly before looking back at him. "After you collared Brianna, you started to become a different person." She paused for a moment. "A better person, if I'm being honest."

Sir nodded. "That is an astute observation, Samantha."

She responded with a smile. "Well, you'll be happy to hear that I don't see my brother in you anymore—not even when I try."

"Good," Sir replied evenly. "It was never a healthy comparison."

She huffed with a thoughtful expression. "True…"

Ms. Clark then met Sir's gaze again. "Thank you for being my friend all these years, Thane. Even when I didn't deserve your friendship."

Sir looked at her kindly. "My loyalty to you has never wavered, Samantha. However, my admiration for you has grown with the years."

She frowned slightly. "I will miss you."

Ms. Clark then turned to Brie. "Do you remember our talk when I stayed with you over Christmas?"

Brie nodded. It was the only time Ms. Clark had ever spoken to her as an equal.

"You of all people should understand why I find Australia so appealing."

Brie nodded, remembering their conversation when she was setting up the Nativity scene for Christmas. Ms. Clark mentioned her fascination with the idea of a person being given a fresh start. Brie also vividly remembered Rytsar standing up at the dinner table and commanding that Ms. Clark stop living in the past and make a future for herself.

Smiling at the Domme, Brie told her, "I wish you all the best, Ms. Clark, and I look forward to seeing what you've accomplished when we visit Master Coen there."

Ms. Clark gave her a curt nod and then smiled at Sir. As she turned to leave, Sir stopped her.

"You can call on me anytime, Samantha. Distance doesn't affect our friendship," he told her, giving her a heartfelt hug."

She nodded stiffly when he pulled away, forcing back tears. "Thank you, Thane."

Brie happened to glance down the shoreline and spotted Mary walking with Jason. It looked like the two were having a serious but pleasant conversation. She smiled to herself, excited by the possibility that Mary might finally have found an anchor to cling to.

"Brianna!"

Brie turned to see Celestia waving at her. Brie excused herself from the conversation and left Sir to continue talking to Master Coen and raven.

Celestia was standing beside Marquis, talking to Boa, Master Anderson, and Shey. As soon as Brie reached them, Celestia gave her a tight squeeze and then stood back beaming at her. "You have wowed us all, Brianna. A million dollars going to such a worthy charity…you are truly amazing!"

"Oh, it definitely wasn't just me." Pointing at Marquis, Master Anderson and Boa, she said, "These are the real stars of the show! I can't tell you how many reporters and fans of the film have contacted me personally, simply to learn more about these three."

"I've been running into that as well," Shey said, patting her new husband's muscular chest as she laughed. "All of my old friends want to 'reconnect' suddenly." She glanced up at Master Anderson, grinning. "Makes me grateful we got married before all of this craziness began."

Master Anderson chuckled, wrapping his arms around Shey. "Mighty sorry about that, ladies. I certainly have no intention of stealing anyone's spotlight."

Brie shook her head. "You'll hear no complaints from me! Not when this film is making such a huge difference to survivors."

Marquis looked at Brie while he gently rocked Caden in his arms. The pride in the trainer's eyes made Brie blush. "I appreciate how hard you fought to get to this place, Mrs. Davis. You are an inspiration to us all."

"Hear, hear!" Boa shouted.

Other people nearby started cheering, though they had no idea what was going on, which made Brie giggle. As she stood there talking with the five of them, she noticed how loving and easy Shey and Master Anderson were with each other. Recalling her own honeymoon, Brie couldn't help wondering if the newly married couple's African safari had left them with more than just good memories. It made her smile, knowing how much Master Anderson claimed to detest babies.

Brie glanced around, looking for Rytsar. Although she had caught glimpses of him throughout the day, they hadn't spent any time together. Scanning the crowd, she saw Captain and Candy, Mr. Gallant and his family,

Rachael Dunningham, Stephanie Connor, Master Nosh and his wife Nenove, and the Reynolds, but still no Rytsar…

She became distracted from her search when she heard the rumble of a biplane high above. Brie looked up and grinned when she realized the plane was making a design in the sky.

Calling Hope to her, Brie lifted her up and pointed to it. "Look at that, sweet pea. The plane is making a picture. What do you think it will be?"

"Doggie!"

"Let's see if you're right."

Brie stared up at the sky as the plane left a thin trail of white, creating a slanted upside-down "J." When it made a second pass mirroring it, she knew what it was but waited until Hope saw it too.

"Hawt!" her daughter cried out.

"That's right, Hope. It's a heart," Brie told her, bouncing her daughter in her arms.

Sir walked up with Antony, looking up at the plane as it continued to write in the sky. This time, however, it began making letters.

Hope called out each one in her sweet voice as it was formed.

"I."

"S."

"L."

"E."

Brie's jaw dropped as soon as she recognized the final letter. At that moment, she heard Rytsar's voice directly behind her.

Turning around, she saw the sexy sadist with the shaved head, strong jaw, and those riveting blue eyes staring at her hungrily the way a lion might stare at a tasty treat.

"It's time, *radost moya.*"

Isle Adventures

Eleven hours later, Brie was standing completely naked, staring out at the crystal blue waters of Fiji from the white sandy beach of their isle. Her arms and legs were outstretched and bound between two palm trees.

Rytsar stood behind her, his hot breath on her neck. "Are you ready for the caress of my 'nines, *radost moya*? I have waited patiently for the day when you could accept my unique expression of love again."

She listened with her heart racing as he continued.

"Although I enjoy causing you pain…" He traced his finger over her right temple. "I do not wish to cause you harm here…" He then traced his fingers across her left breast over her heart. "…or here."

Kissing the back of her neck lightly, he asked with a seductive growl, "Do you want to submit to my cat o' nines?"

Brie swallowed hard as she watched the gentle waves roll onto the shore. This was the biggest challenge she had faced since the devastation Holloway caused to her soul.

It was the one thing left that had been stolen from her.

Am I willing to embrace this?

With her heart beating even faster now, Brie nodded.

Recognizing her fear, Sir walked up to her and cradled Brie's chin in his hand. Leaning in, he kissed her deeply before stating, "Your safeword is your lifeline. Nothing will happen today that you do not want."

She nodded to him.

Kissing her again, Sir stepped back and encouraged Brie. "Enjoy, téa. Accept the love he has to offer you…"

Not being a masochist at heart, Rytsar's sadistic form of affection had always tested her limits. But Brie refused to be limited by *any* remnants left by her captivity.

She heard Rytsar move back and position himself directly behind her as he waited for her command. Closing her eyes, Brie said with courage and trepidation, "Love me, Rytsar…"

She heard the nines cut savagely through the air as he warmed up, but she kept her thoughts focused on the sound of Rytsar's breathing. Feeding off the sexual energy created by the three of them being together, Brie smiled as she waited for the first stroke of his 'nines.

"Feel my love and passion for you, *radost moya*!" Rytsar stated huskily.

Brie screamed out in pain and triumph as his first lash exploded in a fiery caress of wicked knots. Along with the jolting sting of his whip came the ache of painful desire.

"Color, *radost moya*?"

Addicted to the way Rytsar made her feel, Brie swallowed down her fear, answering positively, "Green."

He chuckled softly, pleased by her answer.

The next stroke blurred out all thought momentarily, reminding her once again of how sharp and all-consuming the pain of his whip was. Tears rolled down her cheeks.

"Color?" Rytsar asked again.

Brie could feel the tingling as the endorphins rushed through her bloodstream, the intensity of it stealing her breath away. Taking a moment to answer, she said, "Green, Rytsar."

Confident in his skill and her fortitude, the Russian unleashed his dark passion on her then, caressing her body with his painful expression of love while he spoke to Brie in his native tongue. Rytsar told her how profoundly he loved her and how deeply he admired her courage.

Brie gratefully accepted the pain Rytsar delivered, harnessing the power behind each stroke to carry her higher into subspace. In that moment, she fully connected with his sadistic need to give her pain—and her desire to receive it for his pleasure.

When the rain of his lashes finally ended, Brie was left trembling and quietly sobbing to the background song of the ocean waves gently crashing on the shore.

Both men descended on her then, desperate to connect with her physically. Their lips kissed her body with ardent passion, while their loving hands explored her quivering body.

With her back still burning with Rytsar's dark love and her body responding to both men's impassioned caresses, Brie threw her head back and looked up at the blue expanse of sky above her as she fully embraced her climax, her release coming in wave after glorious wave.

Still weak from her session with his cat o' nines, Brie shuddered in ecstasy when Rytsar bit down on her throat, captivating her with his dark and powerful masculinity.

Releasing her throat, he told her, "I will wait for you inside and prepare the bath while your Master tends to you."

She listened as Rytsar left her, heading into the lush vegetation.

Sir returned to her side, murmuring in her ear, "You are the definition of grace and courage, babygirl." His words of praise caused delightful goosebumps to rise on her skin.

Lightly tracing the burning lash marks on her back, he told her, "I have never been so inspired…"

Brie moaned in pleasure and gratitude when she felt the cooling sensation of the salve Sir smoothed over her back. His touch was gentle and light as he tended to her aftercare.

The sensation of his cooling touch contrasted beautifully against her burning skin—the sensual contact arousing her. "Your touch is magic, Sir."

Brie purred as she turned her head and smiled, telling him, "Your touch alone has the power to make me come."

"Then come," he whispered in her ear, causing tingles of desire to course through her body. Brie moaned passionately, her pussy aching with an intense need in response to his ardent command.

Looking out at the setting sun, Brie watched as the Fijian sky filled with brilliant colors. She let out a poignant gasp when Sir grazed his fingers over her breasts.

It was an act of joyful surrender whenever she gave in to the electricity of Sir's touch. Brie had known the enchanting power of it from the very first moment he touched her. It was something she would never stop craving.

With a heart full of passion and submissive adoration, Brie cried out, letting the whole world know the deep and abiding love she had for her condor.

Now and for eternity…

THE END

I hope you've enjoyed the final Brie's Submission book, ***Craving His Touch***

Reviews mean the world to me!

To celebrate this last book in the series, I have a special scene just for YOU.

Read it now by going on this link to sign up to my newsletter:

Go here to get the sexy "Hayloft" scene between Sir, Brie and Rytsar NOW!

https://geni.us/CHTBonusChapter

If you are already signed up, click on the same link!

*****

Need more of the Submissive Training Center?
Start with *The Rise of the Dominants* Boxset
Grab their story!

*****

COMING NEXT

If you, like me, hate the idea of never hearing these characters' voices again, I have created a Patreon where fans of Brie who have the means to support my writing can make a monthly pledge based on the tier they want.

Each tier has special rewards as my thanks!

Your support would help ALL Red Phoenix fans who want to catch up on Brie, so that I can continue her story sometime in the future.

Go here if you want to support the next Brie Book in the future!

https://www.patreon.com/RedPhoenixAuthor

*Keep reading to get the EXCLUSIVE scene that is my gift to you 🖤

COMING NEXT
New Book?

If you, like me, hate the idea of never hearing these characters' voices again, I have a solution. Fans of Brie, who have the means to support my writing can make a monthly pledge on Patreon based on the tier they want.

Each tier has special rewards as my thanks!

Your support would help ALL Red Phoenix fans who want to catch up on Brie, so that I can continue her story sometime in the future.

Go here if you want to support a future Brie Book!
https://www.patreon.com/RedPhoenixAuthor

Exclusive Gift For YOU!

Read the scorching hot moment between Sir, Brie, and Rytsar in the "Hayloft Scene" after the wedding which never made it into the book.

Read it now by going to this link to sign up to my newsletter:

Go here to get the sexy scene NOW!
https://geni.us/CHTBonusChapter

If you are already signed up, click on the same link!

Need more of the Submissive Training Center?
Start with *The Rise of the Dominants* Box Set
Grab their story!

Reviews mean the world to me, my friend 💜
I truly appreciate you taking the time to review
Craving His Touch!

ABOUT THE AUTHOR

Over Two Million readers have enjoyed Red's stories

Red Phoenix – USA Today Bestselling Author
Winner of 8 Readers' Choice Awards

Hey Everyone!

I'm Red Phoenix, an author who also happens to be a submissive in real life. I wrote the Brie's Submission series because I wanted people everywhere to know just how much fun BDSM can be.

There is a huge cast of characters who are part of Brie's journey. The further you read into the story the more you learn about each one. I hope you grow to love Brie and the gang as much as I do.

They've become like family.

When I'm not writing, you can find me online with readers.

I heart my fans! ~Red

To find out more visit my Website

redphoenixauthor.com

Follow Me on BookBub

bookbub.com/authors/red-phoenix

Newsletter: Sign up

redphoenixauthor.com/newsletter-signup

Facebook: AuthorRedPhoenix

Twitter: @redphoenix69

Instagram: RedPhoenixAuthor

I invite you to join my reader Group!

facebook.com/groups/539875076052037

SIGN UP FOR MY NEWSLETTER
HERE FOR THE LATEST RED
PHOENIX UPDATES

FOLLOW ME ON INSTAGRAM
INSTAGRAM.COM/REDPHOENIXAUTHOR

SALES, GIVEAWAYS, NEW
RELEASES, PREORDER LINKS,
AND MORE!
SIGN UP HERE
REDPHOENIXAUTHOR.COM/NEWSLETTER-
SIGNUP

Red Phoenix is the author of:

Brie's Submission Series:

Teach Me #1

Love Me #2

Catch Me #3

Try Me #4

Protect Me #5

Hold Me #6

Surprise Me #7

Trust Me #8

Claim Me #9

Enchant Me #10

A Cowboy's Heart #11

Breathe with Me #12

Her Russian Knight #13

Under His Protection #14

Her Russian Returns #15

In Sir's Arms #16

Bound by Love #17

Tied to Hope #18

Hope's First Christmas #19

Secrets of the Heart #20

Her Sweet Surrender #21

The Ties That Bind #22

A Heart Unchained #23

Whispered Promises #24

Beneath the Flames #25
Craving His Touch #26

*You can also purchase the AUDIO BOOK **Versions**

Also part of the Submissive Training Center world:

Rise of the Dominates Trilogy
Sir's Rise #1
Master's Fate #2
The Russian Reborn #3

Captain's Duet
Safe Haven #1
Destined to Dominate #2

Unleashed Series
The Russian Unleashed #1
The Cowboy's Secret #2
A Master's Destiny #3

Other Books by Red Phoenix

Blissfully Undone
* Available in eBook and paperback

(Snowy Fun—Two people find themselves snowbound
in a cabin where hidden love can flourish, taking one
couple on a sensual journey into ménage à trois)

His Scottish Pet: Dom of the Ages
* Available in eBook and paperback

Audio Book: *His Scottish Pet: Dom of the Ages*

(Scottish Dom—A sexy Dom escapes to Scotland in the late 1400s. He encounters a waif who has the potential to free him from his tragic curse)

———————————

The Only One
* Available in eBook and paperback

(Sexual Adventures—Fate has other plans but he's not letting her go…she is the only one!)

———————————

Passion is for Lovers
* Available in eBook and paperback

(Super sexy novelettes—*In 9 Days*, *9 Days and Counting*, *And Then He Saved Me*, and *Play With Me at Noon*)

———————————

Varick: The Reckoning
* Available in eBook and paperback

(Savory Vampire—A dark, sexy vampire story. The hero navigates the dangerous world he has been thrust into with lusty passion and a pure heart)

eBooks

Keeper of the Wolf Clan (Keeper of Wolves, #1)

(Sexual Secrets—A virginal werewolf must act as the
clan's mysterious Keeper)

The Keeper Finds Her Mate (Keeper of Wolves, #2)

(Second Chances—A young she-wolf must choose
between old ties or new beginnings)

The Keeper Unites the Alphas (Keeper of Wolves, #3)

(Serious Consequences—The young she-wolf is captured
by the rival clan)

Boxed Set: Keeper of Wolves Series (Books 1-3)

(Surprising Secrets—A secret so shocking it will rock
Layla's world. The young she-wolf is put in a position of
being able to save her werewolf clan or becoming the
reason for its destruction)

Socrates Inspires Cherry to Blossom

(Satisfying Surrender—A mature and curvaceous woman becomes fascinated by an online Dom who has much to teach her)

By the Light of the Scottish Moon

(Saving Love—Two lost souls, the Moon, a werewolf, and a death wish…)

Play With Me at Noon

(Seeking Fulfillment—A desperate wife lives out her fantasies by taking five different men in five days)

Made in the USA
Monee, IL
08 April 2023

31582735R00173